EBONY MOON

BOOK 1: PRISMATIC MOONS

CAIT GRIFFIN

Elusive Blue Fiction
.COM
a passion for story

Ebony Moon
Cait Griffin

Published by ElusiveBlueFiction.com

For my parents.
You never stopped believing in me. Or my writing.

NOVELS BY CAIT GRIFFIN

Prismatic Moons series

Ebony Moon, Book 1

COMING SOON!

Prismatic Moons series:

Blood Moon, Book 2

Azure Moon, Book 3

Kendra Martin hadn't been to her Grandma Em's house (or Gem as they called her) since she was a little girl. Even though Gem was gone now, the Victorian farmhouse still held its old magic.

Fish scales, white spandrels, and its many gables made the old place look like the blue gingerbread house she remembered, set in the Indiana countryside beside an algae-covered pond with a pair of swans and a handful of mallards.

Standing on the wraparound porch at sunset, the air smelling sweet with fresh-mown grass and the faint scent of wild roses from the hedge beside the gravel driveway, Kendra felt strangely at home.

When she'd left her waterside Baltimore apartment this morning, she'd dreaded the return to Indiana. Of all the consulting jobs she could have landed, she hadn't expected one to bring her home, to the place where she grew up. She specialized in change management and when her high school pal, Toni Ambrose called, she had to come back here.

Toni's dressmaking business was booming, even celebrities requesting her dresses and whispering that she was the next Vera Wang. Besides, Toni's business employed almost a third of the small town and Toni refused to move her production facility. This was Kendra's chance to give something back to the place where she grew. To keep the town of Chauncey alive by keeping Toni's dressmaking business here.

"Welcome home, Kendra," she said and unlocked the empty house's front door.

The familiar creak of the screen and rasp of the old oak (painted red) and beveled glass door took her back two decades. So many times, she'd shoved open that door, shouting for Gem, smelling the warm scent of oatmeal cookies sweet with butterscotch chips even before grandma had stepped out of the kitchen.

She fumbled along the wall for the light switch and snapped it on, washing the hallway in pale gold light.

Her red heels clicked against the worn parquet floor, dusty from so many years of sitting empty. Her last memories of Gem's life rushed back as she walked across the old creaky floor, calling back remnants of her grandmother's illness. Her claims of seeing strange people in the house, odd lights across the pond—creatures in her garden.

Dementia, said the doctors.

Kendra's mom tried to get Gem to come live with her in Pennsylvania, but Gem refused to leave this old place, the house where she grew up with its gabled roofs and Victorian garden. Gem cared for that garden like a small child until the day she died.

She winced, remembering the day she found her on the floor in the kitchen, a little copper watering can still gripped in her fist.

For as long as she could remember, Gem had tended this garden like a favorite child. But sometimes, she seemed almost afraid of her hallucinations. Strange winking lights on Fletcher Pond, shadowy figures lurking in her garden.

But Kendra never felt scared in this wonderful old place.

She flicked on another light and walked through the parlor with its cherry wood chairs, covered in sheets, and antique Victorian couch. She remembered these cream-colored walls and striped mauve chairs, steady tick of the grandfather clock. The room used to smell like sandalwood and gardenias but all she smelled now was must and stagnant air.

Nothing a good cleaning wouldn't cure.

She knelt on the blue jacquard Victorian couch and cracked the windows, letting in June's crisp night air. A little summer breeze would make the place feel normal again.

More like home.

Kendra walked back into the narrow hallway through the kitchen and into the sitting room at the back of the house. That faced the garden. A red and white kitchen with those copper pots and gelatin molds hung over the white stove. The dark walnut cabinets were dusty and cobwebby as she brushed off a spot for her purse.

Built in 1899, this old house had seen a lot of life within her walls. Surely, she could handle a little more change—only for the summer.

Mom never wanted to sell the old place. Once a year, she came out from Pennsylvania to check on things and settle up with Maddie Cowger, the woman next door who watched over the house. Kendra dropped her purse on the counter and rushed across the white ceramic tiles toward the back door. To the one magical place she'd dreamed of seeing since she'd boarded that plane in Baltimore.

The garden. Her favorite place in the whole world.

She turned on the porch light and jerked open the back door, flinging it wide. And rushed down the wooden steps into the most magical place she'd ever spent her childhood summers.

It was a gut punch.

Boxwood hedges and pale pink English roses were gone. No huge hydrangeas and dinner plate dahlias clustered along pebbled walkways that once wound through herb gardens and beneath the long white pergola dripping with wisteria and clematis toward the back gate. No hollyhocks and sunflowers turned their faces to the sky to wave gently above a patch of heirloom tomatoes and melons.

Horsetail weeds, dried brush, and dandelions had long overtaken the winding pathways. The manicured, shaped boxwood hedges were scraggly, overgrown bushes blocking the pathway as they crowded thick patches of weeds mixed with thistle, Queen Anne's Lace, and goldenrod.

The stepping stones had disappeared, velvety green grass blanketing the ground. She sighed. Along with those magical glass spheres and ceramic faeries that had once graced the delicate flowers and herbs.

The little glass ornaments and spheres that had given Gem's garden that magical, otherworldly appeal were missing, but she knew Mom hadn't gotten rid of them.

Kendra remembered Gem hauling them up to the attic every fall, right after she'd harvested golden gourds and bright orange pumpkins from tangles of brown vines and leaves.

No, the orbs must still be in the attic.

First thing tomorrow, she'd pull them out and return them to their rightful places in the garden.

Beyond the white fence framing the backyard loomed dark, misty Fletcher Pond. The trailing branches of a massive willow tree touched black water.

She remembered its rich algae green tint and the pair of swans that glided across its verdant mirrored surface. Swans mated for life. She hoped nothing had happened to one of them.

Nothing looked sadder than one lonely swan.

The Fletcher house had weathered badly over the years. Gone was the neat, well-kept field of velvet green grass that had stretched between Gem's Victorian and the old, dilapidated white ranch house when she was a kid. She groaned. The yard was overgrown with weeds, clover, even tiny purple and white violets. And the over-the-top, gaudy display of lawn ornaments looked scary in the growing darkness. A row of pink flamingos, lawn jockeys, and plastic deer and geese filled the yard.

Had someone bought the Fletcher place?

Well, she couldn't do much about the Fletcher house and yard but Gem's garden was a different matter.

She'd restore it to the wonderful sanctuary that she remembered. Her gift to her grandma. Besides, it would give her something to do on her off hours. Toni Ambrose's business plan would only take up so much of her time. She looked forward to digging in the dirt and growing plants again.

She missed those full-sized Indiana gardens that her mother and Gem had planted and maintained. Her pitiful little patio garden in Baltimore had nothing more than petunias, lavender, and cherry tomatoes. But here? She grinned. There would be English roses bigger than saucers, pale pink and climbing over trellises and the pergola again. Wisteria clinging like grape vines. And little boxwood hedge squares of rosemary and lavender and basil.

She went out through the short, faded wooden gate at the edge of the patio, white paint peeling away, and walked around the house to the silver Volkswagen to grab her suitcase. After she'd unpacked her clothes, she'd unpack Gem's house a bit, making the summer livable here. She looked forward to the discoveries awaiting her in the attic.

Tomorrow, after meeting with Toni, she'd make a trip to the garden stores. A good pair of garden gloves and a spade for starters, and as many pounds of topsoil as she could carry. Some well-chosen plants and seeds would get a perfect start on her new Victorian garden.

Maybe this summer would be her best one since she'd broken up with her boyfriend, Brian and left her middle management hell job?

Brian didn't like change—at all. He preferred that Kendra be predictable and routine.

But Kendra didn't like predictable.

She liked to shake things up now and then, but even the slightest change made Brian green around the gills.

What had he expected? For God's sake, he was dating a change management consultant!

The breakup made him crazy for weeks. She sighed. Weeks of calls, texts, and desperate voice mails. He blew up her phone so much that she had to block his number and ghost him.

At first, she felt guilty, but their relationship felt more like outings with a friend than a romance. It had no spark, not even a few embers. And without that spark, that burning ache where she thought of no one else, she hadn't seen much future between them. Especially when he started trying to control her life.

She wanted passion and commitment but she didn't want to settle for a pale grey suburban routine. She didn't want to hurt Brian but she couldn't handle his need to anticipate and control everything and every situation—including her.

She carried her red suitcase inside and up the musical whine of stairs to the three bedrooms. She flicked on the light switch as she carried the soft-sided suitcase into the back bedroom with its tall, transom door, high ceilings, and ornate crown moldings. It had been her room whenever she'd stayed with Gem. The celery green walls and pale maple floors were cool in the summer heat that clung to the house.

She set the red suitcase in front of the small closet door. The bed had been freshly made with crisp white linens beneath a blue and green patchwork quilt. A cool breeze fluttered the lace curtains that whispered above the steady whine of the white ceiling fan overhead.

She plopped down on the bed and slid off her red suit jacket, hanging it on the nearest bed post. She laid back against the quilt that smelled of rose water and a trace of moth balls.

Maddie Cowger had aired out the house for her and made the beds. She'd asked her to turn on the utilities for the summer as well. She'd invite Maddie over for some iced tea, cookies, and catching up. After all, Maddie had been her mother's best friend growing up and Kendra thought of her as the aunt she'd never had.

She sat up and kicked off her red heels, studying the painting of the Atlantic Ocean that hung on the wall above the cherry wood chest-of-drawers. The cool blue waves and beige sand, dotted with hints of mint green beach grass, were soothing as she rose from the bed to unpack her suitcase.

In this room, she felt like a gangly teenager again, upset with her too-dark brown hair, full eyebrows, and near-sighted mud-brown eyes. But she'd filled out since then and discovered highlights and contacts. She wasn't a classic beauty but she looked nice in a pair of jeans and she'd learn to appreciate her dark hair. She pushed a wavy lock of dark hair behind her ear and padded into the hallway.

She stopped in front of the narrow staircase beside the black and white bathroom to the right. The dull white pedestal sink and clawfoot tub were original to the house. To the left of the bathroom was a shallow alcove with three steps and a narrow walnut door.

The attic. She smiled. Where Gem kept her gazing balls and other magical things.

Kendra opened the narrow door leading up to the attic and heat roiled out. She tugged on the string, the bare bulb burning pale above the staircase. Her stocking feet whispered against the worn wooden steps until she stood in the small space with its iron daybed, still draped in a faded ivory bedspread, and a maple dresser beside. The unfinished walls showed its bare wood joists and rafters as she wound around stacks of boxes and antique furniture. The old radio cabinet from Gem's childhood stood dark against a walnut drum table and a large box that read, *dishes.*

The room smelled musty, like wet newspapers and dust, the wood floor dull and rough against her feet.

On the other side, an old round mirror, the surface worn and pocked, leaned against a makeup vanity with a broken leg. It was blond wood and had that art deco styling. Two floor lamps with dirty, cream-colored shades sat beside stacks of cardboard boxes. But the pale gleam of confetti lights sparkled in the corner, catching her attention.

A tall wicker basket sat in one far corner beside an old rusty bed frame and the shimmery lights wavered against the wall in soft pinks, golds, and blues. From the bright bulbs mounted in the ceiling.

They looked like faerie lights, soft among the dust motes floating in the light that washed across the unfinished floors. The dusty air had a faint hint of lemons as she approached the wicker basket. The light looked ethereal, brighter than the other lights in the house.

She peered over the basket's rim, a grin spilling across her face. Nestled in cheesecloth were four shimmery orbs. Gazing balls and witching orbs. Made of hand-blown glass. Brought over on the boat from Ireland by Gem's mother.

To trap evil spirits, Gem always told her. They had a special magic, she'd claimed. The witching balls warded off the bad while the gazing balls reflected back the good.

Propped against the wall was one of Kendra's favorite childhood memories. She bent down, examining the grey, fired clay face.

She grinned. Kind, passionate eyes gazed out of a leaf-covered face. The Green Man!

The Green Man symbolized life and renewal. He watched over the living and protected them from harm. Gem's favorite symbol. The garden wouldn't be complete without that warm, protective face gazing out at the boxwood hedges, flowers, and herbs.

"I knew you'd be up here," a voice called from the stairs.

Startled, Kendra nearly hit her head on a beam as she stood up and turned toward the stairs at the familiar voice.

"Maddie, you scared me to death!" She hurried across the small attic toward the blond, fifty-something woman in a blue chambray shirt and long flowered skirt.

Maddie held out her arms and hugged Kendra. "It's been a good many years, Kendra," said Maddie, letting her go as she gripped her hand, squeezing. "I swear, you look just like your mother."

Kendra nodded, smiling as her gaze fell to her black-stocking feet. "Everybody tells me that."

"How's your mom and dad?" Maddie asked.

"They're both good. Mom said to tell you hi and that she missed you. She's hoping to come out this fall for a visit."

"I'll hold her to that," Maddie said with a wink. She cast a gaze around the attic. "So, what you were hoping to find that couldn't wait until morning?"

Kendra sighed and let go of Maddie's hand. "I miss Gem's garden. It's so sad to see this place without it, so I thought I might at least dig out the gazing balls. Bring back some of that magic. So, it won't look so sad tomorrow morning."

Maddie wiped the back of her hand across her forehead. "I'm afraid it'll take a lot more work than putting out some glass spheres."

"Let's make some tea and turn on the air conditioning," said Kendra, motioning her down the stairs.

"I'm all for that," said Maddie.

"Would you help me carry some things down first?" Kendra asked, moving toward the wicker basket.

"Sure," said Maddie and followed her through the maze of boxes.

Kendra hefted the wicker basket into her arms, the kaleidoscope of glass spheres fluttering their colors across her face as she nodded toward the Green Man mask leaning against the wall.

"Could you carry Green Man down?"

Maddie chuckled as she picked up the clay cast that was about two feet wide. "You and that mask. I should have known."

"What does that mean?" Kendra asked, carrying the basket toward the stairs.

"When you were a little girl," said Maddie, following her downstairs. "You used to talk about your Green Man and how he took care of your garden. You'd invite him to tea and thank him for all the flowers. When you were nine, Em took that mask off the wall and you had a fit, telling her how important he was to her garden."

Kendra laughed, remembering the summer when she'd walked into the garden and saw the Green Man missing from his familiar spot at the side of the house. She'd always loved those intense eyes and warm expression. The casting was old and had come from Ireland along with the gazing balls. She'd never seen another depiction of the Green Man like it—attractive, alluring. Every other Green Man she'd seen had the eyes wrong or the lips too thick, a laughing expression instead of kindness.

No, this Green Man casting was a one-of-a-kind and it captured her view of the Green Man like no other. Gem put him back that very afternoon and he hung there until she died.

"I can't help it. He's as much a part of Gem's garden as these gazing balls. It's not complete without him."

She led Maddie downstairs and into the kitchen where the older woman laid the Green Man mask on the counter. After setting the basket beside the back door, Kendra opened the refrigerator, old and white but still worked. The cold air washed over her as she discovered a big pitcher of iced tea sitting beside a quart of milk. Crisp yellow slices of lemons floated in the clear, warm-brown tea.

"Maddie, you're awesome!"

Maddie grinned and reached for tall glasses dotted with tiny daisies on a shelf above the sink.

Kendra slid out the pitcher of tea and carried it to the small dining room table, covered with a white lace tablecloth as Maddie set down two glasses and Kendra filled them. She pressed the glass against her lips and the cold, sweet tea was summer and childhood against her tongue. She rarely drank iced tea these days, opting instead for Frappuccino's and Diet Cokes.

Maddie leaned back in her chair and ran her hand across the dusty windowsill.

"Gotta remember to dust these sills this week."

Kendra waved her off. "I'll take care of that. It'll give me something to do while I'm here."

"How long you home for, Kendra? Your Mom said you had a consulting job."

Kendra nodded and set down her glass. "Toni Ambrose's dressmaking business has grown beyond her parlor store downtown. And online business is booming. She hired me to help her transition to a bigger operation."

Maddie smiled. "I always knew that girl had something special about her." She studied Kendra a moment. "Kind of like you."

"Me?" Kendra said with a laugh. "I help people get organized and figure out their next steps, that's all."

"No, it's more than that," said Maddie. "You're so much like your grandmother. Emmaline Martin had that calming way about her, could take the fire out of any situation."

Kendra frowned and ran her index finger down the sweating glass of iced tea. "That sounds exciting."

"I don't mean that in a bad way, Kendra. You have a soothing personality, that's all."

"Thanks," she said and took another drink of iced tea. She gazed out at the overgrowth and weeds in the backyard. "I'm going to bring it back, you know."

"Em's garden?" Maddie asked.

Kendra nodded and looked past the weeds at the Fletcher Pond. "Who lives in the Fletcher house these days?"

Maddie snorted. "Oh, I'm sure you'll find out soon enough."

"What's that supposed to mean?" Kendra asked, frowning.

"Let's just say Mr. Fletcher is...well—different."

She'd never actually met the owners of the Fletcher place. Was it a new generation of Fletchers living there?

Gem always said they were private people and she rarely saw them. Not the neighborly sort, she'd always said after telling Kendra to stay away from the pond. As a kid, she'd been chased away from that pond a couple of times but had never stuck around long enough to meet the owner. Probably old and decrepit by now.

"What do you mean, different?"

Maddie shrugged and set down her glass of tea. "He keeps to himself, doesn't say much to anybody. And that place of his is a jungle." She leaned forward and lowered her voice. "Not to mention those strange lights on the pond."

Seemed like someone who liked his privacy. With four acres of forest, a pond, and a quaint but messy ranch house, the old man had a reason to value his privacy.

"I'll keep that in mind," said Kendra, rising from her chair.

Lights on the pond? Had Maddie seen them too? Everyone thought Gem had been demented.

"You saw the lights? What Gem saw?"

Maddie nodded, looking away. "I did and I do," she said, "so don't go making anything out of it. I didn't see shadows and creatures in her garden." Maddie was quiet for a moment. "But I believed her when she said they were there."

"So did I, Maddie," said Kendra, feeling her throat tighten. She'd never believed Gem was demented.

Kendra stared at the Green Man mask a moment. He needed to be in his rightful place. Tonight.

She moved over to the counter and picked up the mask. The back door creaked as she opened it and went out into the old garden. Maddie followed, carrying the wicker basket of gazing balls. Kendra carried the Green Man casting over to the side of the house where it had always hung. She smiled. The rusty nail was still there. Lifting the casting, she placed the Green Man back on his nail and he stared out at the forlorn garden with a calming, pleasant gaze. Soon, he'd have dahlias and lavender to look out at, along with some basil and thyme and rosemary, too.

With Maddie's help, she set out the blue and purple and silver gazing balls in the darkness. The copper, weather-worn stands had a creamy green patina on them and were still in the same places that Kendra remembered as she set each ball in place. She and Maddie stood on the patio, staring at the colorful glass balls reflecting the dandelions and Queen Anne's Lace. It was a start.

Lights flickered across the pond. *Lightning bugs?*

She glanced at Maddie who turned away, pretending to ignore the lights.

"This garden meant a lot to Em," said Maddie, laying a hand on Kendra's shoulder as they walked toward the back door. "She'd be so pleased you were bringing it back to life. She kept seeds, y'know? From the tomatoes and melons."

Gem saved seeds!

Goliath tomatoes almost as big as her head and Tigerella tomatoes with their soft yellow stripes. Kendra remembered the buttery sweet melons—called Moon and Stars melons, or something like that. Jenny Linds and Pocket Melons, too. Victorian women carried the little pocket melons in their pockets because of their fragrance, Gem told her once. The velvety, orange-striped melons gave the whole garden a honeydew-jasmine scent and Kendra loved that scent blended with the spicy aromas of basil and rosemary.

"I hope she kept the melon seeds," said Kendra. "I'll check her potter's bench in the garage."

"I'd better get on home. If you need anything, call me or stop over." She put her arms around Kendra and hugged her. "It's good to have life back in this house again. Even if it's only for the summer."

"Thanks for everything, Maddie," said Kendra, sliding her arm around Maddie's waist. "I'll cook supper for you some night. We'll eat on the patio and watch the swans on Fletcher Pond."

"Sounds good, Kendra," said Maddie, letting her go. She moved toward the garden gate and paused a moment. "Welcome home."

Kendra waved at her as she left through the gate. She paused a moment to stare out at the Fletcher Pond and the flutter of lights growing into a plume of light.

What was that? Fireworks?

Her arms prickled with gooseflesh. Gem always talked about strange lights on Fletcher Pond. This was the first time she'd ever seen them.

What would the summer hold for her and Gem's sleeping garden? Kendra grinned. She couldn't wait to find out.

2

S hade Fletcher ran for his life.

His breath ached in heaving gasps. Weeds slashed at his legs and forearms. Sharp tang of cut grass nearly choked him as he sloshed around the pond's edge.

Evening settled across the Indiana countryside like a musty, soaked saddle blanket. Heavy. Stifling with heat and humidity.

The bass hum of arriving Watchers rumbled against his chest.

He sucked in a breath. Ducked the hail of lights that tore past him. Burning.

Heat from the plum-sized glowing spheres singed his cheek.

He stumbled, nearly pitching into the pond. Caught himself.

Every new moon, they came—the Eidolon. They slipped into this world from his own, trying to destroy him. And the magic he carried.

He shared their bloodline and their dark abilities, his gift stronger than any they'd ever seen. His exile was the only thing protecting his mother's people from annihilation.

Pivoting in the dew-damp grass, he turned toward the bright gold porch light shining at his front door.

More lights crackled past his head, scorching an angry line across his forehead.

He fell, chin slamming against the hard ground.

Swallowing a curse, he scrambled to his feet. Dodged another rush of gold lights that careened toward his face.

"Is that the best you can do!" Shade shouted.

He swung his arm in front of his face, blocking the Watchers' assault.

"You've already failed again!"

He lurched away from the pond, rushing toward the porch.

And his axe.

It lay propped against a green and orange lawn gnome that stood beside an empty, white wooden flower box, a can of Budweiser in the gnome's extended hand.

He envied that gnome.

Shade lunged for the axe as another trail of lights burned across his forearm.

"Cowards!" he shouted, wincing as tendrils of pain throbbed down his arm. "Face me—if you're man enough."

He swung the axe into the haze of lights buzzing around his face like wasps.

Dozens of glowing yellow lights disappeared with a crackle, the sparks dissipating in the growing darkness.

With axe raised high, he rushed off the porch and into the cool, dewy grass.

Another cloud of lights peeled off the pond and surged toward him.

He gripped the axe tighter, waiting for them to come within striking range.

Sweat trailed down the side of his face, stinging the burns left by the last Watchers. He sucked in a breath, gritting his teeth against the pain.

Block it out. Walk it off. Can't let them see they'd hit the mark.

Again, eerie yellow lights hummed toward him. Like the thrum of power lines, the whine sharpened, sounding shrill against the buzz of cicadas.

Heat pressed against his face, the light blinding.

Watchers raced toward his eyes.

He swung the axe through the glow trails.

For a moment, everything went dark, sparks winking out.

He raised the axe again, propping it on his shoulder. Waiting for the next rush of Watchers.

He was the rightful king of their realm and his: Eidolon and Katori. He carried both bloodlines, including one that burned with a dark—and uncontrollable—energy. But without a rare Katorin magic to temper these energies, he would rule neither. The magic that had once united both realms was now tearing them apart.

Without balance, Shade could never wield his inherited gifts. While he searched for that balancing magic, his people hid—and died—in villages, in the wilds, and in disguise. Waiting for the day when Shade could return to defeat the Eidolon. He was Katori's last hope. The last of his line to inherit this rare gift.

But he could only face these enemies when he could control the wilding.

Helplessness ached through him and a thousand *what ifs* drove him mad when he closed his eyes at night. Katorins were dying while he tried to find tempering for his magic.

It made him ache all over.

He gripped the axe tighter, gritting his teeth against the burn of the wood handle against his palms.

Guilt gnawed at him.

He knew the pain and torture his people suffered in his absence. But without that tempering magic, he couldn't stand against the Eidolon with any hope of defeating them. Without that magical focus, he and his people were an easy mark for Eidolon assassins. Here—for now—they were only shadows. Dangerous but vulnerable.

Every ebony moon, more of the Eidolon slipped through to hunt him down. The crossover stunned them, kept them in this hazy Watcher form. Long enough for Shade to destroy them.

They were only shadows, muted versions of their true form. Only in his realm would they die a real death. Unlike Shade. Even muted, they could kill him here. Without the human world's protective veil, he stood no chance of surviving them.

He swung the axe through a cloud of Watchers that descended on him. Sparks showered him, disappearing beneath the wash of porch light.

He was weary of the constant fight, the endless search, and the running. Constantly moving. Constantly hiding.

The Katorins sent him across to protect him. His magic was their last hope. Except for Watcher attacks every new moon, he was safe here.

It was a long, lonely existence, cut off from family and friends. He wanted an end to his exile and his people's suffering. He felt like a coward hiding and running from them here.

And the Eidolon were growing stronger.

If he didn't act soon, they would overwhelm him. Like the others they'd already hunted down and eliminated.

An eerie whine rose from the pond's frothy edge.

A flood of Watcher globes hovered above the pond's satiny surface.

Wash of light blinded him.

He turned, axe raised.

Electric streaks of white slashed through the darkness.

He shifted. Sliding left.

Watchers rushed at him again.

Two more waves of Watchers shot toward him. He swung the axe, connecting again and again with the haze of lights.

Sparks flew. And then went dark as the night turned eerily quiet.

Exhausted, he staggered toward the porch and sank down on the first step.

The axe fell against the ground. He'd beaten back this wave. For now.

More would come through as the night deepened. It would take them a while to send more assassins against him.

He grabbed the can of Bud out of the gnome's hand and snapped it open. The beer was cold against his throat. He leaned against the wall.

It would be a long night.

Until the first sliver of moonlight appeared in the night sky, the Eidolon Watchers would slip through. His presence drew them like moths to flame. But tonight, he had a whisper of hope.

For the first time in years, the Martin house had life in it again.

His endless search for the rare Katorin bloodline had led him around the world and through time. To this countryside.

And Emmaline Martin.

He'd felt her tempering magic in that garden she'd cultivated. But almost immediately, he'd felt the magic leaving her. She was old and gravely ill. Soon after he met her, she died.

Shade was devastated. She had a beautiful and remarkable soul and he missed her calming presence in the human world.

But tonight, after he'd given up hope, he felt the magic return to her house.

One of Emmaline's relatives.

He was certain of it. And this time, he was determined not to lose his connection to that tempering magic. The connection that his wilding craved.

This time, he'd convince this new human that carried Emmaline's magic to journey back to Katori and stand with him against the Eidolon.

Shade rose from the porch and picked up the axe that lay at his feet.

His shoulder ached as he propped the axe against his left shoulder and walked toward the pond.

He had to know. Had to see who walked the floors of that century-old farmhouse. Needed to see who lit the night with a new, stronger energy. A force that ached through him.

Fireflies winked softly in the inky darkness, trying to find one another as he followed the water's edge toward the Martin house. Toward the scalding glare of lights shining across the field between his house and Emmaline's blue Victorian. Like a beacon.

He wanted to get a better look at the new tenant. Needed to see the face behind the magic that he'd sensed all day.

With slow, quiet movements, Shade unhooked the white, wrought iron gate into the back garden. It squeaked a moment's protest as he slipped through the heavy gate.

The face on the wall of the house startled him. Soulful eyes staring through leaves.

Almost like a mirror.

He stepped away from the house's back wall and moved onto the back porch. And peered in the window.

His breath caught.

The slender, dark-haired woman was captivating with her honey-warm brown eyes, tight red skirt, and black silky tank top that hugged her body. Waves of dark hair crowned her head as she paced through the living room, barefoot, a cell phone pressed against her ear.

Full pouty lips, bright smile, and large, wide-set doe eyes. And long, shapely legs that reminded him of a spring fawn.

The young woman had that Fey look about her, tall and lithe, almost waifish. The fluid movements of her body were lyric—like poetry. He watched her laugh and dance across the old house's creaky wood floors.

She was lit from within—like his mother's people.

Shade stumbled back from the window, trying to catch his breath. The sight of her was electric. Intoxicating.

The shrill shriek of Watchers echoed in the distance like the shriek of a hawk.

Light flashed in the night.

He turned his head toward the flash. And stared at the shivers of white light that darted across the pond like electric dragonflies.

Cursing, Shade hurried out through the old garden gate.

He ran toward the pond, axe raised.

He couldn't let the Watchers get a foothold here. If he didn't destroy them quickly, the lights would coalesce into shadows. Shadows were much harder to fight—in darkness.

Already he felt their heat burning toward him as he swung the axe.

Faint cries shattered the lazy summer night as he dispatched more Watchers.

Lights rained down on him like a plague of locusts, searing his forearm. Scorching his cheek. Branding his forehead with a faint jagged line.

Shade cocked the axe and swung it hard. Sending the Watchers back to the abyss. Or from wherever the Eidolon had called them.

But he hadn't been fast enough.

Three shadowy shapes rose around him. Darkness rushed in and swallowed the afterimages of lights streaking through the indigo darkness.

"Shade, you're looking well," a voice said behind him. "For a man about to die."

Carvahl.

Shade felt the anger rise hot in his cheeks. He turned, axe raised. Facing the man that had been hunting him for hundreds of human years.

Carvahl was always the first to make it through after sacrificing a ton of Watchers. Always ready to destroy what he couldn't possess. Always ready to backstab and cheat—whatever it took to get his way. He couldn't wait to face this man when he returned to Katori.

He had a lot to settle with this monster.

"You haven't the talent, Carvahl."

"And you haven't the focus," said Carvahl, his voice a hoarse whisper across the distance. "It's that weak Katorin blood of yours. Not pure shadow. It bleeds red—such a shame. Especially to your poor father. How long has he been in the oblivis now? How much longer do you think he'll last there? Alone...hungry... desperate."

Shade gritted his teeth, holding back the rush of insults on his tongue. And swung the axe.

Carvahl laughed when the blade missed a hazy shape that slid like a moon shadow across the grass.

Two other shadows shifted toward Shade.

He stiffened, pivoting left then right. Axe raised to strike again.

The blow came from behind.

Shade stumbled forward, the axe nearly flying out of his hands. He struggled to regain his footing.

He turned and swept the axe blade in a wide circle. Metal whispered through the darkness, cutting through it as Carvahl laughed at him.

"So inept. In magic and defense. Your father always was a pacifist."

Shade's axe sliced through the air. Finding its mark.

A shadowy shape shattered and began to lose substance. Like smoke, it drifted across the pond toward Emmaline's house.

One Eidolon shadow form dispatched. The first of the night.

"My father hates the killing—something the Eidolon crave. And he hates what the ruling family has become. What you carry out in their name." Shade spit on the ground. "Someday, my father will walk across your graves when you're all gone from the world."

Carvahl laughed at him again. "You're such a dreamer, Shade. The last hope for your people and here, you sit while more of them die every day. And you don't lift a finger to stop it. Come back to Katori and defend your people like a man."

Rage trembled through Shade.

He swept the axe through the mist, missing Carvahl as his shadow rushed across the grass.

Just out of Shade's reach.

Something sharp slammed into his shoulder. Shade stumbled, the axe falling out of his hands.

Dazed, he couldn't see the shadows in the darkness. Couldn't find the axe handle in the cool, dark grass.

The soft splash of water touched his ears and the darkness rippled.

An Eidolon shadow.

Fiery pain tore through his gut. He doubled over as the razor-sharp waves cut through him. And he was on the ground.

The hairs on his arms stood on end with the electric charge that thrummed through the air like heat lightning.

Dark energy vibrated around him as he struggled onto his knees.

And felt the rush of magic. Smelled the cloying burnt char that permeated the night.

He tensed, dreading that first blow. Until his foot hit the axe handle.

He lunged toward it.

Something heavy pressed against his right arm, immobilizing it.

He swung out with his left fist, connecting with something solid.

The force dissipated.

He snatched the axe handle out of the grass, pulling the weapon toward him. With both hands firm against the smooth wood handle, he raised the axe.

Dark Eidolon energy built in painful waves.

Shade slammed the axe into Carvahl's shadowy form with every ounce of his strength.

"Give up, Shade—stop torturing your people."

The Eidolon shadows shattered into flecks of darkness, skittering through the night like falling ash, and fell into the pond.

Shade shouted, plunging the axe into the last trace of shadow that misted the air around him.

It broke into pieces like Carvahl's shadow form.

And for the first time in hours, the night was silent again, charred scent softened by cool, fragrant sweet grass. Steady scritch of cicadas calmed him as he sank down on the pond's bank, watching the ghostly outline of swans float past on the algae-covered pond with a brood of cygnets. His chest heaved, burns throbbing as he huddled in the cool grass and cradled the axe handle against his chest.

"Everything okay over there, Mr. Fletcher?"

Shade glanced up from the grass.

A police car sat at the end of his gravel driveway, blue and red lights flashing, doors open. A squat, balding man in a dark blue uniform stood in the scalding haze of headlights. He pointed a flashlight at Shade and the thin beam caught his face.

He groaned, eyes watering, and sat up straight, letting the axe fall into the tall grass beside the pond.

"Everything's fine," he said, glaring as he struggled to his feet. "Why?"

The cop probably thought he was drunk or deranged—maybe both. His neighbors mostly stayed away from him and his land, mistaking him for some weird, angry lunatic who partied a lot.

He'd keep playing that part if it kept these irritants out of his business and off his property.

"Got another report of a loud party over here, Mr. Fletcher."

Shade rolled his eyes as he limped over to the officer.

"Had a few friends over. Sorry they got loud. I've already told them to go home."

Back to Eidolon where they belonged. Until he found the help he needed to return home and fight them in the flesh.

The stocky, uniformed officer pointed a finger at him. "I'm not going to cite you this time, Mr. Fletcher. In the future, please be more respectful of your neighbors. And tell your friends not to be so loud next time, okay?"

"Yeah, sure thing, officer," he said in a gruff voice, running his fingers through his long, dark bangs. "Sorry for the trouble."

Next time, he'd be quicker with the axe. The more Watchers that got through, the wilder his party got.

The officer cast another glance at the pond then back at Shade. "What was that you were doing by the pond anyway?"

Shade bit his lip, knowing how ridiculous he must have looked right now, like some drunk madman fencing pink elephants or something.

"Tai chi," he said finally.

"Have a good evening, Mr. Fletcher," said the officer as he started down the driveway toward his car, flashlight beam bobbing across the gravel drive. "Take my advice and sleep it off, huh?"

"Good night, officer," Shade called, waving as the officer climbed back into the driver's seat and closed the door.

In a moment, the engine growled to life. Gravel popped against tires as the dark cruiser backed out of his drive and hummed away into the darkness.

Cursing under his breath, Shade bent down and retrieved the axe.

He dragged it behind him, body aching as he walked toward the house. He set the axe inside the door and turned toward the country road that wound past his and the Martin house as the asphalt curve disappeared into darkness.

He glanced around at the houses along the secluded road.

The only house around with a light on was the Martin house. He smiled. Whoever the new occupant was, she seemed to like her world quiet and orderly. Two things that didn't include him.

Guess he needed to get her attention.

Shade walked over to the storage shed beside his house and used his key to open it. The little shed smelled like potting soil and mildew. He moved past rakes and shovels, stepping over the faint outline of a garden hoe and around a big plastic garbage can. He yanked the string on the bare light bulb and flicked it on, illuminating a blue milk crate on the floor. The crate held several cans of spray paint.

Grinning, he found two cans of hot pink, glow-in-the-dark spray paint and carried them out of the shed.

He set the spray paint cans on the porch and sat down on the steps beside them. He picked up the axe and draped it across his legs, watching for the rush of more Watcher lights. They would come again soon.

He grinned. But between visits, he had a little *thank you* note to deliver to his new neighbor. For sending the cop to his doorstep.

3

L ight filtered through the white lace curtains. Kendra groaned and turned away from the window, bed creaking, feather pillow cradling her head. The mint green sheets and lavender and forest green quilt smelled crisp with rose water and lemons. She snuggled deeper into the covers.

Outside, the annoying honk of car horns grew louder and more insistent. On an isolated county road? Where a tractor and two cars were a traffic jam?

Unable to ignore the squawking horns, she got up, white cotton nightshirt settling against her thighs. This had always been a quiet, reclusive corner of the world.

Why was it suddenly so noisy?

First, that loud party at the Fletcher place last night—complete with fireworks (July 4th was a month away). Followed by dancing around the pond and fist fights.

In the flicker of lights, hazy images of a tall, dark-haired man rushing around the pond flashed in the night. He was alone. With an axe.

Creepy. And more than a little weird.

She'd gone out to the edge of the yard to investigate—yeah, she was *that woman* in the horror films. An axe murderer was sighted at the campgrounds? She'd find him!

But from her garden gate, she'd heard other voices out there in the night.

Two men trading insults and a ton of drunken bravado. Then the fireworks started again and more fist fights.

Another honk startled her. What was that about anyway? And at seven in the morning!

She fumbled into a pair of blue flip flops that she'd set by the bedroom door. Her white nightgown brushed her knees as she walked down the creaking staircase, sunlight filling the house, dust motes dancing in the early morning glow.

Two more honks resounded through the quiet dawn as Kendra glanced out the front window.

And nearly fainted.

"Oh. My. God!"

She threw open the front door and rushed out onto the Victorian's front porch. Her mouth gaped and she could only stare, spandrels and corbels casting intricate, swirled shadows across the portico.

Hot. Pink.

Her entire front lawn had been spray-painted hot pink!

A mixture of shock, fascination, and fury burned through her. Then she noticed a little white sign on a wooden stake hammered into the center of the yard.

Beep! The shrill horn startled her.

She looked up as a beat-up, white Ford pickup rumbled past the curve. A grizzled old man in a black T-shirt honked at her and waved as he drove past.

Kendra rushed into the yard, flip flops swishing, and pulled up the sign and its post. She turned it around.

Honk if you like my yard. She glowered at it. Written in hot pink spray paint.

Furious, Kendra tore the cardboard sign in half and glanced around for the joker who'd messed up her lawn.

The bang of a screen door resounded through the quiet summer air that now smelled like hot spray paint and dry grass.

She glanced toward Maddie's place to her left. Maddie ambled off her Craftsman bungalow porch in a pair of Navy shorts and a white T-shirt. Smiling. Carrying a white mug as she strolled down the Victorian's concrete walkway, careful not to step in the hot pink grass. Kendra smelled the warm scent of coffee and milk.

"What happened over here?" Maddie asked, her smile widening into a grin.

"I have no idea," Kendra snapped, waving the pieces of white cardboard in the air. "But I think I have a good idea who did this though."

Maddie took a quick sip of coffee. "So do I, but you first," she said, nodding at the yard.

Kendra held the pieces of the sign together and Maddie chuckled when she read it.

"Whoever's living at the Fletcher place did this! I'm sure of it!"

"So, am I," said Maddie with a smirk, "but why do you think so?"

Kendra crossed her arms, nightshirt fluttering in the warm morning breeze, and glanced down at the hot pink grass.

"To get even for my calling the cops on their wild party last night," she said in a quiet voice and squinted at Maddie.

"Cops?" Maddie's eyes widened. "You called the cops on Shade Fletcher?"

Kendra held a hand over her eyes to minimize the sun's brightness and finally nodded.

"If you'd heard the commotion and partying coming from that place last night, you'd have called them, too."

Maddie took another drink of her coffee and finally nodded. "I've called them before. Glad it's not just me. That man's crazy." She chuckled, poking the toe of her sandals into the bright pink grass. "Crazy smokin' hot—with a hilarious sense of humor."

Kendra rolled her eyes. "That's a matter of opinion."

She sighed. Great, she'd have to deal with this idiot all summer.

Or worse. Some psychopathic, axe-wielding graffiti artist she'd made angry.

"He's harmless, so don't worry. Did I mention he was smokin' hot? 'Coz he is. Tall, dark, and demented with rugged good looks and piercing ice-blue eyes. He keeps to himself."

Kendra flapped her arms toward her hot pink grass. "You call this keeping to himself?"

Maddie propped a hand on her hip. "Not exactly, but he's never bothered anyone—much...beyond a harmless prank or two. For sale signs in people's yards, spray painted lawns—that kind of thing. I wonder if he's the one who took my gazing ball last night."

"Your gazing ball?" Kendra asked with wide eyes.

"Yep, had a green one in the front yard by my wooden bird bath. Found an empty pedestal this morning when I got up." Maddie chuckled. "And when I saw your yard...I figured it was more of Mr. Fletcher's pranks."

Cold fear rushed through her stomach. If that man so much as touched Gem's gazing balls, she'd string him up by *his*...thumbs.

Or whatever was handy.

Kendra ran around the side of the house and fumbled open the garden gate. Maddie followed, calling after her.

"Kendra! What's wrong?"

Kendra ignored her, hurrying into the garden. She stopped a few steps inside, a sigh of relief hissing from her lips.

Gem's four gazing balls peered back at her from the garden's brown and green jungle of overgrown vines and weeds. She released the breath she'd been holding and turned toward Maddie.

"Wanted to make sure he hadn't taken Gem's gazing balls."

She stared across the pond. At the red brick and white ranch house, dark and nestled among tall maples and evergreens that shielded the house from sunlight. The sun's rising light cast heavy gold rays across the pond and the willow tree that drooped beside it, dragging its delicate branches through the water. Two swans with a line of little ones behind them slid across the pond's algae-green surface, two blue herons, and four or five mallard ducks dotting the other end of the pond.

No sign of her crazy neighbor though. Probably sleeping off his drunken stupor and the high from huffing all those paint fumes.

"Maddie, do you have a lawn mower?" Kendra asked.

Cutting the grass was the only way she knew to get rid of this awful pink paint.

Maddie shook her head. "I pay that kid, Ricky Tait down the lane. He mows my lawn every summer. Want me to call him for you?"

"Yes, if you wouldn't mind."

"No trouble," said Maddie. She took a long sip from her cup and leaned against the Victorian house's blue siding. "He'll probably charge you twenty bucks. It's a big yard."

Kendra nodded and crossed her arms, the sign fragments tucked under her arm. "No problem. I'll be sending the bill to Mr. Fletcher."

Maddie snickered. "That'll get things off to a good start."

"He started it and he should pay for the damages he caused." Kendra walked back out the gate, around to the front door, Maddie following. "I don't have time for this. I've gotta be downtown by eight thirty to meet with Toni and her staff."

"I'll see if Ricky can have this—hot pink character to your yard mown off by the time you get home tonight."

Kendra smiled at her. "Thanks, Maddie. You up for some Chinese food tonight? I'll pick up some takeaway on the way home."

"Sure. As long as it's not too spicy, I'm not picky."

"Thanks for your help, Maddie," Kendra said with a wave and hurried inside.

She carried Mr. Fletcher's sign into the kitchen and tossed the pieces into the trash. And then hurried upstairs to take a shower.

As soon as the warm water caressed her shoulders and neck, she'd forget all about Mr. Fletcher and his poor taste in colors. She had better things to worry about, like distribution channels and marketing for Toni Ambrose signature clothing. And top soil and heirloom melons. She looked forward to working in the garden tonight after supper.

Kendra hurried into the master bedroom with its pale peach walls, mint green curtains, and cherry wood bedroom set. Into the small on-suite bathroom. White fixtures. Black and white tiles. Same pale peach walls.

The room smelled like lemons and old newspapers as she slid out of her nightshirt and hung it on a hook behind the door. Then she noticed the towels. Maddie had piled thick yellow and green towels on a white wicker stand under the round, porthole window.

"Thank you, Maddie," Kendra said with a smile and turned on the shower.

Everything she needed for her stay had found its way into drawers and cabinets and cupboards. Maddie had outdone herself and her caretaker duties.

In Baltimore, Kendra had made a list of what she needed, including a bag of Starbuck's breakfast blend. She'd meant to send it to Maddie before she got here but never got a chance. Maddie had taken care of everything though, to her surprise, as if she'd seen the list. Including the bag of Starbuck's coffee.

Maddie probably remembered seeing the bag of coffee in Gem's cupboard every time she'd visited. She'd have to pick up a special gift for Maddie, to thank her for making the place so livable after it had set empty for months and months.

When steam fogged up the gilt oval mirror over the white pedestal sink, Kendra grabbed two towels and laid them beside the tub. Grabbing a comb, she climbed into the clawfoot tub and pulled the white shower curtain closed. She popped open the tube of sun-ripened raspberry shower gel and lathered her face and body with the summery scent. After washing her hair with coconut shampoo and using conditioner, she rinsed off and climbed out of the shower. She turned off the water and combed out her hair over the tub then wrapped it in a towel.

But there was no blow dryer.

She groaned, remembering hers still lying on the bed in her Baltimore apartment.

Sighing, she dried off with the second towel, wrapping it around her body and stepped in front of the mirror. She'd have to pull her hair back today and let it air dry.

She glanced toward her duffle bag underneath the window, makeup bag inside unzipped with products spilling out. Beside her cedar rose blush was a black blow dryer lying beside the makeup bag.

She frowned. She hadn't packed that hair dryer. It was still back in Baltimore.

Maybe she'd thrown it in the bag at the last moment and forgotten. Not noticing it until now?

She plugged in the dryer and unwrapped the towel from her dark locks. She ran long fingers through her ringlets, working in a quick application of sculpting foam and dried her hair. She unplugged the dryer and laid it on the yellow towel and reached for her makeup.

She gave the dryer one last look and hurried toward the bedroom closet. She slipped into a silky sheaf dress in pale aqua, light and sleeveless for the ninety-plus-degree weather and pulled on spiky black sandals. After brushing her teeth and slipping on some dangling chalcedony earrings, she grabbed her purse and briefcase and hurried downstairs. She snagged the house keys off the kitchen counter and rushed out to the silver Volkswagen she'd rented. With one last scowl at the hot pink yard, she drove off toward downtown Chauncey and Toni Ambrose's boutique.

KENDRA PARKED ON THE SQUARE BY THE WHITE-DOMED, GOTHIC courthouse with its statues, round two-tiered fountains, and black wrought iron fences. She walked across the one-way street and south side of the square. O'Riley's bakery stood at one corner with its white facade and blue neon sign. She sniffed the air for a trace of cinnamon. She'd grown up on O'Riley's cinnamon rolls and tea cookies with their colored sprinkles and powdered sugar.

At the other end of the square was Heartland Bank with its grey-green malachite-like marble and turn-of-the-century architecture. Little gargoyles perched at the top of the metal scrollwork. In between the bank and the bakery was a CPA's office, Razor's Edge barber shop, and the purple and teal nook that was Toni Ambrose's boutique. Ambrose in gold script curled across the picture window that was draped with silky purple and teal fabrics. A delicate silk dress in lavender floated in the window. Its gossamer folds gave the dress a dreamy quality.

The ornate, gold-painted door had a Closed sign on it, so Kendra knocked twice until footsteps ticked toward the door from inside. Someone unlocked the door and held it open. Toni Ambrose.

"Kendra! Good to see you."

Kendra stepped inside and Toni re-locked the door. She hugged her high school pal.

"You haven't changed a bit, Toni," said Kendra, holding her out at arm's length. "A little thinner though."

Toni had always been an envious size four in high school but now, she looked leaner—and a little more chiseled. Her oval face had a few more angles than Kendra remembered, wrist and collarbones a little more prominent. Her maple complexion made her look about fourteen, especially when she pulled her chocolate brown hair back in a pony tail.

Toni wore a gorgeous ivory shift, form-fitting and tailored with almost faerie softness. Her clothes had always had an ethereal quality, delicate like cotton candy. She'd never seen anything styled like them before.

"So, who's the latest celebrity to buy one of your dresses?" Kendra asked, following Toni through the racks of dresses setup in a gilded Victorian parlor with swan-armed fainting couches in rich eggplant purple and teal loveseats.

The gold boutique racks that linked the shotgun-style space looked almost bare and Kendra wondered if Toni had enough stock to fill them.

Toni led her to a purple velvet Victorian-style settee that stood on one side of the room, a marble coffee table in front of it, paisley fringed lamps and two teal and purple-striped side chairs. Huge gold framed mirrors, with ornate scrolled frames, hung on both walls above an old black and white fireplace. Inside the fireplace were two rows of purple candles on a black rack. The scent of lavender was strong as she gazed at prints of midsummer's night faeries and fabled women. The Lady of Shallot, Circe—Ophelia.

Toni sat down on the settee and laid her hands in her lap. "I got an order yesterday for two dresses from Kate Winslet. And one dress request from Jessica Alba."

Kendra grinned. "I'm so proud of you, Toni! When you called me about changing the scope of your business, I dropped everything to come out here. But it sounds like you don't need my help."

"But I do," she said, motioning around the small store. "I can't keep the dresses on the racks. Right now, that's my biggest problem. Filling orders and stocking these racks and shelves."

"I noticed," said Kendra, glancing around. "Looks like you need to step up production and get some better distribution lines."

Toni nodded as Kendra pulled out a small tablet computer out of her briefcase and turned it on, tapping out some notes.

"What about the orders you mentioned?" she asked, glancing up at Toni.

"I've got boutiques from New York to Seattle to L.A. requesting my line for their stores," said Toni, looking anxious. "I can't fill them all."

Nodding, Kendra typed more notes. "Where is your production facility?"

Toni sighed. "All over town. I've hired every seamstress I know to assemble the dresses but there aren't enough."

Toni needed a business plan and better facilities. She needed to hire full-time staff to produce the quantities of clothing she needed.

For two hours, over Darjeeling tea and cookies from O'Riley's, Kendra assaulted Toni with questions. One of the sales clerk's unlocked the door and turned over the closed sign, Kendra rose from the settee.

"Thanks for the information, Toni. This gives me quite a bit to get started. The first thing I'm going to do is draw up a business plan for you."

Toni's eyes widened and she laid a hand against her chest. "That sounds expensive. I don't exactly have a lot of capital, Kendra. Only some clothes and a dream."

Kendra slid her arm around Toni's shoulders and walked toward the door, briefcase and purse in hand.

"I know. After I come up with a plan, I'll make some calls and find out what's possible. How much it costs. When I have everything down on paper, I'll present all the options to you. Then we'll start sorting out what you like and what you don't. We can do this in stages —whatever you're comfortable with, okay?"

She opened the door and the bell rang as she stepped out onto the sidewalk—and into the heat.

"That sounds great, Kendra. How long will this take?"

"Two or three weeks."

Toni smiled and hugged Kendra. "Thank you. I owe you big time. I know I could never afford your fees—"

Kendra let her go. "Consider it a return on investment."

"Investment?" said Toni, scrunching her face.

Kendra nodded. "I'm investing in my hometown—and a good friend." She pointed toward the window. "And maybe if you like my plan, you could float me a dress like that one."

Toni glanced at the dress in the window. "Size six, right?"

Kendra nodded. "You may be the next Stella McCartney, Toni."

"Get out of here," said Toni, grinning now but in a moment, the grin faded and a serious almost frightened look touched her face. "That's my dream, you know. To be a top clothes designer."

"You'll get there, Toni. You've got talent and vision. Keep doing your thing and let me worry about the business stuff."

"Thanks, Kendra. I'll call you in a couple of weeks."

Kendra waved and hurried across the street to her car. She laid the briefcase in the back seat and climbed into the driver's side. Starting the car, she headed onto Main, intending to head west to Gem's house but changed her mind. She drove toward the bypass and the gardening store.

IT WAS AFTER ONE O'CLOCK WHEN KENDRA PULLED INTO THE DRIVEWAY of the old blue Victorian house. Ricky Tait, a lanky sandy-haired teenager, buzzed across her lawn on his riding mower. Tang of cut grass, spray paint, and gasoline filled the air as she stepped out of her car, briefcase in hand. Long, shaggy hair hung to Ricky's shoulders, white ear buds hanging out of his ears. He wore a green T-shirt and cargo shorts. Kendra waved at him, pleased to see the Pepto-Bismol-pink grass disappearing.

Grinning, Ricky waved as he passed her on the riding mower. she stepped over the flecks of green and pink littering the driveway and hurried to the front door. She went inside and changed into a red Green Day T-shirt, grey shorts, and red Keds. And returned to her car.

She grabbed her purse from the front seat and set it on top of the car as she popped the trunk. Hefting out a twenty-pound bag of potting soil, she frog-marched it around to the backyard.

She set the bag on the stone path and returned to the car for the thick paper sack that contained a spade, a trowel, gardening gloves, and seeds. And two old English tea roses that she'd bought. She had another twenty-pound bag of topsoil in the trunk but decided to get that out tomorrow. After she'd put in a good eight hours on Toni's business plan.

With a rose bush in each arm, paper bag handles in her right hand, she carried everything to the back yard. She set the roses on the porch near the French doors that led inside to the sitting room and returned to the car. After closing the trunk, she went inside through the kitchen and into the garage. The ninety-three-degree heat and humidity had baked the small garage into an oven as she stepped over the remnants of oil stains on the cement toward the potting bench in the corner.

Already, sweat threaded her upper lip and coated her face as she lifted the lid on the bench. The potting soil bin was empty, dust and cobwebs inside. She opened the cabinets underneath, finding various sizes of dirt-encrusted clay pots, dusty green tomato stakes, a spool of green wire, and a thick, round spool of jute.

"C'mon, Gem," she said under her breath. "Maddie said you had seeds in here."

Kendra rummaged through the line of drawers on the bench. Nothing but dust and dirt from decades of potting plants. She closed the lid, looking behind the bench for sacks or packets—anything that looked like seeds—but found nothing.

Once more, she opened the bench lid that had a big tray for potting. But the corner of brown paper caught her gaze. She pulled the brown-wrapped package out of the slot. A grocery bag, cut and folded over like an envelope and then tied with jute. In shaky blue pen was the word "Melons." She shook the packet and heard rattling.

Seeds! She'd found Gem's seeds!

Kendra explored the nooks and crannies of the bench, finding five packets of seeds. All the strange and unusual plants that she remembered from her childhood.

Kendra cradled the little bundles against her chest and carried them inside the house. She spread them out on the old kitchen table. There were melons, tomatoes, lettuce (Tom Thumb and oakleaf), and pumpkins.

With careful tugs on the jute, Kendra untied the melon packet, spilling little paper-towel-wrapped bundles onto the table, each one labeled and rubber-banded. Jenny Lind, Moon and Stars, Pocket, Emerald Gem, and Rocky Ford.

One by one, Kendra opened all the packets until she'd gathered the seeds that she wanted to plant into a small white cereal bowl.

She carried out the bowl of wrapped seeds and a cold can of Coke to the back yard. She studied the empty garden for a moment. The yard needed a lot of clearing to get it ready to plant, she realized with a sigh. Returning to the garage, she retrieved a hoe and attacked the overgrown weeds and dead plants lining the small, square backyard.

IT WAS AFTER SIX O'CLOCK BEFORE KENDRA HAD THE BACK HALF OF THE yard cleared. She dragged the bag of soil out to the cleared land, still hard with dirt and clay despite the hour she'd spent hand-tilling it. She tore open the bag and emptied it over the hard soil.

The rich, loamy smell filled the humid air as she spread the black soil, wiping back sweat as she worked. Her hands hurt from so much tilling, the hoe's wooden handle rasping against her palms until they ached. After she'd spread out the dirt, she dragged the hoe back to the house and propped it by the door.

Exhausted, she set the bowl of seeds on the table and tossed her empty Coke can into the recycle bin under the sink. After peeling off her gloves, she laid them in the sink. She filled a glass with cool tap water and drank until it gave her headache.

The knock on the back door startled her.

She nearly dropped the glass as she turned around. A tall, dark-haired man with haunting, glacial blue eyes stood at her back door. He wore olive shorts and a light blue T-shirt that hugged him in all the right places. His face was chiseled, shadowed with a hint of beard, full lips, and an almost Greek nose. A shudder rushed through her, her voice lost as she opened the door.

He stared at her, long and lingering as let out a hiss of breath. And those melancholy, intense blue eyes bore through her like winter electricity. She stood there, mouth bobbing.

Get a grip, already, she told herself and sucked in a breath of air, fighting to regain her voice.

"Can—Can I help you?" she asked finally.

He didn't speak, just stared at her and she felt an electric attraction burn across her skin. Something she'd never felt before.

Finally, the faint hint of a sigh touched his lips. Then a grin curled across his face as he leaned against the door frame.

"You've gotta be related to Emmaline Martin," he said, crossing his arms.

Kendra smiled. "She was my grandmother. Did you know her?"

The man nodded, his gaze falling to the door jamb a moment then flicking back to her with renewed intensity. He pointed over Kendra's shoulder. "Drank a lot of iced tea at that kitchen table. She was a good woman. Lots of life in her."

"She was a wonderful lady and we all miss her terribly."

The man glanced behind him, pointing to the backyard with his thumb. "Going to spruce up the place?"

Kendra nodded. "Gem loved this garden. I want to bring it back for her. Fix the damage that maniac did."

The corners of his mouth quirked. "What maniac?" he asked.

"The crackpot who spray-painted my lawn hot pink last night."

"What'd you do to him?"

What did *she* do to *him*? As if.

"Me?" she cried, pressing a hand against her chest. "I didn't do anything to him! Didn't you hear that wild party last night? The fights and the fireworks?"

He shrugged. "Kind of jumping to conclusions, aren't you?"

Kendra felt anger sting her cheeks as she glared at the man, hands on her hips.

"And what am I supposed to think?"

He reached out and pressed a purple wildflower into her hair, behind her ear. She squinted at him. She hadn't seen any flowers in his hand.

"Nothing—until you have the facts."

"The facts?" She balled her hands into fists. "It was loud enough to wake the dead over there!"

The man stepped back from the door and pointed toward the pond. "Over there? By that pond?"

Kendra nodded, crossing her arms. "Yes, practically in my back yard."

That handsome smirk pulled at the corners of his mouth again and she felt her anger dissipate, lost in that smile.

"What's your name?" he asked, his voice soft and buttery.

"Kendra Martin. Why?" What an odd time to ask her name.

He held out a black strap and she realized it was her purse.

"If you're Kendra Martin, this must be yours. Found it in your lawn boy's hands. I made him put back the money. If I were you, I'd make sure all your credit cards are there."

She snatched the purse out of his hands, not sure what to think.

He could have made up that story to steal her money and credit cards and blame it on Ricky Tait. She stared at him, her eyes narrowing.

"Thank you for returning it to me," she said, her voice softening. "I forgot I left it on top of the car."

"No problem," he said. "Glad I could help."

"What's *your* name?"

He grinned at her and took a few steps away from the door. "Shade," he said, suppressing a laugh. "Shade Fletcher."

Kendra couldn't stop her mouth from falling open, her attraction wilting in the face of the fury that rushed over her.

"Fletcher? Shade *I ruined Kendra's lawn* Fletcher?"

He bowed and started walking backward toward the open gate. "Ruined is a little harsh. I only spiced it up a bit."

Kendra rushed outside, pointing a finger at him. "You owe me twenty dollars, Mr. Fletcher!"

"Since I saved you at least seventy and a stolen Visa, I'd say we're even, wouldn't you?"

That smirk returned to his face and she wanted to punch him.

"If I hear anymore wild parties in my backyard, Mr. Fletcher, I promise you I'll call the cops again."

He held up both hands. "Can't make any promises, Kendra. May I call you Kendra?"

"No, you may not," she snapped, hands on her hips. "Now get off my lawn! Er, property!"

That arrogant smirk remained as he turned away toward the pond. She watched him walk away and despite her anger, she enjoyed the view.

Okay, so Maddie was way off when she said he was smokin' hot. He was Greek god, Godiva-chocolate, give me an oxygen mask gorgeous. And even the Lady's finest chocolate truffles paled by comparison.

She let out a breath of air when he was finally out of sight, feeling weak in the knees.

She'd keep an eye on Mr. Fletcher tonight.

If he so much as threw a beer can in her yard, she'd settle it herself. Let the cops come in later to clean up the mess. Although, that man would probably have the hottest mug shot in the country. Front or back.

Kendra hurried inside to wash the potting soil off her hands. She'd run out for some Chinese takeout and call Maddie over. Her next-door neighbor would want to hear all about her first visit from Shade Fletcher.

4

Shade felt shaken and nervous when he entered the front door of his white and red brick ranch house.

The memory of Kendra Martin lingered like the heady scent of lilacs.

She'd been smoky and electric this afternoon, silky long legs, chocolate brown hair, and that pert nose. Her oval face looked sculpted against those wide-set, big doe-brown eyes and he wanted to explore her full, bow-shaped lips with his mouth.

He pulled in a breath, leaning against the closed door, remembering her face a mask of sweat, hair in damp dark ringlets, and the fire that burned in her eyes. Aimed right at him.

Yet for all her anger and his attraction, he felt a calming effect in her. A tempering of the dark energies that raged within him.

He sighed. Something he'd searched this entire world for and finally found.

She had the tempering magic!

He walked across the carpet of moss that led into the ranch house's family room, now a thick forest of oaks and maples. The tree branches stretched to the top of the room's vaulted ceiling as vines draped the walls, covering a framed print of an oil-painted forest. The scent of soil and cool leaves filled the air as he sat down on the wooden bench he'd placed underneath a low-hanging branch.

The trickle of a stream echoed through what had once been a dining room, twisting and rushing through the center of the house and out the back door. The air smelled deep-forest sweet, a breeze cool and soft against his face. He'd taken the doors off their hinges and opened all the windows. Confined spaces made him edgy and it drove the greening within him wild with frustration.

Everything he touched sprouted leaves or grass, blossoming and growing. The greening was part of his wilding magic. Another magic couldn't control because of the Eidolon dark magic within him.

From the front of the house that faced the road, everything looked normal and sheltered by forest to anyone passing by it. But inside, the house was only a shell, the roof riddled with holes to let in the sun and the wind. The front-facing facade concealed his abilities. Magic that no one would understand. Especially if they saw the inside of this place. Here, in this world, it was even more uncontrolled and wild than it had been in Katori.

And this time, he didn't have the option of moving to a new location. This time, after what seemed an eternity, he'd found the tempering magic that made his magic whole. And a deadly threat to the Watchers that hunted him.

He possessed a number of Katorin gifts (like the greening), many of them admired by his mother's people, those he was destined to rule. But they all knew the darkness that raged against those gifts. His Eidolon side. His father's people. Their dark ways warred inside him for release. But using that dark magic made him no better than the Eidolon hunting him. For Katori's sake and his, he had to hold back the temptation to indulge in those dark magics—if he could ever focus them.

With those dark magics, he could tear the life force from a living body and turn it to dust. He could enslave Eidolons and Katorins and these easily distracted humans—like the Eidolon had already done to so many. And he could be just like them if he stopped resisting the dark magic inside him.

No, worse—he could rule them.

That's why the Eidolon wanted him dead. Before he learned to master this magic warring inside him.

Shade leaned against a tree trunk and closed his eyes a moment. He felt weary, a sensation he wasn't used to and couldn't remember feeling.

The constant fight over the centuries had exhausted him. He longed to close his eyes and let it all go, but the Katorins would perish if he gave in and indulged the magics that burned within him. If he could focus and control them. He had to smother that temptation as long as he could—especially now that he'd found the tempering magic.

The Eidolon and Katorins both feared him.

Both races wanted him dead rather than allow him to return to Katori with near absolute power. He had to show the Katorins restraint and control over the magics warring inside him. But how could he do that when his Katorin-side magics were out of control and his Eidolon magic was a raging, dark river he couldn't summon without tempering.

Tonight, in Kendra Martin's presence, he'd felt that strong tempering magic pulsate from her, calming and focusing the opposing magics he carried.

And like him, she had the greening.

He'd felt her magic infuse that old house until it thrummed across the fields and vibrated into his bones. Until he had to see her with his own eyes, feel the presence of his salvation.

He'd waited centuries for her. He'd traveled from the darkest reaches of Africa through the dark ages of Europe and into the dark alleyways of the New World. He never dreamed that he'd find his match in the middle of a cornfield in backwater Indiana. Now that he'd found her, he had to find a way to show her the Katorin heritage that she carried.

And the magic balled up inside her that waited for release.

He sighed. And if that wasn't enough to make her run screaming, he had to convince her to stand with him against the Eidolon. Before they discovered her and tried to destroy her, too.

He sat a long while in the cool shadows of the forest he'd conjured, knowing he had to contact his mother, give her a sliver of hope, a slim promise that his father might escape the oblivis and return to her. Tonight, he felt a tremor of hope that he might return home to see his mother, his sisters, and his only brother, Jaxon.

During the new ebony moon, he could contact his mother using a scrying surface. Allowing him to see through time and the distance— all the way back to Katori.

He rose to his feet and moved over to a tall wooden bookshelf covered in moss and draped in vines. From the top shelf, he slid out a thin, polished sheaf of obsidian. It weighed nearly twenty pounds as he carried it in both arms out the front door and onto his small porch of vine-draped, rusty wrought iron.

Velvet wash of twilight settled against the pond, turning the sky a deepening cornflower blue as a cold chill raked his shoulders. The new moon would rise dark again tonight in the warm, summer night sky, the air smelling like heat and grass, faint smell of toasted grain on the wind.

With the obsidian slab cradled against his chest, he grabbed an old axe leaning against the door and walked into the twilight. Toward the pond.

Lights snapped on along the isolated county road in this quiet countryside, including Kendra's.

He smiled, watching her move past the windows of the old blue Victorian farmhouse. Willowy and bright-faced, he imagined her in that tight red skirt, black stockings, and heels, phone pressed to her ear.

The back door slammed and Maddie Cowger, the next-door neighbor, headed out of Kendra's place and back to her own little grey ranch house on the other side.

Maybe Kendra would eventually forgive him for painting her lawn hot pink? He did rescue her purse from that grubby kid on the riding mower. Thought he'd help himself to her cash and anything else of value.

He felt the rustle of leaves against his palms as he reached the pond's edge. He laid the obsidian in the grass as small white daisies coiled around his hands. He let them fall to the ground as he gripped the axe handle. He sat down in the grass and laid the axe across his lap as he gazed across the still pond.

At the Martin house. Waiting for nightfall.

The Watchers would return tonight with the dark and he'd beat them back to Eidolon. Again.

But what if they discovered Kendra tonight? Before he was ready or able to protect her?

Before she'd mastered the magic hiding beneath her humanness?

Kendra had no idea how much power she'd inherited from Emmaline Martin. The moment she came within proximity to him, those powers had awakened. And she had no idea.

Probably hadn't even noticed it yet.

A single thought made things appear because she'd summoned them. A touch of her hand and the ground greened with life.

Something about that old house held power. Stirred the Fey blood running through her ancestry. He wasn't sure about its source but he'd felt its strength, its presence long after Emmaline had drawn her last breath. Even after she'd left the house for the last time, he still felt the pulse of power lying fallow, waiting for a return.

Kendra's return?

He wasn't sure. It was a human energy, something he didn't recognize, something from the old green country. A place where he'd once spent centuries, a land where he'd hidden in its forests and beyond its streams and plains while he searched for the tempering magic.

They called him Green Man in those Breton and Celtic villages.

He'd used his gift of uncontrolled greening whenever they had their backs to the wind, renewing their crops and protecting their forests from cutthroats.

As the edges of darkness hardened against the grass, a voice whispered to him on the wind, a taunting voice across the distance.

He scowled. Carvahl.

The man would try again to come through in Watcher form tonight, projecting his image across the span of worlds to this one. Trying to destroy him. Carvahl would be stronger tonight, but so was Shade.

Because he'd found Kendra's tempering. He had to convince her to use it—to help him focus his own magic.

After all these centuries, Kendra Martin was his chance to return home and stand against these murderers. His chance to take back his homeland.

"You give yourself far too much credit," the voice in the dusk called to him.

He glanced down at the obsidian slab. Carvahl glared at him from the dark mirrored surface. Long, narrow face, angry dark eyes, thick hair cut short and shaggy against his tanned skin.

Almost elven in form but dark, shadowy.

Carvahl had aged since the last time Shade had faced the usurper of Eidolon's throne. Through treachery and scheming, the only way Eidolon got things done now.

A way that Shade was still a part of...a way that he struggled against every day.

"You look old, Carvahl," Shade said with a smirk. "Isn't it time you passed your obsession to kill me onto someone younger? More capable?"

Carvahl's dark eyes gleamed with a faint silvery light.

Preparing to send his shadow self across the distance. Already, his form had lost a hint of its solidness, growing almost fuzzy and out of focus.

"I've waited this long," said Carvahl, emotion ebbing into a droning growl. "Not even you can stop us forever. And sooner or later, we'll gather up what's left of your scattered people...and destroy them." He laughed, his voice thick and dark. "Your father asks about you every day, Shade, calling from the depths of the oblivis. Give yourself up and give him some company. He's so lonely after all these years down in the pit."

"Eat dirt, Carvahl," Shade snapped, glaring. "I'll see you in that cavern by the time this is over. Or in Hell."

"You grow more desperate with the passing days," said Carvahl, his voice softer now, the silvery glow blotting out his hard brown irises. The silver light ringed his head now, washing across his face and moving downward. "What you seek doesn't exist. Katorins and Eidolon are oil and water. Nothing will make them mix within you, Shade. Nothing."

Shade grinned. Until today. Until he'd stood within an arm's reach of Kendra Martin, he might have agreed. He clutched the axe in both hands.

"Bring it on, Carvahl. I'll knock you back through again—just like last night."

Carvahl's body trembled, his form fading beneath a Watcher's silver wash of light.

Shade scrambled to his feet, axe raised, ready to strike at the first spheres of light that emerged through the veil of darkness.

Energy hummed across his forearms, the hairs standing on end as he felt the electric rush building like a thunderstorm.

The flash behind him startled him.

He pivoted, axe raised.

Hundreds of little winking lights filled the air.

He swung the axe through the pulses of light.

One by one, they crackled and went dark. Exploding like firecrackers. More Watchers exploded as Shade cut through the cloud of lights with the axe blade.

Another cloud of lights rose from the pond.

Shade smashed through them, extinguishing their light with his axe. They popped like gunshots, causing a momentary rush of light then darkness.

He'd only destroyed half the lights when the next plume lit the sky like heat lightning.

Something felt wrong.

Too many lights rushed toward him now. Too fast.

They'd never come through like this before, so many, so fast! He couldn't let them gain form. If too many achieved physical form, he'd have to retreat from this place. Like all the others. He wasn't proud. He'd run before. But he couldn't let them discover Kendra who knew nothing about Watchers or Eidolon—much less Katori.

Shade rushed into the clouds of lights, beating the air with the axe until a crush of gold lights exploded around him.

One of the Watchers slipped past his axe and began to coalesce into a shadow against the growing darkness.

He gritted his teeth, arms burning as he whipped the axe into another wash of tiny lights crowding around him.

The slash across his back slammed him into the ground. Dazed, he struggled to his feet, the pain sharp.

"You're as arrogant as your father, Shade," Carvahl's angry voice echoed from the shadows. "It's what landed him in prison."

Shade shouted and lunged at the growing shadows, axe slicing through the night. Sparrows took flight. Ducks scattered around the water's edge.

He fell into a stand of seedlings near the pond and hit the spongy ground. Pond water seeped into his shirt as he scrambled up, axe raised.

A cloud of Watchers flitted across the pond toward him.

Shade fanned the lights with the axe blade.

They popped like live wires, sending tendrils of smoke into the night sky.

Even as he stepped up his battle against the Watchers, he felt more of them gaining form.

Presences massed in the darkness like vampires.

He'd been too slow tonight.

Until the sun rose, he was their prey. Had his sluggish response cost him everything?

Talons raked his shoulder.

He gasped, nearly dropped the axe. He fell to one knee as the searing pain consumed him.

"You've gotten rusty, Shade. And you're weak. Too much Katorin poison in your veins."

Carvahl's smooth laughter carried on the breeze that blew across the pond.

Leaves rustled. Shadows whispered.

Shade ran toward the porch. Eidolon surged behind him, shadows on shadow.

"I gave you the chance to stand at my right hand, Shade."

Carvahl's voice was nearly against his ear.

"At the right hand of evil? No thanks."

He veered right.

Careened back toward the pond as a new plume of Watchers rose in the night again.

"You could have ruled it all as my second but you betrayed us."

Something moved to his right.

Shade ducked and thrust the axe handle upward, catching something solid in the darkness.

A muffled cry touched his ears.

He bolted. Turned. Set himself, axe raised.

As a cloud of lights swarmed him.

He chopped at the glow. Lights crackled, exploding in sparks.

A sharp blow slammed between his shoulder blades. Air wouldn't fill his lungs.

He gasped, falling to his knees, unable to draw the axe into a swing.

"You know I'll never let you reach Katori alive, Shade," said Carvahl, the voice at his ear now and something pressed against his face.

Claws raked across his neck.

He jerked his arm up, warding off a slash that might have cut his throat.

Warm stickiness dripped down his neck, streaming down his forearm. He fell into the grass, still clutching the axe.

"Fight them, Shade—fight them!"

The achingly familiar voice cut through the gouging pain.

He crawled through the cool grass toward the obsidian slab lying beside the pond. His mother's desperate gaze stared back at him, shocked and frightened.

"Shade!" she cried, reaching out as if she could stretch her fingers through the obsidian and touch his face. "Hold on. You're our last hope."

"And finally, that hope will be extinguished."

Carvahl's voice was deadly close now.

Shade rolled onto his back, axe in hand, as shadowy shapes mobbed him.

A dull whine buzzed in his ears like insects. Dark energies built inside him. He thrust the axe blade up as claws cut across his chest.

And cleaved the shadowy shape in two. It popped in a fiery burst and dissipated into smoke.

"You can't get all of us before sunrise, Shade," Carvahl said, his voice a whisper now.

Shade felt Carvahl moving with the night.

The Watchers had gone dark. He had no idea how many other Eidolon had gained shadow form. Besides Carvahl.

Carvahl would pick his moment. He wouldn't rush into an attack like the other Eidolon, eager to brag that they'd tasted Shade's blood.

Shade lifted his axe, swinging at the shadowy ripple to his right.

An Eidolon shrieked, falling away into smoke.

Fire burned down his right arm. A deep gash.

He screamed and dropped the axe. Wincing, he clutched at the bleeding wound on his forearm and staggered to his feet.

As his axe rose from the grass. Damn.

"It's over, Shade," said Carvahl, laughing as Shade's axe glinted in the faint glow of lights along the country road.

In Eidolon hands.

Shade backed away.

He'd failed his mother and her people. He'd failed his father, too. All these years, he'd fought for them. Battled princes of Eidolon. Assassins. Stayed alive when so many others fell.

Now, Carvahl would keep the throne. And Katori would fall. Because he'd gotten tired and weak.

The axe blade smashed against the ground as Shade side-stepped the blow.

Throbbing pain pounded through him as he stumbled backward, away from the axe as it fell toward him again.

"Thanks for keeping it so sharp," Carvahl taunted as Shade backed away toward the porch. "It makes killing you much easier, Shade."

Shade cursed under his breath, stumbling over a rock, and nearly falling. He regained his footing and dodged the axe blade again.

"I've waited centuries for this moment!" Carvahl shouted.

He didn't see the edge of the porch.

His heel smashed against the boards and he fell against the wooden glider.

For a moment, the night rushed in but the porch light gleamed overhead as he shook off the pain.

Until shadows engulfed its feeble light. Strangling it.

Carvahl's hazy form stood over him, axe raised over his head.

"Goodnight, Shade"

Carvahl laughed as the axe fell toward Shade's chest.

5

The half-empty white carton of sesame chicken sat beside the nearly empty carton of chicken and broccoli on the dining table, faded walnut covered in a red tablecloth. Its curved Queen Anne legs were dull against the gleam of copper pots that hung on a copper rack above the white stove.

Kendra spooned out a glob of sticky white rice onto the white Corelle plate and passed the carton to Maddie. Maddie gazed out at the backyard through the kitchen door a moment then dropped a spoonful of white rice onto her plate.

"Pass me the sesame chicken," said Maddie, setting down the carton of rice.

Kendra set down her wooden chopsticks and handed Maddie the carton.

"I should try those," said Maddie, pointing at the chopsticks. "They'd be a great diet aid. I'd never get the food into my mouth."

Kendra laughed and picked them up again, setting them between thumb and forefinger. She picked up a piece of chicken and took a bite. The sauce dripped down her chin and she dabbed it off with a paper towel.

"Takes a little practice, that's all."

Maddie set down her fork, grinning. "Like conversing with Shade Fletcher? I can't believe he came over here and talked to you this afternoon."

Kendra smiled, still remembering his burning smile, long mop of dark bangs, and those wild, arctic blue eyes watching her with such intensity. Yet he had a playful look in those eyes. Not the angry, acidic persona she'd expected. Even now, she couldn't shake off that distracting effect he'd had on her. Made every thought in her head vanish.

She couldn't even hold onto her fury at him after he'd rescued her purse and its contents. She'd never felt such an attraction before. It almost gnawed at the pit of her stomach. Like a hunger that no food could satisfy. She'd thought about him all evening. Somehow, she'd have to find an excuse to go over there and say something to him.

Anything! See if this weird ache went away.

"He's something, isn't he?" she said with a smile and propped her elbows on the table.

Maddie nodded. "Handsome devil. Definitely a different sort though."

"You got the devil part right but smokin' hot didn't quite cover it."

He had a knowing way about him that made him different. Like he knew way more than he was telling. He didn't have any sort of accent, no strange hairstyle, no odd mannerisms. What made him seem so different?

"Did he apologize for your yard?"

Kendra shook her head. He'd seemed proud of himself over that. "Are you kidding? I think he came over to gloat about it."

Maddie chuckled and took a drink of iced tea. "Sounds like Fletcher."

"Okay, that and he gave me my purse. I'd left it on the roof of my car and that lawn kid you hired was helping himself to an advance."

"What?" Maddie's mouth fell open. "Ricky Tait was going through your purse?"

Kendra nodded. "According to Shade Fletcher. I counted the money and it was all there."

A sheepish look replaced Maddie's smile. "I'm really sorry, Kendra. I had no idea Ricky would do something like that."

"Forget it," said Kendra with a wave of her hand. She laid her chopsticks on the plate, feeling stuffed. At least for now. "No harm done. Everything was there, including my credit cards."

"So, Fletcher rescued your purse." She crossed her arms, the trace of a frown forming. "That doesn't seem like the Shade Fletcher I know. He never gets involved in other people's business and he's never been the helpful type." Maddie was quiet a moment. "Did you ask him about my gazing ball?"

"No, I was too busy yelling at him about my lawn." Her voice softened. "Before he gave me my purse."

Before she'd looked into those wild blue eyes, before his smile had struck her dumb and mute. She wanted to tell Maddie how devastatingly handsome Shade Fletcher was and how much she wanted to ask him over for supper.

"So, he's not the ogre he tries to make us believe he is," said Maddie, leaning back in the chair as the smile returned to her face.

Kendra shook her head. "I really should find a way to thank him for rescuing my purse." And try to get past his distant, *don't mess with me* facade.

Maddie stared at her a moment, her eyes sparkling. "You're attracted to him."

"Oh, please," said Kendra, rolling her eyes. "He's so not my type. And even if he were, I'd never get past that bad attitude of his."

"You already have. He's never helped anybody that I know of and I know all the folks on this road." Her smile widened into a grin. "I think he's got a thing for you."

"That's ridiculous," Kendra snapped. "The man spray-painted my lawn hot pink."

Kendra rose from her chair, her back to Maddie as she stepped into the kitchen, empty glass in her hand, and opened the refrigerator. She slid out the pitcher of iced tea and refilled her glass.

"And got your attention, didn't he?" said Maddie as Kendra carried the pitcher over to the table. She smiled. "All of it."

"Refill?" Kendra asked.

Maddie waved her off. "No, thanks. I've gotta get home." She glanced at her silver Timex then slid out of the chair, plate in her hand. "Wheel of Fortune's coming on."

Kendra took the plate out of her hand and laid it in the scuffed white sink.

"Thanks for dinner, kiddo," said Maddie. She moved over to the back door. "I'll talk to you later in the week."

"Bye, Maddie," Kendra called as she cleared the table. "Thanks for everything."

Maddie left through the back gate. Kendra heard its squeak as she tossed the empty takeout cartons into the trash can under the sink. After rinsing the plates, she dropped them into Gem's small stainless-steel dishwasher tucked underneath the white cabinets. A birthday gift from Kendra and her mom. She chuckled as she emptied Maddie's tea and set the glass in the top rack. Gem always said her two hands were all the dishwasher she needed. Until Thanksgiving dinner when she and Kendra had a dozen place settings to wash. From then on, Gem said this little stainless-steel dishwasher was a godsend.

Kendra tore off a white sheet of paper towel from the spindle beside the sink and moved back to the table. She picked up her half-full glass of tea and wiped off the table.

The crackle of firecrackers shook the house.

Startled, Kendra nearly dropped her glass. She gritted her teeth, slamming the glass back on the table.

Fletcher was at it again.

Kendra threw away the dirty paper towels as another string of firecrackers exploded across the pond.

She looked out the window. Across the dark pond, sparks flew like a thousand fireflies and spilled into the darkness. Shade Fletcher stood in the middle of the sparks.

What in God's name was that man doing now?

She squinted as the flashing lights hit him just right. He ran around the yard like a mad man, something in his hands. A baseball bat maybe?

She shook her head, turning away from the window. Fletcher was probably drunk and making all that racket to annoy his neighbors again—especially her. He seemed to delight in his pranks. The hot pink lawn. Stealing Maddie's gazing ball. This was probably another one he'd cooked up.

Kendra ignored the racket outside and put the leftover food in the refrigerator. When everything was put away, she turned off the light in the kitchen. She sat down on the plain yellow sofa in Gem's family room.

The room was small, a bay window overlooking the garden. Plain walnut end tables flanked the sofa and separated two blue wingback chairs that sat in front of the window. An old Sony television sat on a simple black stand in front of the sofa. Kendra wondered if Maddie had turned on cable for her. She opened the end table drawer to her left, the whole room smelling like Chinese takeout, and fished out the remote.

A concussion of firecrackers startled her again, the sounds more like explosions.

People shouted but she couldn't make out the words. Another wild party.

She gritted her teeth, flicking the remote's power button. Pat Sajak's voice blared through the room and she stabbed at the volume until his voice was a polite murmur, just loud enough to cover the firecrackers snapping outside.

Another explosion rattled the windows.

Kendra slammed down the remote and jumped up from the couch. Enough was enough.

"You've had it, Fletcher," she said and reached for her phone, intending to call the police.

But something made her stop. No, she didn't need the police to handle this problem. She'd handle it herself. Besides, who knew what Fletcher might do if the cops showed up again tonight.

She slid her bare feet into her black flip flops and went out the back door. She stood at the gate and listened a moment, trying to identify the voices.

Angry voices rumbled across the pond, the cascade of firecrackers making her jump with every pop.

Was it a fist fight? Or something worse?

She grabbed the hoe propped by her door, marched out the back gate, and into the cool evening grass that swished against her calves.

Blurs of movement and more clouds of sparklers fluttered around the pond's western edge. More loud pops of firecrackers grew louder, nearly deafening her as she hurried across the field.

When she reached Fletcher's side of the pond, Shade stood there, swinging a baseball bat at the air.

No, at the sparks in the air.

Had he lost his mind? And where were all the people?

She'd heard their voices, but Fletcher stood alone in the darkness.

Kendra moved toward him. He was at least twenty feet away.

The distant voices were distinct. She couldn't quite make out the words. Except for Fletcher, his front yard was empty of anything but hundreds of dandelions.

A winding gravel driveway rounded the pond's northern edge and ambled left toward the aging white ranch house. It stood between tall stands of mature maples and oak trees, a small clearing in the dense forest surrounded the house.

Again, voices rang out but no one was there. No one at all.

"Shade Fletcher!" she shouted. "I warned you about the wild parties!"

He didn't turn toward her, instead swinging the baseball bat at the air again.

The baseball bat caught a glint of light and sparkled in the growing darkness.

Kendra squinted, a cold feeling settling in the pit of her stomach. It wasn't a baseball bat.

It was an axe.

She froze in mid-step. Shade Fletcher had gone mad...and what was he doing with an axe again?

He stumbled, fell, and pulled himself back to his feet.

Kendra moved closer, fascinated, and frightened as his voice rose in the night. Maybe she should have been afraid? But something about the lights and Fletcher's determination made her more intrigued than anything.

"Bring it on, Carvahl! I'll knock you back through, just like last night."

Who was he talking to?

"You can't get us all before sunrise, Shade."

That voice carried around the pond and Kendra heard every word as if the speaker stood beside her.

She glanced around, trying to find the owner of that voice. But all she saw was Fletcher.

This made no sense.

More explosions shook the ground as she rushed after Fletcher who moved toward his house.

Fletcher was about ten feet from her when he fell to the ground. He cried out in pain, the axe falling out of his hands.

"It's over, Shade," said that voice again as Fletcher scrambled backward toward the porch.

Kendra's mouth gaped, staring. As the axe hung in the air above Fletcher.

That no one held or swung. The axe blade whumped into the ground. Inches from Fletcher's leg.

Chills rushed down her spine. An axe wielded by something unseen? Had she lost her mind, too?

"Thanks for keeping it so sharp," said the voice as Fletcher backed toward the porch. "It makes my job much easier."

She crept forward, hoe braced in both hands as she passed through the twinkle of gold lights. Glittering like fireflies.

She stood three feet from the axe.

Her skin crawled as the horrid thing moved through the air. If she hadn't seen the determination and rage on Fletcher's face, she'd have thought this was another one of his pranks.

Fletcher staggered to his feet. Tripped over the porch's edge and fell.

"I've waited centuries for this moment!"

The axe rushed toward him, no one holding it.

Kendra chased after it.

For a moment, it hung above Fletcher. And plunged toward his chest.

Kendra swung the hoe, deflecting the blade. The axe slammed against the wooden porch, lodging between the boards.

"What's this?" the voice shouted.

She heard it as clearly as her own voice.

But there was no one there!

"What's happening, Fletcher?" she demanded.

His haunted gaze darted toward her and his eyes grew wide. "What are you doing over here?" he shouted.

Kendra's mouth bobbed open, the fear trembling through her now. He rolled left, grabbed hold of the axe, and tore it free from the porch boards.

And ran at her.

She screamed, thrusting the hoe up to block the blow, fearing that axe would cleave through her skull.

But he rushed past her.

She turned, watching him swing the axe, smashing it into the clusters of gold lights floating on the wind. They exploded like firecrackers with every swing.

The noises she'd heard across the pond.

Kendra stood frozen until the last of the lights winked out. He stepped out of the smoky trails that hung in the air, axe balanced in both hands.

"You stay away from me!" she shouted, holding up her hoe again. "You're crazy. I don't know what's going on over here, but you're crazy!"

But he kept walking toward her. When he was within two feet of her, he let the axe handle fall to his side. He stepped so close that she smelled his sweat, saw the rise and fall of his exhausted breaths. Blood trickled down his left arm and his shirt was torn open in three places. That dark hair was disheveled, his face bruised and tired. She didn't understand what he'd gone through, but he'd been in a fight for his life.

She wanted to reach out and caress his cheek, smooth the worry lines pressing into a frown on his handsome face.

"You saved my life," he said finally, unblinking.

Kendra shook her head, letting the hoe fall to her side. "I don't know what I did...or why. It just happened."

He studied her for several moments until a sigh rattled through his chest. He smiled.

"Great instincts, Kendra. Saved my life."

She returned his smile and stepped closer. "Least I could do for a guy who saved my Prada purse."

He nodded, chest heaving, eyes closing. And began to sink.

"Fletcher?" She dropped the hoe and grabbed his arms as he sank to the ground. "You okay? Talk to me, Fletcher."

When he didn't respond, she gently shook him until his eyes rolled open. She slid her arm around his waist, trying to hold him upright, but he was too heavy for her. She braced him against her body.

"You need a doctor," she said with a gasp.

He shook his head. "Only need you," he said in a hoarse whisper.

A shiver of excitement rippled through her. "Me?"

"Yes," he said and squeezed her hand. He lifted it toward the torn shoulder of his shirt and pressed her palm against it. "You have no idea who you are, Kendra Martin."

"Of course, I do," she said, distracted by his touch, by the heat pulsing through her as she felt his bare shoulder against her fingertips. The molded curves of defined muscles and smooth, pale skin. The cool cedar smell of him. "I'm Kendra Alexis Martin, daughter of Joan and Harry Martin."

He nodded, his breathing still rough. "Granddaughter of—of Emmaline O'Riley Martin. Great granddaughter of—Aeryn O'Riley ni Katori." He sucked in a labored breath, eyes looking weak as he held her hand. "Holder of the tempering flame and—the greening. Slayer of the Fallen."

She couldn't stop the laugh that slipped out. Slayer of the Fallen?

Fletcher definitely had a loose screw rattling around in his brain. But it was such an attractive head.

"Try not to talk, Fletcher," she said.

His hand was so hot against hers. So soft, blisters across his smooth palm. She'd expected rough, calloused hands, but the blisters told her he wasn't used to swinging that axe.

"You're a little out of your head."

"No, listen to me," he said with a hiss of breath. He gripped her hand and she felt his anxiousness. "I know it sounds crazy but all of it's true. I'll explain more later—about the lights and the axe." He sighed, letting his head fall back against her shoulder. Those ice-blue eyes pierced her heart as he stared at her. "Didn't want you to find out like this."

Kendra drew in a breath, taking a moment or two to recover from his intensity. And did her best not to laugh at the absurdity.

"Fletcher, how many beers have you had tonight?"

Anger sparked in his eyes. He stared at her for several long moments.

His unblinking stare unnerved her, frightened her, yet she couldn't look away. Didn't want to look away.

"As many as you had, Martin," he replied. "None. You saw the axe. And you blocked it. So, don't go dismissing what you saw to a pint of beer."

His gaze moved past her, frustration shadowing his forehead.

She frowned. "And what *did* I see, Fletcher?"

"The Eidolon," he said with a sigh. "The Fallen."

"What are the Eidolon? The Fallen?"

"The people behind the shadows. Wielders of twilight, dark magic, and friend to none. They're as much a danger to humankind as they are to me and my people."

Seriously?

His deadly serious gaze sent chills down her spine. Had

something unseen really held that axe? Or was she hallucinating from bad Chinese takeout?

Whatever craziness he spouted didn't matter because he believed it. She'd bring it up with him in the daylight. But something about his words gave her a shiver of dread. She'd seen that axe float in midair and nearly kill him.

That wasn't a prank. It was real.

But Fletcher's presence was comforting, the strong feel of his shoulder against her hand easing her anxiety.

"I don't know what any of this means," she said. "I'm sorry, Fletcher but it sounds crazy."

"You'll understand soon," said Fletcher. "I doubt it'll make any more sense, but there's a lot more you need to know."

He sagged against her, nearly a dead weight, but she kept her hand against his shoulder.

"Let's forget all this fallen one stuff and get you inside. You need to rest. And get some bandages on these wounds."

She winced and held open the thin fabric at his shoulder. Deep gouges curved across his shoulder, oozing dark blood. He might even need stitches.

She nudged him to try and stand, gripping his arms, steadying him. He clutched her wrist, staring into her eyes again and she felt herself melt into the intensity of his arctic gaze.

"I can't yet," he said. "Not 'til sunrise."

The man had taken leave of his senses. He needed professional help beyond a paramedic.

"Why?" Kendra asked, shaking her head. "You're exhausted and probably need stitches."

He pointed over her shoulder.

She turned, still holding onto Fletcher.

A flurry of gold lights rose from the pond. Like crazed fireflies, they darted toward Fletcher.

He let go of her arms and bent to retrieve the axe. Hefting it onto his shoulder, he stumbled past her toward the cloud of lights. He swung at them like a mad man.

"Fletcher, what are you doing?"

He ignored her, concentrating instead on the lights.

The air crackled every time his axe connected with the lights. And they kept coming.

Gold lights swarmed him like hornets.

One of the tiny spheres touched his skin, burning him.

He winced, axe in motion, movements stiff and slow. He began to limp.

Kendra picked up the hoe and hurried beside him, swinging at the lights. They exploded into showers of sparks.

Coils of smoke drifted on the wind, smell of ozone strong.

"What are these things?" she asked, hacking at the lights with her hoe.

"Watchers," said Fletcher, his voice tired. "Assassins. They come through on the ebony moon to try and destroy me. And get a foothold in your world."

Ebony moon? My world? Where exactly was this guy from anyway?

"Why do they want to kill you?" Kendra asked.

She swung the hoe in a tight arc, trying not to hit Fletcher.

"I'm heir to both the Katorin and Eidolon thrones," he replied with another swing of the axe. "But the Eidolon would rather see me dead than ascend either throne."

Katorin throne? Eidolon throne? She had no idea what he was talking about. It sounded absurd, but Fletcher believed it. And she couldn't explain away the axe or these strange faerie lights that burned skin and exploded on contact.

"What's stopping you from taking this throne now?"

"I lack control of...of the dark magic I carry," he said.

"Dark magic?" Kendra asked, casting a sideways glance at him.

As a kid, she believed in magic. When she spent summers in Gem's garden. But dark magic sounded crazy.

She swung the hoe at the lights that hovered near her face. Their heat was like a sunburn when the cluster of lights exploded.

"I'm half Eidolon," he said.

Kendra's eyes widened. "Those things I can't see? The thing that tried to kill you?"

He nodded. "I carry those same energies inside me but I can't focus them. Control them." He swung the axe again and the sky darkened as the last of the lights vanished in a puff of smoke. "I can't control the magics I inherited." He sighed, running a hand through those thick, dark bangs. "And without that control, I can't stop the Eidolon from destroying everything I hold dear."

"But aren't they your people, too?" She frowned, not quite understanding any of this craziness.

"My people," he said, almost spitting, and sank to his knees. "They imprisoned my father for sending me through to your world. For saving me. And for joining with a Katorin woman. I love my father, but his people aren't my family. My mother's people exiled me here—to protect me."

"To protect you?"

He nodded. "Until I find a way to control my dark magics, I'm stuck here. And as long as this dark moon fills the night sky, the Eidolon can take form here. The Watchers only last until dawn. First, they come through as Watchers—the little lights you see now. When they reach your world, the Eidolon take shadowy form. And remain here until their projections are destroyed."

She frowned and knelt beside him, her hand on his shoulder. "You do this—repelling them—every new moon?"

He nodded, head bowed, chest heaving.

She didn't understand any of this but something about Shade Fletcher seemed honest and true.

And she'd seen these Watchers with her own eyes. She'd even destroyed them. She'd watched one shadowy form wield an axe and nearly kill Fletcher.

As soon as she got back to the house, she'd question everything that happened out here, but right now, she believed something about Fletcher's story.

"How can you fight them all off? With so many stalking you?"

He shrugged. "It's getting more and more difficult. Tonight, they gained ground on me for the first time." He fixed her with his gaze. "Without your help tonight..."

His voice trailed off and the fear in his eyes cut through her. She barely knew the man, but he looked shaken. Sober. Exposed. But admiration burned in those arctic blue eyes. For her, she realized.

She laid her hand against his face, wanting to ease his pain and fear.

All of this sounded like a bad drug trip, but he looked so haunted and vulnerable at that moment—and that was incredibly attractive. She couldn't help herself. She wanted to touch him.

"Thank you," he said in a whisper.

She leaned toward him. Gently. Slowly. Kissing his lips.

He kissed back, his mouth covering hers like a drowning man gulping for air.

The connection was fiery. Electric. Thrumming.

His arms slid around her, pulling her hard against him.

She melted into his embrace. But the intensity overwhelmed her, frightened her.

She pulled back. "I'm sorry," she said. "I—I'm sorry."

It was all she could say. She'd only wanted to comfort him, but there was nothing casual about Shade Fletcher. It was too much. The emotions built like flood waters. Surging through flood gates.

She had to climb out or drown.

"No, it's my fault," he said. "This connection—between us. It's intoxicating." He sank back in the grass, watching her from beneath thick, dark bangs. "I know all of this is a bit overwhelming." He nodded toward the pond.

"A bit?" she cried. "The hot pink lawn I could handle but this..." She gestured at Fletcher's axe. "Shadow people and exiles and dark magics and other realms—way more than I'm prepared to handle, Fletcher."

He nodded. "I know. It's too much. You should go home and get some sleep. And forget all of this."

She shook her head, wanting only to kiss his fiery mouth again. She fought the urge as she sat down in the cool grass beside him.

"Afraid I can't forget any of this, Fletcher. And I couldn't sleep, knowing you might be out here getting slaughtered."

He rose on his elbows, watching her, studying her as she gripped the hoe. "What's that mean?"

She slid the hoe across her lap. "It means I'm staying put until morning. To ease my conscience."

"You barely know me. Why would you stay out here and risk your life?"

She shrugged, watching his wild eyes lighten. "To make sure you don't spray paint my lawn hot pink again—the moment I go to bed."

He chuckled. "I'm out of hot pink and I'm little busy right now."

"Will they come at you like this again?" Kendra asked, motioning toward the pond.

He gripped the bridge of his nose with thumb and forefinger, his right hand gripping the axe handle.

"That was the bulk of their forces for now. Takes them twenty-four hours to regain the energy to come through in Watcher form again. And they can only come through in close proximity to their target."

At last, he looked up at her, a smile brightening his haggard face.

"And tomorrow night, a sliver of blessed moon will appear in the sky again."

The hoe's wooden handle rasped against her palms, burning little blisters across her hands.

"Is that good?" she asked.

He nodded. "Yeah. Watchers can't come through again until the next ebony moon."

"Good," she said. "Then we hang on until morning, right?"

Fletcher glanced up at the clear, starry sky. "It'll be a long time before morning. Sure you're up for it, Martin?"

She rolled her eyes at him. "I'll be fine. You worry about that shoulder of yours."

"This one?" he asked, holding open the gaping tear in the fabric.

Kendra nodded, but her mouth fell open when he revealed thin red scars where oozing gouges had been only moments ago. She pointed at the wounds.

"How could they heal so fast?" she demanded.

The corners of his mouth quirked. "Part of your gift, Kendra."

"Fletcher, I ruin Band-Aids trying to apply them. I don't have those kinds of skills. I'm only a change management consultant that likes to garden."

None of her skills had prepared her to deal with Shade Fletcher and his wild stories. She could have handled it if he'd simply been crazy. But he wasn't. Besides, she'd seen things she couldn't explain. The healed wound was too much.

Had she really done that or was Fletcher just playing with her?

"Like it or not, it was your doing, Kendra," said Fletcher, sitting up in the grass. "You've got the greening. You'd have discovered it in a few days anyway."

"How?" Kendra asked, brow furrowing.

Fletcher pointed across the pond toward Gem's Victorian house. "Through that old house."

"How do I have this...this greening as you call it?"

"Gotta be from Emmaline," said Fletcher, groaning as he rubbed his sore shoulder. "She's part of the Katorin bloodline."

"Like you?" Kendra asked.

"Like me," he said with a nod. "Except I'm half Eidolon."

She tugged on the thick grass blades. "Half shadows and half what?"

Fletcher was quiet for a moment and Kendra wanted to know what he was thinking. Until this afternoon, she'd never even met the man. How did that happen anyway?

She should be at home sleeping instead of out here in the dark with her crazed, axe-wielding neighbor. She smirked. Sultry, smokin' hot, axe-wielding neighbor. Through the tears in his shirt, she'd caught glimpses of his well-toned abs and pecs, felt his lean body against her, tasted that sexy mouth.

"Half Katorin," he said finally. "And protector. Katorins protect life with their magic, but the Eidolon destroy and assassinate what they can't control. If my father hadn't been useful to them, they'd have already killed him."

Kendra wasn't sure how much she believed about Shade Fletcher's stories, but she'd deal with that in the daylight.

Lights floated up from the pond and Fletcher tensed. With the axe handle tight in his hands, he rose unsteadily to his feet.

"They're back," he said through gritted teeth.

Kendra rose from the grass, wishing she'd worn tennis shoes instead of these stupid flip flops. She raised the hoe into the air as lights fluttered toward her like locusts.

6

By morning, Shade and Kendra had destroyed the remaining Watchers that came through the veil.

The night had been sobering. It was the first time he'd failed to fight off the Eidolon.

Even now, he worried how many had gained shadow form when his back was turned.

If Kendra hadn't been there...he would be dead.

He wondered if there were other halflings left like him, those carrying the energies of both Katorin and Eidolon—even though Eidolon magic rarely manifested in halflings. Ice blue eyes were difficult to hide in shadow.

Three others like him came through the veil—right before his parents sent him through it.

All three were dead now. Like the scores of others sent through since the war began. But none had manifested Eidolon magic. Only him.

Exhausted, every muscle screaming from exertion, Shade sank down in the dewy grass as the sun rose. A cardinal's insistent chirp echoed from a nearby spruce. He smiled and leaned over Kendra

Martin's sleeping form curled up in the tall, damp grasses and hugging the hoe against her chest.

She saved his life tonight.

He slid the hoe out of her grasp then brushed a wisp of dark hair out of her face, dirt smudging her chin.

His chest ached as he ran his thumb across her chin, wiping away the dark soil. She was so beautiful. He wouldn't have cared if she'd been a troll because he needed her tempering magic, but he'd never expected her to be...so beautiful. And he never expected to feel this way—about the woman who tempered him.

He'd never expected the fierce attraction that he struggled with even now. A woman who had already saved his life once. She had no idea that she'd be expected to do it again—on the other side.

In his realm.

Sliding his arms underneath her thin frame, he lifted her from the cool grass, the heat not yet baking the fields, and carried her around the pond. The smell of sweet grass and dew, with a hint of roasted grain, hung in the air. His arms and legs burned from the night's work, the dull throb constant as he carried her across the field and through her open back gate. It squeaked as he closed it behind him.

She never stirred. She was exhausted.

He remembered when Emmaline Martin lived here and the wondrous garden she'd cultivated. That quiet sanctuary had been such a magical place back then, when few Watchers pressed through the veil. They had many other Katorins to hunt down in those days—and weren't aware yet that Katori's and Eidolon's heir to the thrones had been exiled here.

Back then, Emmaline thought no one saw her magic. She thought that no one saw the faerie lights floating through her garden or heard the music that only those of the gift heard. At twilight, tiny Fey creatures roamed and played among the herbs and flowers as other magical creatures like griffins and unicorns visited. Even the faerie queen passed through once with her entourage. All of those magical beings had been displaced when Emmaline—and her garden—died.

He was heartened by the rose bushes that Kendra had bought and the bags of top soil she'd already spread, weeds culled. She had to remember this garden from her childhood. Maybe she wanted to bring back that little corner of magic? It was the only place where Shade had felt at home since he'd left the druids and crossed Europe, heading east through Bulgaria and Transylvania to understand the darker human magics—like his own. And find that tempering control he required. He sighed. Or at least find peace from the warring magics within him.

He'd traveled with wizards, hunted with werewolves, dined with vampires, and drank with witches. Many of them anguished over their afflictions, as they called them. A few reveled in their gifts and gave him the simplest and most useful advice.

Accept these gifts and go on. So, he did.

Shade shifted Kendra's weight against him and stepped onto the small wooden deck, his footfalls hollow against the greying boards.

He knew the best and worst of humans. He shared a quarter of their heritage from his Katorin lineage. He resonated most with the Fey. Not those of royal blood but the common faerie folk. They were creatures of twilight, caught between the light and the night. They weren't perfection and sunshine. Like him, they carried darkness within them. And they had human-like emotions.

All creatures carried some thread of darkness alongside their light, but most didn't carry equal measure of both (as he did). And the cost of those shadows was usually high. Vampires paid a high price for their immortality and the dark nature of that price fascinated him. Those of faerie paid a price, too. Living as Methuselah with nowhere to cross over at the end. He was long-lived like the Fey and he understood the cruel streak that ran through them, brought on by envy of the humans sharing their world.

He understood that envy, but not because they were travelers to worlds the Fey could never touch.

No, he envied humans because of their ignorance.

They went through their daily lives and routines oblivious to the other realms that ebbed and flowed—rose and fell—around them.

Instead, they connected in quiet ways to their own here and now without detection.

Living in the moment was something he longed to do. Since he'd passed through the veil, he spent most days analyzing his past and planning for the next ebony moon. And the next. While the present slipped away.

Humans ignored what they didn't understand, dismissed what wasn't convenient or comfortable, and went about their day. Battles raged among the magical races, sometimes nightly in some parts of the world. Humans were so swept up by the minute details of their own lives, by their ability to concentrate on one thing—as only a human could do—they never saw most of these conflicts.

Shade felt it all shift and move around him. He felt the presence of magic in all its forms, including the blackest. All of it exhausted him, set him on edge for days at a time and he was powerless to ease the tension. Part of his inability to control the flow of magic through him, around him—within him.

He balanced Kendra's sleeping form against his chest and tried to open the door.

Locked.

Shade mumbled a word or two in the Eidolon tongue and pressed his thumb to the lock.

Click.

First try, he realized with a grin.

He'd never been able to focus even the simplest Eidolon spell, but this time, it worked on the first attempt. Was it Kendra's presence or dumb luck? He gripped the doorknob and turned it. This time, the door opened. He carried Kendra inside.

The old house looked different at Kendra's hands but it gave off that same sense of safety he'd found so comforting. He carried her past the yellow couches (Emmaline preferred florals), into the hallway, and up the stairs. The familiar warm creak of those stairs made him smile, remembering Emmaline Martin's frail but determined steps and her Fey ways. After all, her mother had come from the old country. The place of druids and faerie.

He stopped at the top of the stairs, glancing right then left at the bedrooms on either side of the stairs. A red suitcase stood against the wall of the master bedroom, painted a soft peach. He carried her into the peach room.

The room smelled crisp with fresh lemons, soft with rosewater, and warm with sunlight that pooled on the maple wood floors as he turned down the green and lavender quilt. He laid her on the bed, slid off those crazy rubber sandals humans always wore and draped the quilt across her.

He adjusted a mint green pillow underneath her head and brushed a kiss across her lips.

A charge surged through him at that brief connection, the force of his magic meeting hers. Like a magnet. Like lightning.

He straightened to his full six-foot-two height as a trace of light floral fragrance wafted up from the sheets.

He smiled. Lilacs after a spring rain.

It was her scent, he realized. Some sort of cologne, but it reminded him of Katori, of his mother's color-changing lilies. For a moment or two, he sat on the edge of the bed, watching Kendra sleep with the peacefulness that only children and humans shared.

"Sleep well, Kendra," he whispered.

A promise, he knew, as he spoke the Katorin words and summoned the paler energies within him. For a moment her body glowed with a faint pink light, his Katorin magic washing over her.

She would sleep a restful, healing sleep now. Something he desperately needed.

He left her on her side, underneath the quilt, the steady rise and fall of her chest comforting as he walked down the stairs and out the back door. He smiled at the gazing balls placed around the garden-to-be. Rich amethyst, vivid blue, and a dark teal gazing ball, reflected the world back in a fish eye view.

An empty pedestal stood beside a young Japanese maple with its feathery red leaves and he wondered if Kendra would place another of Emmaline's old gazing balls there. It was an ideal spot. The shiny orbs brightened the landscape and sprinkled a little Katorin magic through the garden.

Shade headed across the field toward the pond, his body aching. When he was halfway back to his house, he turned around, casting one more look at the blue Victorian.

Even from this distance, he felt the force of Kendra's tempering presence on him, soothing the dark energies roiling against his Katorin heritage. He looked forward to the garden's return. She would soon discover that she had her grandmother's greening magic.

Kendra had no idea she was part Fey and part Katorin. At her hand, magical creatures would return to this place, hidden from those who didn't believe, thriving among those who had patiently awaited their return.

Like him.

He needed their influence and guidance now more than ever. He had to prepare for his return to Katori and the battle he couldn't avoid, learning to command the Eidolon darkness inside him. Somehow, he had to teach Kendra about her own magic and convince her to help him. She had to stand with him against the Eidolon or all of it was lost. After they consumed Katori, they would enter Kendra's world, hell-bent on ruling the humans, too. Taking their resources. Enslaving anyone they couldn't control.

It would happen right before the humans' eyes and they wouldn't even realize it until the battle was already lost.

He had to become teacher and student, learning to control his own magic for the first time since it had appeared in him. And if it allowed him to spend time with Kendra Martin, he looked forward to every moment.

Shade stepped onto his porch and went inside the house, eyes closing from lack of sleep. He'd been up all night and needed to sleep soon but not before he spoke to his mother.

Sparrows twittered from the trees in his living room, soft moss carpeting the old wood floors as he walked into the kitchen. Scent of pine and shadow was strong as vines entwined the cabinets, ivy covering the countertops. A blue bird sang as it landed on top of the ivy-covered refrigerator when he opened the door. Pulling out a beer bottle, Shade twisted off the cap and pressed the bottle to his lips.

He walked into the living room, stepping around the yellow and red maples. River birch with their white bark clustered around the fireplace as he collapsed onto the moss-covered recliner.

Gentle trickle of a stream filled the room as it wound its way through the family room and dining room. His eyelids drooped at the lulling sound of the stream and he laid his head back against the soft moss. The air smelled crisp and clean. The faint whiff of Kendra's light floral scent—lilacs and lilies—wafted up from his clothes.

Beside him, on the tree stump end table, lay a polished obsidian slab. He'd left another out by the pond. Obsidian reflected back unseen magic and ley lines that ran across the landscape. Those lines connected him with other realms, including his beloved Katori. Where his mother and sisters waited for his return. He wondered if his youngest brother, Jaxon, still blamed him for Father's imprisonment.

Shade took another sip of Oberon beer and set it on the stump. After taking a few moments to gather his thoughts, he lifted the obsidian slab from the table and laid it in his lap.

Summoning his Katorin energies was easy. Focusing them was hard, a skill he lacked. Something he hoped Kendra could teach him in time.

It took Shade over an hour of concentration and missteps before he managed a hazy image across the obsidian slab. His breath caught, throat tightening as the bruised face of his mother, Mallora, appeared on the mirrored surface. He hadn't seen her face in months. He frowned at the swollen cut that curved above her right eye. She looked weak and unsteady.

"Mother! What happened to you?"

"Shade?" She squinted at him, smiling, her eyes welling with tears. "Shade! It's been so long...how are you? Is it safe for you to talk? I've been so worried."

He reached shaky fingers toward her face, wanting to ease her pain. Her curly mahogany hair was tied back from her squared face.

Her wide-set hazel eyes seemed bright, like the yellow maple leaves drifting down around him.

Was it hope or a mother's relief?

"For now, it's safe," he said, eyes stinging with moisture when he saw the faint bruising across her cheekbone. "Now, tell me what happened."

She smiled at him, brushing away tears. "It's nothing. A close call with the Eidolon guard, but I'm fine."

"Are you sure?"

It tore at him, knowing that even if she wasn't fine, there was little he could do to stop it. Not from his exile. He balled his hands into fists and struck the arm of the chair. The spring green moss cushioned the blows, muffling the sound.

"Yes, my son—for now, we're okay. Don't worry about me. I know how to hide from them. I was a little too slow in my escape."

His eyes narrowed, at last understanding what she'd done. "You slipped into Eidolon to see Father, didn't you?" His voice was sharper than he'd intended, but the thought of her risking death to see Father made him crazy.

Nodding, she bowed her head. "I had to see him. It's been months, Shade—I had to know he was still alive."

Shade sucked in a breath and grabbed the bottle of beer. He pressed it to his lips and took a long, numbing swig. Father must have been furious with her for taking such a risk.

"How is he?" he asked finally.

It tore at his gut knowing Father was there because of him.

"Braeden's thin but hopeful, Shade. He insisted I give you a message if I could."

Shade swallowed hard. "I'm listening."

"He sends his love and hope that you'll someday stand beside him against Carvahl and his troops. He says he's holding on for that day."

Shade squeezed his eyes closed, fighting the sting in his eyes and the knot in his throat. He took another hard pull from the beer. Guilt burned through his stomach. The man had sacrificed himself to get Shade out of Katori, away from the Eidolon—his own people. Shade alone carried equal measure of Eidolon and Katorin energies. His siblings had been spared the scourge of Eidolon darkness.

He wondered if sometimes they wanted him dead like so many others. His threat to the Eidolon realm was very real and because of it, the Eidolon hunted his family. Even if he'd never been born, Katori would still be scattered to the winds by the Eidolon. They'd long overtaken Katorin cities and villages, disappointed and angry when they realized that Katori wasn't a place. It existed in its people and as long as the Katorins fought back, their realm could never fall.

"If you get the chance, tell him..." His voice cracked and he pulled in a quick breath to hide it. "Tell him I love him, okay?"

"Of course, Shade," she said, reaching out to him. "He knows you love him."

Shade nodded, his throat too tight to speak.

"I wish I could be there to fight them," he said finally through gritted teeth. "It's my—"

"Don't you dare, Shade," his mother said, her voice rising. "Don't you dare blame yourself. Braeden and I refused to give you up to those fiends."

"But if you had, maybe the war wouldn't still rage?"

His mother shook her head, hazel eyes turning hard with anger.

"Understand me, Shade, son of Braeden, Katorins don't sacrifice their children. If only you understood the gifts you carry and the hope they represent."

Shade ran a hand through his dark hair, wondering what his mother saw when she looked into his Eidolon blue eyes. He felt like a coward, turning his back on his family, but finding Kendra was a new hope for all of them.

"I've found her, Mother," he said, grinning as her eyes brightened.

"Found who, Shade?"

"The tempering. A woman who has the tempering. In her presence, I focused a simple Eidolon spell. I mastered it on the first try, Mother."

Tears welled in her eyes and slid down her cheek. "Is it true, Shade? After all this time?"

He nodded. "She has no clue about her lineage or the magic she carries. I'll have to teach her to use it." And convince her to help him, something that wouldn't be easy. He wouldn't mention that yet though.

"Oh, Shade—I can't believe it...after all this time, there may be an end to this."

"I hope so, Mother. Maybe I can finally stand up to Carvahl? Within Katori's walls. Defeat his forces. Forever."

"It's my constant prayer, Shade."

"How are the girls? And Jaxon?" He hoped their hatred had softened with the years. He couldn't blame them. After all, he'd taken their father away from them, caused him to be imprisoned.

"Jaxon is his usual sullen self and your sisters are well. Missing you."

He missed his youngest sister, Meriel, most. They'd been close as children and adulthood hadn't changed that relationship. He knew she loved him no matter what.

"Give them my love, Mother," he said finally. "Especially my Meriel."

Mother smiled. "She'll be thrilled with your news, Shade."

"I can't wait for the day when I can return."

He would prove their trust in him hadn't been misplaced. He would stand against the Eidolon and if need be, he'd offer his life to free Katori forever.

"So do I, Shade. Until then, stay well and safe. I love you, my son."

He smiled, touching her image on the cool obsidian.

"I love you. See you soon."

"Soon, Shade," she said as someone stepped beside her.

Thick mahogany hair, a face in profile, whispering in Mother's ear.

He squinted. His sister, Malise? The rush of pain across Mother's face sent a shiver of dread through him.

"What is it?" he asked.

"It's Serilda," she said.

Shade remembered her from a Katorin village, remembered her

pale blue eyes and curly nut-brown hair. She was like him, part Katorin and part Eidolon. Like him, she'd been sent through. He'd met up with her three or four times over the human centuries, deciding it best to stay apart and not draw too many Watchers. It was Katori's best chance for survival.

At the flood of tears streaking down Mother's face, Shade knew.

"She's dead, isn't she?"

Mother nodded.

"How?" Shade asked.

But he knew that answer, too.

So many Eidolon had swarmed through last night, more than he'd ever seen before. They had probably overwhelmed Serilda in the same way they'd nearly overtaken him.

"The ebony moon brought too many through," said Mother, shaking her head. "Serilda fought hard, Shade."

He nodded. That meant he was the last Eidolon halfling. All of the Watchers would focus on him now.

"I had the same experience last night," he replied. "I got some last-minute help. Otherwise, I might have..." His voice trailed off when the worry lines deepened across his mother's face.

"What happened last night?" she demanded.

"More came through than I'd ever seen before," said Shade, trying his best to downplay the situation. "Lucky for me I'd made contact with another halfling."

This statement seemed to ease his mother's fears. "The woman with the tempering?"

He nodded. "Together, we destroyed Carvahl's shadow self. I'm safe until the next ebony moon."

"What will you do next time?" she asked, the color washing out of her cheeks.

By the next new moon, Carvahl would hit him with everything he had. Now that he was the last.

Before then, Shade hoped to raise an army of magical creatures to stand against the Eidolon. Here and on the other side...on his side of the world. From vampires to the Fey, he would call them, but he was powerless without Kendra. He had to convince her that everything was at stake. That everyone would lose if the Eidolon gained control.

"Raise an army," he said. "Next time, Carvahl will hit me with everything he's got—now that Serilda and the others are gone."

"I fear for you, Shade," she said in a strained voice. "I fear for all of us."

It was only a matter of time before the Eidolon captured the rest of his family. And rounded up the remaining Katorins. His family and the others had run, staying ahead of the death squads so far, but with the other Eidolon halflings gone, they would all have to go into hiding.

"You've got to disappear for a while," said Shade, leaning toward her image in obsidian. "You've got to hide everyone until my return."

Mother nodded. "We'll leave Gwydon tonight." She stared down at the ground for several moments, the tears still trailing down her face. Finally, she looked up. "After tonight, you won't be able to contact us, Shade. Don't even try."

He wouldn't. It was too dangerous. "Guess this is goodbye for a while." He offered his most self-assured smile. "Until I show up on your doorstep."

"I pray for that day," said his mother. "Take care of yourself Shade and don't lose hope. The day is coming when the Eidolon rule will end."

"All my love," Shade said in a quiet voice.

"And mine to you." She blew him a kiss as her face faded into the mirrored darkness.

Shade covered his eyes as the images stopped flowing across the obsidian. Right now, all he felt was guilt and shame.

People died—and kept dying—while he struggled to focus his magic.

How many could he have saved? How many might have been spared if he'd only given himself up? What mattered now was Kendra. Through her, he could summon others.

With her by his side, he could face Carvahl.

Shade had one month until the next ebony moon. One month to train Kendra and one month to train himself.

When Carvahl returned, he would try to bring the whole of Eidolon through beside him. To kill Shade on this side like he'd destroyed the others—before Shade became a formidable enemy in the flesh. But he would defeat Carvahl here in the human realm and then pass through to Katori. He would face him within the old city walls.

For Serilda and the others that Carvahl slaughtered, he'd make that monster pay.

7

K endra awoke to sunlight and a soft bed, the familiar scents of lemon and roses settling around her. Until she jolted up from the mattress.

How did she get back here? To the house?

She remembered nothing except the endless flashes of light and Shade Fletcher beside her, along with the steady crackle of exploding firecrackers.

All of it seemed like a dream now and she wondered if she'd been here all night. But when she climbed out of bed, she wore blue shorts and yesterday's grubby grey T-shirt. Her flip flops lay beside the bed.

Had Fletcher carried her back here last night? That made her smile.

She slid out of her dirty clothes and tossed them into the clothes basket. After snagging her blue robe off the bedpost, she padded into the bathroom for a long, hot shower.

She turned on the water, letting it steam up the bathroom. So, what if the temp climbed to 95 degrees today! With buckets of humidity. She wanted a hot shower.

When she closed her eyes, those flashes of yellow light were afterimages in the darkness, exploding into showers of sparks at the edge of Fletcher's axe.

Last night had been so surreal. What did it all mean?

After a slight temperature adjustment, she shucked off her robe and climbed into the shower. The warm water rushed over her bare skin. She closed her eyes, remembering Fletcher's lean, toned body, haunting blue eyes, and playful smile. Those smooth hands running down her arms, cupping her chin. He'd battled those lights for hours with nothing to show for it but blisters.

She didn't understand what the lights were but she'd understood his desperation. No, she felt it. She'd never felt such a pull before, such a strong attraction to a man. To Shade Fletcher.

Kendra ran raspberry shampoo through her dark hair then conditioner before foaming shower gel across her body.

Maybe last night was a big joke Fletcher played on all new people? Laughing hysterically while she told her neighbors about strange creatures from an unseen world. To make her look like a real idiot—like that hot pink lawn.

Anger trembled through her body as she rinsed off conditioner and soap. He was probably laughing his ass off right now—at her. At how naïve she was for believing in faeries and shadows.

Who'd believe a wild story like that anyway?

Her mood darkened. Or maybe he was trying to get laid?

Dripping wet, she climbed out of the shower. She meant to set a couple towels by the tub. Wiping water out of her eyes, she turned toward the old oak cabinet on the wall. And tripped over two fluffy blue towels.

She grabbed one, wiped her face, and wrapped it around her hair. After drying her body with the other towel, she hung it across the white shower curtain rod.

She stared at the towels a moment. *How did they end up by the tub?*

"I know I didn't grab any towels last night," she said to her foggy image in the mirror, reaching for her robe and a comb.

It didn't make sense.

No more sense than Fletcher's shoulder wound that had healed before her eyes. And the shadow people—especially the one holding the axe.

He'd called them the Fallen. People of twilight—friend to no one.

She dismissed the thought and got dressed. It was hard to take a guy seriously about anything when he'd spray-painted her lawn hot flamingo pink. Besides, she didn't have time for shadows and pixie lights. She had a business plan to write. She wouldn't be in Indiana long anyway.

By August, she'd be back in Baltimore and Shade Fletcher would be a story she told over too many glasses of wine. With regret.

KENDRA SPENT THE ENTIRE DAY ON TONI'S BUSINESS PLAN, MAKING A barrage of phone calls and gathering pricing on distribution, shipping, and upscaling to a larger production facility. She took a break and ate a tuna salad sandwich.

But she didn't remember seeing that deli container of tuna salad.

Maddie must have put it in the fridge yesterday along with the garden-ripe tomatoes on the windowsill that she sliced.

By six o'clock, she set aside her ThinkPad and laid back on the yellow sofa. She'd gathered a lot of preliminary cost information. Tomorrow, she'd do research specific to the fashion industry. She had a few friends who worked in the business. She'd tap them for information tomorrow. But now, she needed a break.

She rose from the sofa in cut-off shorts and a purple and white layered tank top. *No suit and heels for this job*, she thought with a grin and slid her feet into her red Keds by the backdoor. She grabbed the lime green gardening gloves off the counter and went outside.

Time for a little greening therapy, as Gem used to say.

For the next two hours, Kendra planted rose bushes. And planted a bunch of Gem's wrapped seeds in the rich black soil she'd spread yesterday. She planted flower and melon seeds and drenched the soil in water. Afterward, she walked through the cleared paths, spade in hand, missing the mossy cobblestones that had once made a winding trail through the garden.

She passed yesterday's tilled dirt beds, imagining towering

delphiniums and coneflowers beside peonies and lavender. And tall stands of dinnerplate dahlias in burgundy, yellow, and purple. All the flowers she remembered from her childhood. She imagined all of them in their familiar places along the paths as she made the grand circle past the blue and green gazing balls gleaming on their stands.

Her heart dropped. Except the one under the Japanese maple. It was missing.

She rushed to the concrete pedestal, looking around it, behind it, under the maple's feathery growth of red leaves.

But the gazing ball was gone. She felt sick.

Maddie said her gazing ball had gone missing, too. Had someone stolen them right out of the yard?

Someone like Fletcher. She frowned. Playing another prank. Spray-painting lawns and stealing lawn ornaments? Really?

Anger rose hot in her cheeks. How many other lawn ornaments were missing in the area? She glanced across the pond at the dark ranch house. Would she wake up one morning to find forty gazing balls rolling around her front lawn?

"Damn it, Fletcher, if you're playing some kind of joke, it's not funny!"

Nothing stirred at Fletcher's place except the two swans gliding in graceful circles around the pond. She hurried up the garden path but stopped at her favorite Green Man sculpture against the house. He stared at her with kind eyes and a leafy expression.

"I wish you could tell me who took it," she said and hurried toward the patio.

"The Eidolon."

Kendra jolted at the familiar voice. She whirled around, spade raised.

Shade Fletcher stood at the gate, arms crossed, ice-blue eyes haggard as he leaned against it. Stubble shadowed his jaw, giving him a handsome, disheveled look. Her heart skittered into her throat. He wore a yellow short-sleeved camp shirt, unbuttoned, and olive cargo shorts.

"What did you say?"

He flashed an enticing smile. "You heard me," he said in that arrogant tone. "The Eidolon."

Kendra matched his stance, crossing her arms and mimicking his tone. "How would you know?" When he didn't answer, she filled the silence. "So why are you here? Come to gloat about the little joke you played on me last night?"

His brow furrowed. "Joke? What joke?"

She shifted her weight, hands on her hips. "Oh, come on! The little game with the fireworks. Bet you thought I'd look pretty stupid telling my neighbors about—shadow people, didn't you? Well, it didn't work!"

He gestured toward the pond. "You think last night was a joke I played on you?"

"Like my lawn," she said with a nod.

He laughed, but Kendra saw the annoyance in his gaze. "I guess I deserved that after the lawn prank, but believe me, Kendra—all of that was very real."

Kendra rolled her eyes. "Sure it was."

Fletcher held open his shirt. "You think this is my idea of a joke?"

Dozens of thumb-sized burns covered his smooth chest and those eight-pack abs. She gasped at the deep and angry claw marks curving across his shoulder, stomach, and left side. The shoulder was partly healed but the other wounds looked puffy and swollen. And painful, she realized as he winced and let the folds of his shirt fall back in place.

After he'd fastened the last button, he pointed to her legs and left arm. "You have the burns, too. Explain that."

She stared at the faint red, nickel-sized burns that dotted her legs and arms. Five or six. Not like the dozens that covered his chest. She stepped closer to him.

"I—I can't."

"I can," he snapped, his gaze hard.

She stood inches from him now, her Keds nearly touching his loafers.

He sucked in a breath as that hard, angry gaze faded.

"They're from the Watchers."

She nodded. Seeing the look on his face made her believe him. He looked humble. Shaken. Like he had last night in the fiery glow of the exploding lights.

"I remember," she said softly, unblinking, and stared into his eyes, losing herself in that arctic blue.

He smelled like cedar. She inhaled the cool, intoxicating scent, remembering his lips against hers. She fought an impulse to lean up and kiss him hard on the lips. If he made the slightest move in that direction, she'd be in his arms and she feared what might happen next.

"What were you talking about when I walked up?" Fletcher asked, squinting at her.

For a moment, she couldn't find her voice. She let out a breath and glanced at the Japanese maple. The empty pedestal brought it back.

"Someone took my gazing ball," she said.

He frowned. "Gazing ball? What's that?"

"A glass lawn ornament. These are special. They belonged to my grandmother."

He nodded, quiet for several moments and pointed at the other lawn ornaments. "Was it like those other mirrored spheres in your garden?"

Kendra nodded.

"Nice garden, by the way," he said, a smile lighting his sharp-edged, chiseled features.

Nice dirt maybe, Kendra thought. "Thanks. It's a work in progress but it will be."

Fletcher grinned and pointed. "What are those tall purple flowers? I've never seen them before."

"What flowers?" Kendra asked, turning around.

She stumbled, falling against Fletcher as a shocked cry escaped from her mouth.

Delphiniums in blues, purples, and whites stretched toward the deep blue sky, purple and burgundy dahlias as big as her head. A sea of coneflowers waved in the breeze beside a bank of lavender infusing the air. Blue wisteria and pale pink English tea roses climbed the restored pergola over the patio. Velvet-petaled roses the size of tea cups and wisteria blossoms bunching like grapes. Beside the patio, peonies in deep pink, dewy white, and rich burgundy wept heavy blossoms onto the ground.

Beyond the blooms, melons and tomatoes sprouted yellow flowers, vines trailing across the ground toward the—her breath caught—toward the mossy cobblestones lining the path. The air warmed with flower scents and something else—spices?

On the far side of the patio, beside the white picket fence, a bed of herbs grew tall, framed with boxwood. Chives, dill, basil, rosemary.

Tears welled in Kendra's eyes as she rushed down the path, beneath the trailing vines that formed an arch above the path. This was Gem's garden! Exactly like she remembered it.

Kendra recalled curling up beside the waves of lavender, reading her favorite books: *Mandy* and *The Secret Garden*. Gem's garden was like stepping through the pages of those books into her own private place. Into her own magic.

But she grew up, Gem got old, and the garden faded away. When Gem died, thoughts of returning to this old house and its fallow garden hurt too much. But Kendra's mother couldn't let the place go. She'd grown up here and couldn't bear to see it in someone else's hands. Gem made this place special. She'd dreaded being here without her grandmother.

But she was here now. Kendra felt her in every mossy stone, smelled her lavender scent in the blossoms, and heard her musical voice (raspy with the years) in the rustle of leaves.

The hand on her shoulder startled her. She turned around. Fletcher, smiling, ice-blue eyes warm. She gripped his forearms.

"Fletcher...what's happening here?" she asked, searching his face for the answer. "I planted those seeds right before you showed up at my gate. I just planted them. How can this be happening?"

He brushed a lock of dark hair out of her eyes and gripped her hands. "There's magic in you, Kendra. Doesn't this prove it?"

She shook her head. "I—I don't understand."

"You have the greening," he whispered. "And more—like me. You were meant for a life beyond the one you live, Kendra."

She frowned. "I like my job."

"But you're capable of so much more." He motioned toward the lush garden. "Isn't this proof?"

"This was my grandmother's garden. It's identical. It's her magic, not mine."

He smiled, shaking his head as he let go of her hands and cupped her cheek. She inhaled another breath of warm cedar, her body trembling at his touch.

"Change it," he said.

"What?" *How could she change it?* She'd planted flowers and vegetables. *How could she change the layout?*

"Change it," he repeated, his voice a little louder. "Plant a new flower, a new tree—anything." He pressed his index finger to her forehead. "When you plant it here first, you'll find it in your garden."

She nodded, closing her eyes a moment as she focused on tall, droopy tulips—fuchsia. She imagined the slender, reedy stalks that drooped with elegance into tight, heavy fuchsia blooms.

When she opened her eyes, Fletcher was grinning at her.

"What?" she said, not turning around. "What is it?"

"Tulips," he said with a grin. "Deep pink—kind of like your lawn. I have good taste."

She laughed, grabbing hold of his arms as she turned around. A thick stand of tulips nestled against the white trellis board, large blooms drooping like rabbit ears.

"How did I do that?" she said with a gasp.

How had she materialized tulips out of thin air? Her knees felt weak.

Fletcher's grip tightened on her arms, to keep her from pitching over into the grass.

"It's the greening, Kendra. I told you. Part comes from your grandmother's Irish roots. But the other part...that's Katorin."

Kendra's mouth fell open. "What other?"

"The tempering magic. Softens things. Sharpens and focuses

them. Even makes things appear when you need them—don't tell me you haven't noticed that yet?"

It was crystal clear now, sending shivers down her back. The tuna salad. The towels. The Seattle's Best Coffee that she preferred—even the hair dryer she'd left in Baltimore. All of it. Had she...summoned those things or created them out of the air?

"I left my hair dryer in Baltimore," she said with a nervous laugh. "But when I stepped out of the shower, it was there beside the sink. Even the tomatoes I ate at lunch hadn't been there until I imagined them."

Fletcher laughed, his eyes as bright as the summer sky. "The Katorin in you amazes me." He sighed, a wistful look in his eyes. "Makes me homesick for the old days."

"The old days?" Kendra asked.

He nodded. "Before the Eidolon imprisoned my father. Before my gifts matured into a threat—when we were all still together. When Katori's cities and marketplaces were full and alive. When she still had wonders to see." He bowed his head. "Most of it's gone now. As long as my family still lives, I'll keep trying to restore my world."

She laid her hand against his face and he leaned into it, nuzzling her hand. He seemed a little lost, a little broken up, and a little beaten but he wasn't quitting. She felt the strength of his resolve beat in time with his pulse.

"And without the tempering, my gifts are useless," he said with a heavy sigh that shook his body.

He pulled away, eyes darkening.

"Without the tempering?" she asked. "Without the magic you say I have?"

Fletcher nodded, gazing at the ground. "Yes," he said and looked up. "I need a Katorin with the tempering gift to help me focus my own energies." His voice was barely above a whisper now. "Without it, Katori is lost. And so am I."

A chill touched her arms, turning her skin to gooseflesh as she studied his face. What did that mean? From the laid-bare expression on his face, in his eyes, she realized he was asking something of her.

She had no idea what he needed, but it was obvious that he needed her help.

"That's why you've come here," she said, her gaze not leaving his eyes. "To me."

He nodded. "It's a difficult thing I'm asking of you. I won't lie, it's dangerous and..." He looked away, his eyes narrowing. "And it might get both of us killed."

A cold wind brushed across her face. *Get us killed? Was it more than those lights on the pond?*

He was the most handsome man she'd seen in a long, long time and she wanted to know him better. But risking her life for him? Not her idea of a first date.

"Fletcher..." She held out her hands, struggling to find a response. "I—I don't know what to say. I barely know you and you're asking me to risk my life for something?" She laid her hand against her chest. "I'm a change management consultant and I handle change pretty well, I think. But this is a bit much even for me. I don't even know what you're asking me to do, but you're not making it attractive by telling me it could kill me."

He shrugged. "You have to know everything up front. It's only fair."

"And what is everything, Fletcher?" she asked, hands on her hips.

"The Eidolon will return on the next ebony moon. The shadow people." He sighed. "It will be a force so large...I can't even hope to defeat it alone. Carvahl will throw everything he has at me because I'm the last. And...without help—the tempering—I won't survive it."

Kendra released the breath she was holding. That was everything all right.

He pointed at the garden. "This place was once a haven for those of the old magics, Kendra. Dark, light, in between—they all came here. Met here. Danced by moonlight here." At last, some of that lightness touched his eyes again. "They'll return to the magic when they feel it. And I'll be here to enlist their help against the Eidolon. But for all their abilities, it won't be enough. The Eidolon want to control everything, including worlds beyond the veil." He pointed at the ground. "This world."

"What does that mean?" she asked.

"It means when they kill me, they'll sweep over your world, subduing the magical beings on your fringes and winding their way into the oblivious humans of your world. And without creatures who can detect them, the Eidolon will rule your world, too. And destroy it."

"My world?" She shook her head, feeling overwhelmed now. So much for change management. This was too much. "Fletcher, do you have any idea how crazy this sounds?"

"To those who ignore the magics around them, yes, it's crazy. But to you, to someone who thinks of something and it appears. To someone who imagines a garden and it materializes out of the dust and the soil...no. The battle is coming, Kendra, whether you fight in it or not."

She tried to shake off his words of doom and destruction, but everything he'd said so far rang true. She'd imagined the garden of her childhood and in minutes, it had grown up around her.

"But if I have this magic like you say I do, then why haven't I done this my whole life? Why only now?"

He laid a hand on hers, squeezing. "It's my magic that's awakened yours, Kendra. When the wilding meets the tempering, the union is powerful. Usually, both magics are found in one person in some measure. Halflings."

"Halflings?" she cried.

He nodded. "Mine is all wilding—and the greening—with Eidolon darkness strengthening it. Makes it overpowered and wild. Yours is all tempering and greening. Together, we're terrifying to the Eidolon. Because the uncontrollable dark magic inside me becomes —controllable. And a weapon. That's why they're trying to destroy me." His face turned pale, his mouth stretching into a taut line. "When they finally sense your magic, Kendra...they'll come for you, too."

A warm breeze rushed through the garden and she felt a chill in it, an ache of truth in Fletcher's absurd story. She was a six-figure, nationally recognized consultant and in high demand to up-and-coming businesses. Listening to this strange (and gorgeous) man tell her stories about faeries and shadow people and some crazy magical battle looming. In realms beyond anything she'd ever imagined or daydreamed among the stands of lavender in Gem's garden.

Something *had* awakened in this old house, something she didn't understand. In an odd way, it felt real. Normal. And she felt comfortable with it—even destroying Fletcher's crazy Watcher lights last night.

What was this epic battle? And why her? Why now? She was only back in Indiana because she'd gone to school with Toni Ambrose. What if she'd never returned to this place? What would Fletcher have done then?

"But you don't even know me," said Kendra, shaking her head, her voice softer now. "What if I'd never come back here?"

His fingers brushed against her cheek, his voice a ragged whisper. "I would have found you."

Chills rushed down her arms and spine, warmth spreading through her belly. "How?" she asked.

"I've felt your presence for a long time," he said, smiling. "At a great distance. I've searched for it for so long. But when my back was turned, you showed up on my doorstep."

He leaned toward her, his mouth covering hers in a deep, urgent kiss.

She smashed her mouth against his, grabbing hold of his face, wanting her body against his as his arms slid around her waist. It was firecrackers and lightning strikes as she ran her hands underneath his shirt, exploring those ridged stomach muscles and lean sinews. His mouth tasted like warm spearmint.

His fingers stroked her neck, running down her back and bare arms in blistering strokes. With an intensity that made her gasp.

She pulled back, fighting to catch her breath, her knees shaky. She wanted to make love to him right here in the lavender. But she barely knew him.

"That was some kiss, Fletcher," she said, still out of breath, a hand against her chest.

"It's the wilding," he said, his voice husky as he took a step back from her. "The attraction is—too strong."

She brushed the hair out of her eyes, her body trembling, heart racing.

"You're telling me," she muttered.

He held out his hands. "I throw myself on your mercy, Kendra. I've searched a long time for you. Will you stand with me against the Eidolon? I don't expect an immediate answer—it's a lot to consider. So much at stake. But we don't have much time. If you agree to stand beside me, we've got to learn to use our magic together. In tandem."

Kendra frowned. "But don't you already know how to wield your own magic?"

He shook his head. "Without your tempering flame, my magic rages out of control. We'll have to learn together—and fast—if we're to survive the next attack. Long enough to stand in the realm of Katori and face the Eidolon throng. Together."

She didn't even like war movies. How was she going to battle these—these shadows? She was a planner not a fighter.

"Fletcher...I'm not a soldier. I can't do this—I can't."

"You're wrong," he snapped. "You wielded that hoe like a broadsword last night, Kendra. All I'm asking is that you use the energies within you against them."

"I don't think I can," she said in a sad voice, seeing the disappointment on his face. "I'm sorry, Fletcher. I just can't do it."

He took hold of her hands and held them in his, finally pressing them to his lips. "Can't you feel the magic within you, Kendra? Doesn't it almost roil at your fingertips when you're so close to my wilding magic?"

She felt the electric surge of current running through his hands into hers. She felt the writhing energies struggling to rise into her palms and join with his. Or had it been way too long since she'd had sex?

Not that long, she thought indignantly. Four months since she and

Brian broke up. All part of change management. She'd managed to find a hobby (gardening) and he'd managed to find a twenty-year-old nail technician.

Or maybe she just wanted Fletcher.

Hello? He was hotter than this year's firemen calendar—January through December combined. Even after he spoke.

All she could do was nod at Fletcher. She felt something she couldn't identify. Couldn't explain.

"If you feel something," he said, kissing her fingers. "Anything—then you can't completely deny my request. Please? Give it a day or two? At least consider it."

She squeezed his hands. "What happens if I say no?"

Why did she ask that question out loud? She didn't want to know the answer, didn't want to know the consequences.

His eyes fixed her with a piercing stare. "Bad things will happen. From the look on your face, I don't think you're ready to hear them."

He let her go, taking a few steps back.

"You're right," she said, holding up a hand. "But I have to know the whole story, Fletcher. Otherwise, I can't make an informed decision."

She cringed. It wasn't like he was asking her how she felt about birth control or stem cell research. It was a simple yes or no question. But it was anything but simple. As much as she wanted to stick her head in the sand and not make that decision, she knew she couldn't. She didn't work that way. As a kid, why had been her favorite question.

She stared at his face, mouth in a taut line, sexy jaw set, eyes intense. She wouldn't like his response.

"If you don't help me, the Eidolon will kill me on the next new moon."

No, she didn't want to know that. No pressure.

He smiled. "Of course, then you're annoying neighbor problem would go away. But the Eidolon won't stop with me. They'll hunt down and destroy the last scattered Katorins. And when Katori falls, they'll cross the veil to your world."

Kendra stiffened. *There, that wasn't so bad. Just your typical, the world will end and it'll be all your fault, you selfish cow.*

He was spinning that story—wasn't he?

"C'mon, Fletcher," she said, hands on her hips. "Aren't you embellishing that story just a little?"

"Am I?" he said, frowning. "You saw the Watchers last night? You tell me."

He'd told the truth about the Watchers but maybe it was all a setup?

"Think about it? For a day or two—please?"

This was serious. He'd said please twice.

"Okay, Fletcher, I'll think about it. Will that make you happy?"

He smiled at last. "For the moment. In two days, have dinner with me—at my place. I'll cook for you and tell you about Katori. Then you can tell me your decision."

A man who cooks. This she had to see.

"All right. I'll have dinner with you but no promises on this magic thing, Fletcher. Okay?"

He held up his hands and backed toward the gate. "Deal. I promise to be a gentleman at all times."

Kendra frowned. Rats. That's the last thing she wanted out of Fletcher.

"If you insist," she said, holding back a sigh.

He glanced toward the Japanese maple and pointed as he opened the gate. "By the way, I didn't take your gazing ball."

Kendra crossed her arms. "I was sure you had it—as another prank."

"Not me," he said.

"Maddie's missing hers, too."

His eyes widened a little. "That's very strange. Both of you missing gazing balls."

She nodded. "Maybe it was the lawn boy playing pranks?"

That worried expression deepened on his face and he chewed his lip a moment, studying the empty pedestal and the other gazing balls scattered throughout the garden.

"You might want to bring the others inside," he said, his voice taut. "In case they return to steal the others."

"Who's they?" Kendra asked.

He shrugged, but that uneasiness still gleamed in his eyes. "Who knows," he said. "But it'd be a shame to lose the others, too."

"You're right," said Kendra. "I'll bring them inside."

He started out of the gate, but Kendra called after him.

"What time is dinner?"

He turned around, walking backward across the field. "How about seven?"

"Fine. I'll bring some wine—red or white?"

A hint of that handsome smirk touched his lips. "Rosé? Like your lawn?"

"Red or white," Kendra repeated. "Pick one."

"Red," he said with a grin. "See you soon, Kendra."

She watched him hurry across the field, but his concern over the missing gazing balls bothered her. What hadn't he told her? It made her nervous as she gazed across the garden. But the lavender and the English tea roses softened her apprehension, scattering it to the wind as she strolled toward the first gazing ball. She picked it up and moved toward the next one, wondering why Fletcher had reacted the way he did.

What was so sinister about stolen gazing balls anyway?

8

Shade kept his fear tucked behind the facade he'd mastered over the centuries as he walked across the dewy grass toward his house. Already, the air was heavy with heat, tang of grass sharp.

Missing orbs meant trouble.

A little thing to most people. A minor theft, nothing to worry over. To Shade, it meant only one thing: more of the Eidolon made it through last night.

And in shadow form, they could hide from him a long time—before trying to assassinate him. But right now, Kendra had plenty to think about without him adding more to her worries.

He glanced around at the late afternoon silence, the soft chatter of birds comforting, reassuring. At any moment, Eidolon could be on him. He needed a warding spell at his door, something to keep them at bay until *he* found them. With Emmaline's garden returned from the dust, the Fey and other magical creatures would soon return. Maybe one of them would agree to set a warding spell around his doorstep?

If he had any sort of focus, he'd do it himself.

How many more orbs had gone missing along these country

roads since the last ebony moon? What did the Eidolon intend to do with these mirrored glass gazing balls?

The possibilities nagged at him. Still, he knew one thing was certain: whatever they were doing, it was creating a weapon. And it was aimed right at him.

A cold chill shivered through him. Or Kendra.

He felt foolish now as he reached the white ranch house's porch. He kicked the wall.

What an idiot he'd been!

For months, they'd chased him, ambushed him at every ebony moonrise. All this time, he thought they wanted to destroy him but a nagging truth roiled in his belly. It wasn't him they wanted to destroy.

It was Kendra. And he'd led them right to her back door.

Dammit! She knew nothing about the Eidolon and wouldn't suspect a thing until their shadow forms were on her, attacking.

Granted, they were weak under moonlight, glowing, and easily destroyed. Only by darkness and the new moon could they shift form to shadow—and stay there for a time. But with the element of surprise, they could kill her easily. In shadow form until that first sliver of moonlight appeared, they were at their most dangerous.

He had to protect her somehow. His world depended on her now.

Besides, when the ebony moon rose again, none of this would matter without Kendra's help.

Tonight, when the light of the moon touched the darkness, he'd go out to Kendra's garden and call out the Fey, the clans, the forest nymphs—even the garden gnomes if it would help. They had to protect her. Starting tonight. He was cousin to them all. They had to help him and protect Kendra. And even if they chose not to, they had to feel the Eidolon threat to their own world by now.

He hurried inside and closed the door behind him, surveying the quiet woods shrouding his living room. He needed to give Kendra some Katorin obsidian—it would act like a mirror to the shadows. He had two or three pieces. He'd get one over to her—now. Before something terrible happened.

Trees and ferns sprouted along the banks of a calm brook that sputtered through the house in a rush of cool water. With the obsidian and some tools, he'd set watch over Kendra from the garden. Until moonrise.

He had to make sure she was safe.

Pale gold leaves fluttered down from the treetops that created canopy, obscuring the once white popcorn ceiling as he crept across the mossy floor. No birds chirped, not even a sparrow soared overhead. The loamy scent of soil comforted him as he studied the trees. He felt a chill. The pattern of leaves on the forest floor had shifted.

Something felt heavy, dark—something that shouldn't be here. In his woods.

He took another step but the snap of a twig across the room made him stop in mid-stride. Fear pooled in his stomach, something dark and fast rushing past in the distance. Disappearing into shadows.

He turned. Nothing.

The axe. He cursed under his breath. Why hadn't he grabbed the axe off the porch?

Because it hadn't been there, he realized.

The axe hadn't been at the door where he'd left it early this morning.

He dropped down on his haunches and listened, studied the lines of trees bathed in shadowed silence and dim yellow light from the floor lamps. No bird calls. No sway of wind through the branches. Not even the ghost of a butterfly among the stand of trees.

Another twig popped.

He crouched low, crawling behind an oak tree.

Pressing his back against the thick trunk, heart pounding into his throat, he searched the ground for a weapon.

Not even a tree limb lay in sight.

Something brushed past him.

He flinched, throwing himself to the forest floor as the blade of his axe slammed into the tree trunk.

Right above his head.

A shrill scream from the oak raked across the room. Shade

flinched, holding his ears as he rolled away from the axe coming at him again. He got to his feet a moment too slow and the axe bit into his shoulder.

The cry of pain tore from his throat as he stumbled, fell, and picked himself up.

The axe blade fell again.

He ran down the dirt path into the hallway, through the trees and beside the brook toward the kitchen, clutching his right arm.

Two carving knives rose out of the misty air surrounding the dark oak kitchen cabinets. Coming at him from the right.

He turned left. The axe bobbed toward his face.

Dammit! That first sliver of moonlight was still hours away.

Without those first rays of the moon, the Eidolon still clung to last night's shadow forms. They'd stay in that form until the next moonrise passed its glow to them.

But it was a long time until moonrise.

Shade leaped into the stream as the knives hissed toward him.

He slogged through the water, legs pumping toward the front door. He threw it open but the move cost him another bite of the axe.

It sliced across his back. Burning. Leaking blood.

He bit back the cry of pain and sprinted off the porch, weapons pursing him.

Three Eidolon, their shadows barely visible against the crisp morning light.

Shade ran toward the wood pile and snatched up a long, slender cut of firewood. Spinning around, he raised the firewood in both hands as the axe fell toward him.

He thrust out the piece of wood, catching the blade in its soft pith.

The blade lodged deep and stuck there.

A voice whispered a curse when the blade wouldn't slide free.

With one hand, Shade grabbed hold of the axe handle, pulling it toward him.

A shadow rushed at him, through him as he wrested away the axe. He freed the blade from the hunk of wood and slammed it against the shadowy form. It crumpled at his feet and he finished it with a painful swing of the axe.

But he didn't move fast enough to avoid the puncture of the kitchen knife as it rammed into his lower back.

The cry of pain wrenched free as he swung the axe around, catching the Eidolon in its wake. It shattered and turned to smoke. His body shook with pain, a gasping breath of air struggling up from his lungs.

One of them was punctured. He felt it in every hitch of breath as he scanned the terrain again.

One more Eidolon lurked out there.

He felt the world rise as he struggled to hold onto that axe, fearing the next attack.

Where was the other knife?

He craned his neck in all directions, realizing he was on his knees now. But the weapon was gone.

Coward had probably retreated to lie in wait for him again. Or they'd meant to incapacitate him enough to go after Kendra.

The raw pain ached through him with every breath as he fought to stand. He had to get to Kendra. Had to protect her from these bastards.

Struggling to his feet, he limped across the field toward Kendra's house. His heart hammered against his chest with every step. He had to get there fast.

His breath caught. Somehow, he had to save her.

9

S hade Fletcher was crazy. Absolutely crazy! Kendra was certain of it.

She walked inside the farmhouse. From the dining room window, she watched him walk across the field. But the sight of her magnificent garden took her breath away! She couldn't believe it was real. Tall spires of delphinium in deep purples, bright pinks, and pure white—the ones she'd loved as a kid—stood beside waves and waves of lavender. And Gem's prized, whisper-pink roses wove a tapestry of pink and green across the pergola. The entire garden had a pearlescent glow to it.

It was more beautiful than she ever remembered as a kid.

But how would she explain this to Maddie? Her neighbor would freak when she saw the backyard. She'd ask a bazillion questions about it. And Kendra had no answers. None. It was a mystery—a magical one.

As she watched Fletcher disappear across the field, she felt a strange sense of longing.

He carried his mystery well, made her want to know more about his wild ramblings. But she couldn't deny everything he'd said. Did she really carry some sort of magic?

Seriously...look at this garden! It was a full-fledged magical miracle. Yet standing here, gazing at the wisteria dripping from the pergola and the dahlias as big as dinner plates, she still didn't quite believe him.

There had to be an explanation.

There was no such thing as magic...was there? Whether magic existed or not, she couldn't explain away the garden. It had been barren dirt and brown, tangled dead vines before she started planting seeds and roses.

She turned away from the window and walked into the kitchen. She stood in front of the stove and closed her eyes.

"I want O'Riley's cinnamon rolls. With extra cream cheese icing. Right out of the oven."

She took a deep breath but let it out quickly when the thick smell of warm cinnamon filled the kitchen. She opened her eyes and yanked open the oven door.

Four cinnamon rolls dripping in warm cream cheese icing sat in a pan on the top rack.

She stuck her hand in the oven. And it was cool. When she touched the pan, it was still warm.

She slid out the square metal pan and set it on the wooden cutting board beside the stove. Grabbing a fork out of the drawer to the right of the stove, she picked up a gooey bite of cinnamon roll and slid it into her mouth.

As rich and wonderful as she remembered them from high school. She took another bite then grabbed a plate and plopped the roll onto it, carrying it to the dining table. She ate the roll and watched the garden, remembering Fletcher's kiss right there under the pergola.

Her cheeks burned at the thought. She wanted a rematch. And she looked forward to dinner at his place.

What was she saying? The guy wanted her to stand up to thousands more of those Watcher lights! And God knew what else.

Was he painting the whole story with doom? That those things would really kill him? She had no way of knowing. Was it all his crazy way of trying to get laid?

Men.

She took another bite of cinnamon roll.

But there had been a hint of desperation in his eyes, like his world was ending or something. A whisper of truth in his words. Maybe he *was* in trouble?

She sighed. Maybe he did need her help?

After finishing the cinnamon roll, she put the rest of the rolls back in the oven and tossed the fork into the dishwasher.

She headed out of the kitchen and up the stairs. To change out of these dusty clothes.

She needed to get out of this house for a while, clear her head a bit. She'd drive out to the mall and check it out, get a feel for the clothing stores and what they stocked in the area. Hopefully the mall had improved from her high school days. Not exactly the hallmark of fashion back then with few stores and no parking but it was better than nothing. Better than driving an hour or so down to Indianapolis every time she wanted to try on clothes.

Kendra hurried into the bathroom to wash her face and brush on some makeup. A little foundation. A little eyeliner and some lip gloss and she'd be set.

"I need a radio in the bathroom," she said as she reached the top of the stairs and gazed around the second floor of the house.

A small black radio perched beside the tall, clear vase of silk yellow roses that stood on a round drum table outside the bathroom. No, she'd prefer hydrangeas in cobalt blue vase and a networked speaker to stream music. In purple. She blinked and the roses fanned out into silk hydrangeas, cobalt glass vase catching the light as the small radio expanded, turning into a dark purple cylinder.

"Perfect," she said with a smirk and grabbed her hairbrush. "I could get used to this."

She turned on the speaker. "Stream my favorite pop playlist."

Kelly Clarkson sang about hazel eyes in edgy tones as Kendra turned the volume down to a low setting and stepped into the bathroom. She picked up her brush off the white pedestal sink and brushed her hair. After washing her face, she slid off her dirty clothes and slid on a pair of jean shorts and red T-shirt out of the blue duffle bag that set on the floor behind the door. When she was dressed, she grabbed a small teal makeup bag out of the duffle bag and began applying makeup.

She leaned closer to the huge mirror over the sink as she brushed on powder foundation, smoothing it out with her fingers.

As she picked up the eyeliner, the stairs creaked.

Her heartbeat quickened as she glanced away from the mirror toward the stairs. Empty. No one there.

She turned back to the round, gold-framed mirror above the white pedestal sink.

Another stair creaked above the music. A little louder this time.

Straightening, she glanced out the door again.

"Turn down the music volume to low," she said to the speaker.

The volume dropped as she moved toward the doorway and stared down at the empty staircase.

"Who's there?" she called. "Maddie?"

No answer.

Anger reddened her cheeks. "Fletcher, are you playing pranks again? I took a firearms class. I know how to use this gun."

The weight in her hand made her gasp.

Her gaze darted toward the eyeliner pencil she'd held: woodland walnut. Gone. The Smith and Wesson gleamed silver and heavy in her palm.

"Hey!" she shouted. "That was my favorite eyeliner!"

She stared at the gun again.

Get rid of it! She screamed in her head until the weight lifted. When she turned to look at her hand, the woodland walnut eye pencil was back between her fingers again.

"Only illusions," a voice whispered against her ear and she froze. "Nothing more."

Fear spiraled through her in chilling waves and she couldn't move. A haze clung to the air, almost like a shadow against the white tiles.

"Who's there?" she shouted.

The knife blade snapped out of the air and fell against her throat as unseen hands clutched her arms.

Her voice strangled in her throat.

"What—what are you?" she said in a hoarse whisper, trembling.

"We are the Fallen. About to rise. Shade was fool enough, arrogant enough to think we sought him. With his tempering gone, he's powerless. Worthless. He was an easy kill."'

Oh, my God...they'd killed Fletcher! She began to tremble.

No, it was a lie. He wasn't dead. This thing was trying to scare her. And it was working beautifully!

But she had this strange magic. So far, everything she'd imagined had materialized. Why shouldn't this work, too?

In her mind, she called up a big hunting knife in place of the woodland walnut eyeliner that she gripped.

No sooner had she imagined a long slender blade with smooth pommel, she felt its weight in her hand.

She raised it slowly at her side.

"So, you think I'm the real power?" she asked the shadows. "Me? Why? If all these things I've summoned are illusions, they hold no power. Like this, for instance."

She plunged the knife toward the pressure against her arm.

The air parted with a shriek, the knife falling away from her throat. The blow to her back knocked her down, hunting knife clattering out of her hand. Something dark straddled her as that knife slashed toward her face.

The blade of an axe met the knife, knocking it away!

The hunting knife skittered across the tile and slid underneath the clawfoot tub.

Kendra rolled away, toward it, and ducked behind the tub.

Fletcher stood in the bathroom doorway, axe in motion. Hacking at the air. At nothing, yet she felt the dark presence in the room.

"Make the shadow glow," she shouted and a faint light gleamed beside her.

"No!" the voice shouted, startled as its body took shape in the glow around it. It looked surprisingly human.

Fletcher swung the axe. Missed as the creature rushed past him. Shade turned, swinging again. His axe blade caught it in the doorway. The creature shattered and sparked into puffs of smoke.

"Fletcher, you saved my life!" Kendra cried as she sprang to her feet.

She ran across the tile toward him as he turned around, chest heaving hard.

He was struggling to breathe, she realized. And he was sinking.

"Fletcher?" she cried, catching him as he fell. She broke his fall against the tile as he collapsed against her. She held him up, but her hand came away red.

Then she saw the gaping wound on his shoulder and felt a deep, jagged puncture in his back, shirt stained red.

"Who did this to you?" she demanded, trying to get him on his feet. "Who, Fletcher?"

"The Eidolon," he said in a thin voice, gasping for air.

His face pressed against her shoulder as she struggled to her feet, pulling him up as best she could. She felt him struggle to rise, helping her get him on his feet.

With both arms around his waist, Kendra led him out of the bathroom and the few steps across the hall to the front bedroom. Yellows and reds warmed the room as she turned down the flowered comforter and laid him on his side. The butter yellow walls were soothing, the air smelling like lemons above the cloying scent of blood as she stuffed pillows around him to support his head and torso.

When he was comfortable, she slid his open shirt off his shoulders. Underneath were two wounds, one of them a deep puncture in his back. The knife had hit his lung. He needed a doctor. Maybe a hospital?

She started to rise from the bed, but he grabbed her arm.

"Don't leave," he said. "Need—your help."

"Fletcher, I've got to get a doctor. Your lung's collapsed."

"Use your tempering," he said through gritted teeth. "While I can still use my—wilding."

Even if she didn't know how?

The look in those distant blue eyes was all pain, except for a flicker of something else. She studied those haunting, large blue eyes another moment, trying to stop herself from falling into them. At last, she recognized it.

For a man who acted like nothing affected him, his eyes reflected a lot of emotion right now.

It was hope. It was need. It was an acknowledgement that he needed her. She felt like she'd broken through another one of his barriers (besides lust).

She nodded and lifted her hand to the bleeding wound in his back. She pressed it to the puncture and he flinched, a cry of pain slipping through his teeth. His muscles corded as he arched his back against a wave of pain. He tried to pull in a lungful of air but couldn't manage a full breath.

Fear trembled through her. He needed help right now or he could die.

She hadn't known him long but long enough to realize she wanted him around. He was gruff and needed a few anger management classes (okay, maybe a bachelor's degree) but something genuine and strong burned beneath his cranky facade. Honest and true.

His stoic acceptance of the pain made her smile as she worked on him. She wanted to delve beneath his mask to the wild spirit that writhed beneath it. With her hands pressed against his bare skin, she felt it fight and struggle against her touch. In a moment or two, the raging energies within him quieted.

She applied more pressure to the wound on his back and he winced as she focused on trying to heal the lung. She bit her lip against the warm ooze of blood trickling through her splayed fingers.

As the moments passed, she felt him weakening, a hint of

distance building in him. He was pulling away, struggling to find his own healing. She understood how hard it was for someone like Fletcher to place himself at another's mercy.

His fast-weakening state alarmed her. She had to stop the bleeding and help him breathe.

The faint echo of the music fell away as a car whispered past on the road outside.

She blocked out everything...time, her own body aches, even whether it was day or not, concentrating on Fletcher's wounds.

When the sunlight had faded from the room, the corners pooling with the first inky washes of twilight, she let out an exhausted sigh and pulled her hand away to examine the wound.

She smiled. It had closed, but Fletcher had already lost a lot of blood. Had this strange magic inside her actually helped his lung?

She watched him a moment, waiting to see if his chest inflated with air. He lay still, his eyes closed and panic rose in her.

"Fletcher?" She gently shook his shoulder. "Fletcher!"

His chest rose, a thin groan escaping. It was painful but he could breathe.

"Yeah," he replied in a rough voice, opening his eyes to stare at her.

"The bleeding's stopped. How's your breathing?"

"Painful," he said, closing his eyes again.

Kendra laid her hand against the wound and concentrated again, trying to ease his pain. She felt light-headed, the sounds muffled, the light dim. And it got worse the harder she concentrated.

When the entire room tilted and went dark a moment, she felt only numbness in her hand. He reached out and took hold of her wrist. His grip was weak and she could have broken it without effort, but she let him hold on. That's when she realized he was pulling her hand away from his wound.

"Too much—you'll pass out. No more, okay?"

She smiled as his eyes rolled open.

"Okay," she replied. "I'll get the first aid kit and get you bandaged up."

He nodded as she rose from the bed.

"Patch me up—enough to get home."

She grabbed hold of the wall as everything tilted a moment. When she got her balance back, she gave him a stern look, her hands on her hips.

"You can forget going anywhere tonight, Fletcher. You're staying right here, so I can make sure you don't die on me."

A weak smirk touched the corners of his mouth. "Why do you care?" he asked.

"If I'm supposed to watch your back on this new moon—I mean, this ebony moon—I'd better start now. Make sure you live that long." She bowed her head. "Besides...you saved my life tonight."

"Guess we're even."

She smiled at him. He looked sexy as hell lying there with no shirt and those ice blue eyes shining back at her, thick dark hair tangling around his face. Smooth, leanly muscled chest. But he was ready to pass out from the pain and blood loss, despite her best efforts to heal him.

"Guess so," she said, crossing her arms. "I like going into things without any debts."

"Me, too, Martin," he said, his eyes trying to close. "Thanks," he said, his voice a whisper now.

"Sleep," she said to him.

And he was gone, his face against the pillow.

10

A bout midnight, Shade awoke to whispers.

Fey voices calling to him, chanting his name—from Kendra's garden. He groaned and tried to sit up, fever pounding through him.

The dagger-sharp pain sliced through his chest with every breath. But the voices persisted. The magical realm of Kendra's world had no doubt felt the Eidolon's ripple of dark magic like a seismic tremor, one signaling the impending earthquake.

Now that Kendra had brought her grandmother's garden back from its slumber, the magical creatures of her world would feel it, too.

The Fey and the wood nymphs would recognize him as the Green Man and they would blame him. They would demand answers from him. An explanation for the sudden turmoil invading their world, not realizing how many centuries the Eidolon had cast shadows here. With the garden's magic pulsing across their realm again, they'd feel the Eidolon's threat again. Like they had when Gem lived here. They would also feel the buildup and release of magical energy. He had to gain their trust and support. He'd need it when the ebony moon darkened the sky.

It was agony to slide his feet out of bed and onto the floor, but he managed, gasping for air against the knife-edged pain in his lungs. He sat up, the room swaying, his heart pounding in his ears. He propped his elbows on his knees, laying his face in his hands to wait out the spinning. When the world settled in one place again, he rose from the bed.

Everything smelled like ointment and bandages, the one across his back thick and tight. It made his breaths a little easier as he struggled for each one. He laid his right arm across his chest to support his lungs as he took a step forward.

Paused. Another step. Paused.

The room tilted and he grabbed hold of the dresser to steady himself.

But the high-pitched faerie call carried, its crystalline notes an insistent plea. He sighed. Sebille, the Queen of Faerie herself, he realized, laying his head against his arms as he struggled for enough strength to rise and pull on his torn, bloodied shirt. He didn't have the strength to button it as he reached the stairs.

Sebille's call was to all creatures of the unseen world, with the unseen gifts. A gathering. Worse—a tribunal.

He moaned. And his presence was requested.

He shook off a twinge of pain as the notes sharpened against his eardrums like razor blades.

No, his presence was demanded. Sebille saw him as the cause of all the turmoil. All the trouble. Groaning, he straightened his body to let his lungs expand.

She was right, of course. It was his fault the Eidolon came through last night.

He'd failed to destroy several of their shadow forms, but they had only temporary residence in shadow. When morning came, after a sliver of moonglow touched them, they would appear in solid form in all their hideous glory. Solid wasn't quite the word he wanted. They were projections of solid forms that lurked beyond the veil.

Back in his homeland.

With shaky steps, he slid into his battered loafers and made it to the top of the stairs. But he paused to gaze at Kendra's sleeping form in the bedroom across the hall. She lay on her side, covers kicked off, a silky red nightgown fluid against her lean, shapely body.

It was Kendra they wanted. And they would do their best to destroy her. He was just in their way. An annoyance until he could focus his magic.

Regardless, it was his fault that the Eidolon had come through, but he hadn't been the first to call them forth. The human and Katorin bloodlines that were oblivious to their unseen gifts had called other Eidolon through, not knowing what they'd invited into their world. Long before he'd set foot in this foreign place.

He had to make Sebille understand that—and understand that all of Faerie was in danger now as were the vampire clans, the elementals, the shapeshifters—even the wizards, witches, and sorceresses. All of them, united or not, faced the swarm of Eidolon.

He hoped Sebille wouldn't kill him for his role in this assault.

The mournful call tore through him in sharp-taloned waves as he made his way down the creaky stairs. He walked with soft, deliberate steps, trying not to wake Kendra with the creak of the stairs. He had to sit down on the steps for a few moments, trying to regain enough strength to walk through the kitchen and out the back door. In a moment, he got to his feet.

As he moved down the remaining dark stairs, the presence of magic roiled across his skin, making the hairs on his arm stand on end from its pulsating, electric energy. He paused on the bottom step. He was in no condition to face Sebille and the others, but she rarely offered choice to anyone.

That was the way of the Fey—and most magic.

When Shade couldn't stand the painful energy raking his skin any longer, he stepped into the living room and staggered through the dark house toward the back door. As he entered the kitchen, the unearthly pale glow of magic gleamed from Kendra's garden. Illuminated like an aurora borealis, the colors shifted and danced in the warm darkness.

He stood there a long time, watching the graceful dance of blue and pink faerie orbs in the gleaming garden. They hung in the air like strings of garden lights and he wondered what the neighbors might think. Of course, they'd lived near Emmaline Martin for years, so nothing probably surprised them now. Kendra knew very little about that side of her grandmother.

Sucking in another breath, like swallowing broken glass, Shade opened the back door and stepped onto the patio.

The pergola lit with gossamer faerie wings from the tiniest of their kind, dressed in silks and fabrics lighter than air. Palest ivory, buttery yellows, robin's egg blues, and powdery pinks. Even the freshest bloom of lilac. The air smelled of ozone and roses as he studied the garden.

A small dappled unicorn the size of a pony stood under the Japanese maple, its snowy mane and shiny silver horn bright against the deep red leaves. In the center of the garden, elvenkind clustered around a bed of sunflowers (Kendra must have dreamed those up after he'd gone), their lithe stalks tall and lean, huge yellow sun-like blossoms turned toward the sliver of moon. The elvenkind's skin was pearlescent, frosted silver with moonglow as they stared at him with stoic expressions, long ears gently tapered to points beneath hair the color of starlight. The intensity of their large amethyst eyes made him uncomfortable. He looked away.

Kendra had added a small weeping willow and two dogwoods in a half moon beside the bed of herbs on the north end of the garden. Wood nymphs in diaphanous draped white gowns flitted between the small trees, their milky, pastel blue skin looked powder-soft and their thick, walnut hair flowed around their shoulders. They had large, wide set wood-brown eyes filled with wonder and conviction, their voices alto whispers on the breeze.

A man and woman sat in blue lounge chairs on Kendra's patio. Their skin held the moonglow, eyes hollow, mouths taut. Hungry, he realized.

They were vampires.

The woman wore a burgundy cocktail dress and pearls around her neck that she flicked with her deep red nails. She was tall and sinewy like the man, her hair a short blonde bob framing her tawny oval face and dark eyes. The man wore a white dress shirt and baggy dark pants, his shaggy wheaten hair tousled by the warm breeze. Their chiseled features made them attractive as a couple.

The man looked impatient, waiting for something to happen. The woman looked bored.

"Ah, look who we have here," said the male vampire, leaning forward in his lounge chair, amusement in his haunted eyes. "About time you showed up."

The woman shrugged then rolled her mahogany brown eyes. "I'm bored, Gabriel," said the woman, still clicking her pearls against her fingernails. "And I want to feed."

The vampire called Gabriel patted the woman on the arm, his eyes steely, determined, yet the hollowness remained—like most vampires.

"We'll go as soon as Sebille has spoken." He grinned, the faint sharp points of his incisors visible now. "I'm sure she has much to say tonight."

"North American tribe?" Shade asked.

Gabriel nodded.

Shade frowned. Only two vampires out of all the clans? They must not sense a threat by the Eidolon. Or care.

"Where are the others?"

"None felt this was important," Gabriel said with a shrug, staring at his squared, buffed fingernails. "I drew the short straw. I'll relay Sebille's message to the clans. Eventually, it will reach the tribes." He smirked. "Eventually. No doubt long after Sebille flays you alive, Green Man. I do enjoy a good bloodbath though, so this night won't be a complete and utter waste of time."

"Glad I'm at least entertainment, if nothing else," he replied.

"The very least," said the woman. Gabriel and the woman chuckled, watching him with bowed heads and upturned eyes.

Shade struggled with another breath, but it caught in his throat as Sebille, Queen of Faerie materialized beneath the trails of English roses. The air was fragrant with lilacs and hyacinths and her gown was diamond bright, the fabric flowing around her as if caught on the wind.

Her hair had the palest blush of champagne, long and coiled in ringlets over her alabaster shoulders. Lithe, willowy body, eyes large and lavender, her features drawn in silk. She wore a crown of starlight that spilled its sparkling dust across her clothing and skin. She stood beneath the pergola, four attendants carrying the silky train that trailed behind her like clouds.

Sebille was like the moon in its crescent form.

The garden fell silent, every magical being bowing in a deep gesture of respect before the Queen of Faerie.

"Well, my Green Man, at last you stand before us." Her voice was a dark chocolate alto. "No matter how much we despise you this night."

Mutters rose throughout the garden as wood nymphs gathered beside the elvenkind, gnomes and faerie folk skittering across the paths to stand beside three satyrs and two unicorns. The vampires rose from their chairs and stepped off the patio to stand beside Sebille, sunglasses perched on their noses.

Shade winced. They all stood as one against him. He leaned against the house, the aches trembling through his body. He was in no mood to fight all of the unseen world this night.

Gabriel spat on the ground, glaring at Shade. "You make me sick, Green Man."

Sebille laid a graceful hand against Gabriel's blousy sleeve. "It's all right, Gabriel. Let me finish please."

The young vampire nodded and remained quiet, his angry glare deepening.

Shade continued to lean against the side of the house, beside the back door, wanting to sit down. It was all he could do to remain vertical but he knew he had to listen. He understood their anger even though he could do little to quiet it.

Sebille raised a delicate eyebrow. "What? No response?"

Shade motioned at her, his arm falling to his side. Couldn't muster the strength. He laid a hand against the wall to steady himself.

"You've a right to your anger, Sebille," he said, trying to chase the weakness out of his voice, but it clung there like lichen. "I'll not argue that point."

Sebille propped her hands on her hips as she sauntered toward the patio, stopping at the first step. Her entourage trailed behind her.

"How dare you patronize me," she snapped. "You've infected our world with a plague of darkness, Shade. How did you think we'd react?"

He lowered his gaze. "The Eidolon came here long before I did, Your Majesty. While it's true they come through to hunt me and others like me, I didn't bring them."

Sebille pointed a finger at him. "But your kind brought them here. It's more or less the same thing."

Shade nodded, bowing his head. "You're right. I won't argue that point either." He looked up at her, his chest tight. "But you all know that matters little in the face of what's coming."

"And what is coming, Shade?" Sebille asked, her mouth turning up into a condescending smile.

"You know as well as I do what's coming, Your Majesty. The Eidolon seek to rule all worlds and after they've finished with mine, they'll come for yours."

Her laughter was like the clink of crystal and the rest of the creatures in the garden joined her, mocking him.

Shade shrugged off their arrogance and short-sightedness. They would learn soon enough how deadly the Eidolon were among them. Only the vampires looked unsettled.

"What if he's right, Sebille?" the woman vampire asked, letting go of her string of pearls. "We know little about these shadow creatures. Only that their presence and power are building. And that they are deadly."

"Lenora, dear," said Sebille, a hardness touching her face despite the pleasant smile. "That's not the issue. The issue is our Green Man's treachery. He's sold us out to creatures that could destroy us!"

A brooding look darkened Gabriel's face. Maybe he wasn't another one of Sebille's puppets after all?

"Seems to me he's running."

The vampire gazed at him and Shade felt his stare pierce him to his soul. Looking for deception, Shade realized. Vampires knew when someone lied. They saw the shadow of lies and knew truth when someone spoke it.

Shade nodded. "They seek to destroy me first," he replied, staring at Gabriel, hoping the vampire picked up his emotion of thanks. "Because I share their lineage. I hold their power in my hands."

"You?" Amusement cast a pale pink whisper across Sebille's cheeks. "Then why haven't you raised your little pinky and destroyed them, Shade? And saved us all from this horrible war?"

Laughter rippled across the garden, the faerie lights floating like fireflies across the patio.

Shade bristled at her comments but held his tongue. Angering the Queen of Faerie further would accomplish nothing.

He held out his hands. "I have no magical focus, Sebille. My Katorin heritage has left me unable to focus my Eidolon magic. Here, in your world, I'm protected until the ebony moon because your cycle of magic follows the moon. Like the tides."

Gabriel frowned and cast a look at Sebille.

"The Green Man. We've always known him otherworldly, with the greening and all—but a halfling?" At last, Gabriel turned back to Shade. "You're part wilding and part darkness. The darkness of these shadow people?"

Shade nodded and pointed to his light blue eyes. "My wilding is obvious," he said. "But combined with the dark magic, it's deadly. The dark magic is rare even among the Eidolon. A gift passed to me by my Eidolon father."

"Then why hasn't he reined in his own people?" Sebille demanded.

"They imprisoned him for helping me cross through to your world. After they labeled me heir to the throne and a threat—and one that must perish. He saved my life and rots in prison because of it." Shade sighed and stepped away from the wall, his legs shaky. "My wilding and the greening are Katorin gifts. If only they had been tempering."

"Tempering? What is that?" the woman vampire asked, face contorting like his gift was an ugly handbag she'd picked up by mistake.

"The more powerful the wilding," he explained, "the harder it is to wield, to control. It and the Eidolon magic have always been kept in check by Katorin tempering. Until the Eidolon hunted down and destroyed all the temperists—and the balance of power. That's partly why I came here. To your world."

Gabriel frowned. "What balance of power?"

"The Katorin magical lines are all but lost. One member escaped long ago. A halfling like me who joined with the humans. That line still exists and I'm trying to find its descendants. With the tempering magic's focus, I can defeat the Eidolon once and for all. But without that focus, the Eidolon will destroy my homeland. And yours."

The mirth left Sebille's face, the garden falling quiet now. He felt them weighing his statements, considering that what he'd said was truth.

"Like it or not," Shade said, his voice rising, "you're all a part of this battle."

"How does this otherworldly situation even affect us when you claim this war will be fought on your soil?" Gabriel asked, crossing his arms.

Shade shook his head. "Ultimately, when I return to Katori with the tempering magic, I'll face the Eidolon in the flesh. But before that night, on the next ebony moon, the Eidolon will send vast forces against your world."

"To destroy you?" Sebille asked, motioning toward him. "That hardly seems a loss. I'll hand you over without pause."

Twitters of laughter touched his ears. From the tiniest faerie folk.

"That may be true," said Shade with a shrug. "But it's not only me they seek to destroy. It's the woman who lives in this house."

"Emmaline Martin?" Sebille asked. "But she left this plane long ago." She crossed her arms across her chest and rolled her eyes. "I assumed you had resurrected this garden to call us to your cause."

Shade shook his head. "No, it's Emmaline's granddaughter. She's got the greening, Sebille. She brought this garden back from its fallow beds. And she carries the tempering flame I need to face the Eidolon. They've found her and they will try to destroy her. She's Emmaline's blood line. One of your own. You won't turn your back on one of the Fey. Even if she is a halfling."

He knew how much Sebille adored Emmaline Martin, treating her almost as a daughter and it hurt her deeply when she learned that Emmaline aged as humans aged. Many times, Sebille had tried to convince Emmaline to return with her to Faerie, but Emmaline felt a stronger need to stay among the humans. The Faerie Queen mourned a long time after the old woman's death, knowing they would never cross paths again. She would take great interest in Emmaline's children and grandchildren.

"Her granddaughter, Kendra," Shade continued in a soft voice, "brought back this garden. Out of love for her grandmother."

Crystalline tears formed in Sebille's eyes. "She restored this wondrous place, this meeting of worlds as it had been. As Emmaline had loved it. I'm grateful to her for this."

Shade took an unsteady step across the patio toward Sebille. "She's in great danger. The Eidolon will try to destroy her on the new moon. They will send a force against her and me, one unlike any others that have crossed the veil before. Alone, we have no hope of surviving it. But with your help—"

"My help?" Sebille laughed again, a hand against her chest as she turned to face the other magical realms standing in Kendra's garden. "He wants us to fight his war for him."

"No," Shade snapped through gritted teeth. "We want your help. Without it, we are lost." He took another step forward until he was at the patio's edge. "I appeal to your sense of justice, of duty, please—help me fight them. Stand with me against them, so I can take this fight back to my world. And hopefully, end it there."

The garden fell deathly quiet.

Shade glanced from the satyrs to the wood nymphs and back to Sebille, but no one responded to his request. As if he'd never spoken. They had no desire to fight a battle with him or help him hold back these shadow creatures.

Finally, Gabriel walked back onto the patio to face Shade.

"This battle," he said after a moment or two of silence. "It's imminent, you say?"

He nodded. "They will set such a massive force against us on the ebony moon...there is no way we'll survive it. Me or Kendra Martin." He sighed, running a hand through his dark hair. "The forces that slip through will bring others until you'll be overrun. The Eidolon will cast their shadow presence into all of your safe havens until they destroy the rest of your worlds."

"And we have only you to blame, Green Man," Sebille said, her hard-edged stare making Shade angry.

"That's what you do best, Your Majesty." His temper flared and he had no chance of getting them behind his cause. "Place blame rather than troops. You have a chance to stop this, but you choose to blame me instead. Like you, I didn't start this fight. But with your help, I can finish it. I can take it back to my world and save yours. But only if you stand with me on the next ebony moon."

"You're asking us to fight the Eidolon alongside you?" Gabriel asked, the intensity of his gaze unnerving Shade.

Would Gabriel suddenly decide to plunge his fangs into his neck while the others looked on in boredom? But he sensed no hunger in those eyes, no craving to consume him. Gabriel craved only answers.

Shade nodded. "Yes, that's exactly what I'm asking. The Eidolon forces will be too vast...I can't stop them all. Alone, I can't turn them from your world and back into mine."

Gabriel studied him for a few more nerve-wracking moments before he turned to Sebille. "Please, Sebille, don't dismiss his request out of hand. Consider what he asks." He cast another long stare at Shade, searching for deception again. "I, for one, would be willing to stand with you, Green Man. If it would send these creatures back to where they came from, I'm willing to try."

"So will I," said Lenora, waving a hand at him. "We'll talk this over with the tribe. See how many will stand with us."

"Thank you," said Shade, smiling at Lenora.

People knocked vampires, but Shade had always been able to count on them when everyone else walked away. Granted, they made him nervous at times and some were little more than butchers, but many of them, like Gabriel and Lenora, had integrity and a commitment to protect others.

He studied Sebille as she moved back beneath the pergola, her lithe form mingling with the faeries of her court. Male and female alike, they materialized in sparkling bursts beside her and spoke in hushed tones. He had no idea what was said, but the number of faerie courtiers grew as Sebille walked down the pergola. He wondered what thoughts traversed her mind right now and he wondered if the vampires' declaration of assistance had swayed her at all.

In the end, Shade walked toward the back door and leaned against the house as he watched Sebille work her way through the fluttering clutch of nymphs and on to the elven folk. Without her translucent faerie wings, Sebille could have been elven with her delicate bone structure and noble features. Where the Fey had alabaster skin, the elvish peoples had silvery skin that had a pale blue or lavender cast. Elves were less flamboyant than the Fey, less interested in play and more concerned with the proper movement of magic through the world. They saw humans as partners, not as playthings like the Fey.

Shade felt the muscles in his shoulders knot as he waited for the Queen of Faerie to respond, to speak about the battle, to even acknowledge it. Gabriel laid a hand on his sleeve.

"Don't write her off yet, Shade," said Gabriel, a slight smile that revealed a hint of his frost-white fangs. "She's considering your request this time. Don't rush her and you might gain her support."

Shade nodded. "I hope you're right. Without the support of this magical realm, we stand little hope of surviving the next Eidolon assault."

"Is that where your injuries came from?" Gabriel asked, pointing toward his back. "I can taste your loss of blood. It was severe."

Shade nodded. "I didn't think I'd live to see the sun rise. Without Kendra's tempering flame, I'd be dead now."

"This tempering must be powerful magic."

"Combined with my wilding," he said, running his fingers through his hair, "it will hold back the wave of Eidolon. They will never consume your world or Katori."

Gabriel nodded. "I hope they never gain a foothold here."

"They're ruthless," said Shade. "Willing to destroy everything in their path to achieve their goal. They've enslaved their own scryves with rare magics, forcing them to send troops through the obsidian gates within temples. Gates meant for exploration, to locate others with Eidolon magic, but never meant to wage war. In their eyes, it's acceptable that a whole world should perish because of one person."

Gabriel frowned. "Don't think I've encountered anything like that in my centuries of life."

"Mine either. That's why we've got to band together and stop them. It's the only way. Fortunately, they can only come through in close proximity to those from my realm. That's how the gates work."

"Good," said Gabriel. "I'd hate to imagine them pouring into every crevice on the globe." He extended his hand. "My tribe will stand with you. I don't care what Sebille decides, we'll stand with you."

Shade choked up, a painful breath catching in his throat as he reached out and shook Gabriel's hand.

"There are others who ignore these sorts of gatherings," said Lenora, walking toward them with a slink in her walk. "Wizards, sorceresses—witches...I will tell them what you need, Shade, and hopefully, they'll stand with us, too."

He nodded. "We need as much magic as we can assemble. The Eidolon force will be huge."

At last, Sebille made her way past the unicorns and sauntered back toward the pergola, her train floating behind her, held in the air by the tiniest of faerie. She'd completed the entire circle of Kendra's garden, speaking with all the magical entities gathered.

"All right, Green Man," she said with a sigh. "It is the wisdom of this council that we should band together against this dark threat. All of faerie will stand with you on the next ebony moon."

For a moment, he was stunned. He'd expected Sebille to put a bounty on his head and deem him an undesirable. A target to all magical beings in this realm.

"Thank you, Your Majesty," he said, his voice tight as he bowed before her. He nearly blacked out with the shift but held onto consciousness as he straightened to his full height again.

She pointed a finger at him. "But if you have lied to us, you will pay a dear price. I assure you of that."

"Of course," he replied, her threat making him feel a little queasy.

The Fey jumped to conclusions and decided what was truth, regardless of the facts.

There was a time when he'd longed for her acceptance, her protection—even her attention once, but he quickly realized that was part of her spell, part of her nature. It made the heartiest of men fall hopelessly in love with her and sometimes, Shade wondered if that had been where Sebille's animosity for him had first developed. He'd never fallen madly in love with her like every other being she'd encountered.

Maybe she'd expected that and when he didn't fall for her, she began to hate him?

"Your Majesty, I have no proper words to thank you," said Shade as he struggled to walk toward her. Every nerve in his body screamed when he dropped down on one knee and took her hand in his, pressing a feather soft kiss against the back of her hand. "Your assistance is invaluable and I will forever sing your praises in Katori."

"If you live that long," she said and shook her head.

"My thanks, Your Majesty," he repeated, letting go of her hand.

A leopard cub appeared beside Sebille and she stroked the cub's soft spotted fur, delighting as the cat rubbed its face against her hand and purred.

"How will you stand against the Eidolon, Green Man?" Sebille asked. "How will you temper your wilding in such a short time?"

He shrugged. "I'll study and practice every moment until the fight arrives." It was all he could do.

"We'll let you get to it then," she said, turning away from him to face the others in the garden. "Assist our Green Man if he asks or your help. Return to this place before the ebony moon rises. I bid you good evening."

She turned back to him and cast a glowering expression at him with the shake of her head before she faded into the sparkle of stardust from her crown. Her entourage disappeared with her as brush and flowers rustled, the wind rising.

Gnomes scampered away, tiny faerie folk rising into the air. They flew toward the sliver of moonglow in the sky and disappeared. The unicorns galloped off into the night shadows until only Gabriel and Lenora stood on the deck, bathed in silvery moonglow.

"We'll return in a few evenings, to see what you need," said Gabriel, taking hold of Lenora's hand.

"I'll bring the wine," said Lenora over her shoulder.

Shade let out a breath. That would at least give him a few days to explain to Kendra that vampires were coming over for dinner.

11

The next morning, Kendra awoke early. She slid out of bed and grabbed her red robe before going into the front room to check on Fletcher. Sunlight washed the room and pecan-wood floors in warmth, falling softly on the bed and Fletcher's sleeping form. The air smelled dusty with a trace of lemons.

She sat down on the edge of the bed. He was on his side facing the door, dark hair tousled, breathing a little shallower than she'd hoped.

A slight rasp clung to each breath and she worried that he might still need a doctor.

She brushed a lock of dark hair off his forehead. His face looked almost boyish despite the day of dark beard shadowing his jaw. It was silky soft, not coarse like human beards. He had a finely sculpted nose and strong, tapered chin. His body was lean, chest smooth and muscled like an athlete. She wanted to run her hands across his chest, explore his beautiful body, tangle her feet around those long, runner's legs.

He was smokin' hot—even if he was crazy.

Last night had been so strange and even now, she wasn't sure she believed what she'd seen with her own eyes. And she didn't understand how she could summon anything by imagining it.

She laid her hand against his forehead. Hot. And damp with sweat.

Fletcher had a fever.

Why did she believe she could heal someone with pressure from her hand? What was she thinking? Especially for a wound that deep. Guilt ached through the pit of her stomach. She should have done the right thing and called 911. He could die.

The thick white bandage was still around his waist, a dark rusty stain on it. Another thick bandage hugged the curve of his shoulder, also blood-stained. They needed changing. His shirt was rumpled at the foot of the bed. Had he just taken it off?

She frowned. Last night, she'd put it on top of the dresser. Had he gone out last night?

His fever-bright eyes rolled open and he jolted.

"It's okay, Fletcher," she said in a half-whisper, stroking his long, dark bangs off his forehead. "Only me. Looks like you've got a fever."

"It'll pass," he said in a raspy voice. "I'd better get back to my place."

He started to rise, but she pressed both hands against his sexy bare chest.

"Oh, no, you don't. You're not going anywhere until you're well."

His eyes darkened at her order. He didn't like to be told what to do. She smirked. That made it so much more enjoyable.

"I can't stay here," he said in a gruff voice, trying again to rise, but Kendra pushed him back against the bed again.

"You can and you will," she said, her voice rising. "I mean it, Fletcher. If that knife wound had been any deeper, you'd be dead now. Not to mention that nasty gouge on your shoulder."

He rolled onto his back and with his left hand he anchored the pillows beneath his head. For several long moments, he stared at her.

"What?" she asked finally, holding out her hands. "Why are you staring at me like that?"

"I was thinking about the Eidolon. And how close we both came to dying."

His words hit her hard. As much as she tried to deny it, Fletcher was right.

"How was I able to summon up that knife?"

"It may be part of the tempering, but I'm not sure. It's not a magic I've seen before."

How many other magics lurked inside her?

All of this talk of magic and Eidolon sent her brain on overload. She didn't have time for it. She was only here for Toni Ambrose, giving her the next steps of a new business plan to expand her company. Growing it into something extraordinary, something Toni hadn't imagined when she made that first dress. All of that was Toni's doing. Kendra was only planning the resources to get her to the next level. That's why she was here—not for this magic craziness.

She stared at his ice blue eyes, trying so hard to read them. She hadn't come here to meet anybody, especially someone as loon-crazy as Shade Fletcher. Not even the garden had been a thought until she saw the desolate backyard and called up her childhood memories.

"You look a little dazed, Martin," he said, patting her arm with his over-warm hand. His body trembled a little.

"That's an understatement," she said. "All of this stuff scares me."

A worried look tugged his mouth into a grimace. "It'll get worse, trust me," he muttered.

"Fletcher, what do you expect from me?" she asked, rising from the bed to pace the wooden floor. "I know nothing about magic."

He shrugged. "Magic just is, there's no thinking required to understand it."

Kendra shook her head, hands on her hips, bathrobe falling open on her silk red night shirt.

"No, magic is Disney films, white rabbits, and fireflies on a summer night. To kids, it's second nature. Adults have trouble focusing on this kind of stuff. It's really hard when the Visa bill's due and you're out of toilet paper and you have a presentation in Cleveland on Wednesday."

"That's really sad, Kendra. Toilet paper?"

She hurried over and sat down on the edge of the bed again, taking hold of his arms to stare into those glacial blue eyes.

"No, it's the way it is. It's not the way we chose it or how we'd even prefer it. Real life intrudes despite our trying to pretend it's not there. With its errands and car payments and household repairs. Super mundane stuff that we all want to avoid but can't."

"And pretending magic is some movie on the Hallmark channel is no different?"

Her eyes widened. *He'd seen the Hallmark channel?*

"Yeah, I get cable," he snapped, eyes narrowed. "Hell, I even stream. I've been in your world a long time, remember?"

She hated it when he was right, but he was. She couldn't ignore this magic any more than she could ignore her job. If she'd ignored it last night, she'd have gotten her throat cut.

"You're right," said Kendra, bowing her head. "But understand, Fletcher, it's not second nature to me. It's hard, okay?"

He nodded, that luscious bow-shaped mouth curving into a smile. She wanted to press her mouth against his and check that fever properly.

"Fair enough," he replied.

She patted his leg and rose from the bed. "Okay, then you stay here while I get some supplies to change those dressings. And a thermometer to see how sick you really are."

That smile widened into a grin. "No magic?"

She glared at him. Okay, all she had to do was imagine them and they'd appear. Why not try it?

"Thermometer," she said and held out her hand.

A small thermometer appeared in her palm.

"No, the other kind that presses against the forehead," she said.

The thermometer disappeared, replaced by a curved blue plastic thermometer with a grey rubber tip that she saw in all the drugstores. It had an LCD screen and an *on* button. She pressed the button. When the screen lit and said ready, she pressed it against Fletcher's forehead and took his temperature. In a few seconds, it beeped. She pulled it away and looked at the screen.

One oh one point seven.

"Fletcher, you've got infection," she said with a frown.

He nodded, sinking back against the pillows. "Thought as much."

"First aid kit with bandages," she said and a white and red case appeared beside her.

Kendra opened the case and pulled out scissors, antibacterial ointment, and a roll of heavy gauze.

"Turn on your side, Fletcher, so I can look at this wound again."

He grumbled a little but turned onto his side. She ran her hand down his graceful, long spine, to the delicious curve of his lower back and took hold of the gauze, cutting it with the scissors. After removing last night's bandages, she peeled back the pad covering the puncture wound. It oozed blood and pus, the edges puffy and red.

"It's totally infected, Fletcher. I need to clean out this wound and dress it better."

"Do it—fast," he said through gritted teeth.

Kendra called up a bottle of hydrogen peroxide and soaked some cotton. As gently as she could, she pressed it to the wound, washing away dried blood and infection. He flinched with every stroke, groaning as she worked, but after a few minutes, it was clean. She applied ointment and wrapped the wound with fresh gauze. Calling up this strange energy inside her, she pressed her hand against the wound.

She closed her eyes and concentrated on healing the infection, knowing how painful the pressure of her hand must be on that tender wound. But Fletcher remained still and silent. Something within the wound, almost a force, seemed to push back at her, resisting her concentration.

She pushed harder. And held the energies longer.

Only when she felt the resistance fade did she let up, pulling away her hand.

Fletcher let out an exhausted sigh and slumped against the

pillows. Had he been fighting her or had it been the wound? Or something else?

She let him rest a moment or two and then made him sit up so she could wrap the gauze around his side, to keep the bandage in place. When she was finished, he laid back against the pillows on his side, allowing her to clean and dress the wound on his shoulder.

This wound looked much better than the other one, requiring only a little cleansing. She swiped it quickly with peroxide and taped a new bandage over the wound. Fletcher's eyelids drooped, his breathing a little easier. She laid her hand against his forehead. Cooler.

To make sure, she pressed the thermometer to his forehead until it beeped. Ninety-nine point eight. Much better.

"The fever's down,"

"Your magic worked again," he said.

She smiled as she stroked her fingers through his thick, dark hair. "Looks like it did."

"That feels nice," he said in a sleepy voice.

Kendra realized she was still stroking his hair and forehead. She pulled her hand away and his eyes opened wider, a faint smirk on his face.

"Why'd you stop?" he asked.

When she didn't reply, he laid his hand on top of hers, running his long, squared fingers across hers. The warmth of his touch spread like wildfire through her, hovering in her belly and she wanted to crawl into that bed with him.

"I've got to take a shower now, Fletcher," she said, sliding her hand out from under his.

"Need some company?" he asked with a smile.

He was too weak to even sit up right now. Even though she'd enjoy a long, hot shower against his soap-slicked body, he was much too weak and injured for that.

She smiled. Yet.

"Nice try," she said. "But no. "I've got to get back to a business plan. When I get out, I'll make you some breakfast, okay?"

He nodded.

"What do magical beings such as yourself eat for breakfast?" she asked with a wry smile.

"Pop Tarts," he replied. "Frosted, otherwise what's the point, y'know?"

She laughed. Figures. It was so Fletcher. "Right. Unfrosted toaster pastries are so unmagical and pointless. Any flavor preference?"

"Brown sugar cinnamon," he mumbled, the words barely audible as his eyes closed.

In a moment, his soft snores filled the room, his breathing much easier. He'd be fine. She patted him on his good shoulder, admiring the curve and definition of those muscles.

Pop Tarts for the Green Man, she thought with a shrug and rose from his bedside to take a shower. At least he hadn't requested Lucky Charms.

AFTER HER SHOWER, KENDRA DRESSED IN BLACK SWEAT PANTS AND A yellow tank top and went downstairs for coffee and Special K. She ate her cereal by the dining room window, mesmerized by her enchanting garden. Gem would be so pleased—magic or not.

Outside, Maddie stood by the gate, her face lily pale, her mouth gaping as she stared at the garden. Kendra cringed as the rusty gate rasped open and Maddie's hurried footfalls echoed outside. The anxious knock filled the house and she rose to open the door.

"Coffee?" Kendra asked.

"Oh my God...Kendra ...how'd you get, I mean—where'd you get—"

"Come in and sit down, Maddie," said Kendra, smiling as she opened the door wider.

Maddie ducked under her arm and hurried into the family room. She wore baggy tan shorts, a white T-shirt, and white Nike tennis shoes.

"I don't know how you did that!" Maddie cried.

She hated to lie to Maddie, but there was no way she could explain this rationally to her neighbor.

"Called a nursery out near Watsonville," she said, walking into the kitchen. "Told them exactly what I wanted and they put it all in." Kendra turned her gaze to the kitchen counter and imagined a hand drawing of her garden, one she might have drawn for a landscaper. "See?" she said, reaching for a dog-eared piece of white paper.

She handed the diagram to Maddie who seemed to calm down.

"Oh, I see," she said, her voice not so shrill now as she paced through the room. "You put in mature plants. Five-year-old trees. That makes sense." She looked up at Kendra, smiling at last. "I'm impressed, Kendra. You did a great planning job."

Kendra grinned. "All part of the service. I wanted it to look like it used to...when Gem was alive. She'd have loved this, wouldn't she?"

Maddie nodded, handing back the diagram. "She certainly would have. It's magnificent."

Kendra set down the diagram and picked up a green coffee mug. She held it out to Maddie. "Coffee?"

Maddie nodded and Kendra set down her own cup to fill the green one. She handed the mug to Maddie and slid the creamer and sugar bowl toward her. As Maddie doctored her coffee, Kendra returned to her cereal.

Her neighbor sat down at the old kitchen table, across from Maddie, and stared out at the garden as she sipped her coffee.

"What a view you have now! Almost blocks out Fletcher's awful ranch house."

Kendra smirked. Almost. But she didn't mind it so much now. She thought of him lying upstairs half naked in her front bedroom. Just her luck he was crazy. She wanted to find out how much—and crawl into bed with him.

"He's not so bad," said Kendra.

Maddie's mouth fell open and she set down her mug. "You can't be serious!"

Kendra nodded, finishing off the last bite of cereal. She slid the bowl out of her way and folded her arms against her chest.

"He uh—saved my life last night, Maddie."

The color drained out of Maddie's face, her eyes looking frightened now.

"Saved your life? How?"

She held in a groan, not wanting to tell her about the intruder. Another lie to her next-door-neighbor but it was better than her thinking that knife-wielding psychopaths were now roaming the Indiana countryside.

"I was working in the garden, trimming those boxwood hedges with an electric trimmer. Got the cord caught around the wrought iron table and grill. Almost pulled everything off the patio and on top of me. Fletcher was there to push me out of the way, but he got hit by the furniture. Got banged up pretty bad."

Maddie pressed a hand to her mouth. "Kendra! Glad you're all right. What about Fletcher?"

"He's better this morning but still needs some recuperation time." She pointed toward the hallway. "He's in my upstairs bedroom."

Maddie gasped, a hand to her chest. "He's here? In your house?"

Kendra nodded. "Like I said, he's not so bad. Saved my life."

Maddie leaned across the table, her voice barely above a whisper. "So, what's he like really?" She smiled. "Bet he looks even better without his shirt."

"Maddie!" Kendra snapped.

She didn't blink or smile. "Well, does he?"

"I can't believe you're asking me that." She smiled, knowing Maddie was right. "And yes, he does. It was a pleasure to bandage his ribs."

Her next-door-neighbor grinned and picked up her coffee cup, not saying another word as she looked out at the garden. But Kendra saw her grin behind the cup.

"So, Fletcher's in your bedroom," Maddie said finally. "No wonder you didn't come to the front door when I knocked earlier."

"As if," said Kendra, rolling her eyes as she picked up her coffee cup steeped with milk and sugar. More like coffee-flavored milk but she liked it that way.

Maddie finished off her coffee and rose from the table. "I'll let you get back to work," she said with a wink, her gaze trailing toward the hallway.

"Goodbye, Maddie," Kendra said in an annoyed tone as she rose to open the back door.

"Call me after he goes home," she whispered and sauntered outside.

Kendra ignored her, closing the door. She rinsed the coffee cups and her cereal bowl then loaded them into the dishwasher. She turned away but stopped and went back to the dishwasher. She grabbed the door handle.

"Clean," she said and opened the door.

Everything inside was spotless. She closed the door again.

"Put it all away."

When she opened the door again, the machine was empty.

"I'm definitely liking this magic stuff," she said and closed the dishwasher door.

"Pop Tarts," she said and opened the cabinet beside the refrigerator. "Brown sugar cinnamon."

A blue box sat inside. She set it on the counter and opened it, pulling out a silver pouch containing two Pop Tarts. She opened it and plopped the pastries into the toaster, pressing down the lever. When the scent of brown sugar and hot cinnamon tanged the air, the toaster spat out the pastries. She dropped them onto a plate and carried it upstairs.

He was barely awake as she entered the room, sitting up against the headboard, his eyes looking feverish. He managed a smile when she walked in with the plate.

"What would you like to drink?" she asked setting the plate beside him.

"Got any milk?" he asked.

She held out her hand.

"Whole, two percent, skim?"

A scowl touched his face. "Skim? That's colored water."

"Oh, I get it. Only real men drink whole milk?"

He shook his head. "No, I only want it to taste like milk." He took a bite of his Pop Tart. "What do you suggest?"

"Any milk but skim," said Kendra, holding out her hand again. "Cold."

The full glass of cold milk appeared, numbing her hand as she held it out to him. He took it but quickly set it on the nightstand.

"That's really cold," he said. He took a few more bites of the Pop Tart before he picked up the glass and drank a tentative sip.

It didn't take him long to drain the glass. He picked up the other Pop Tart and took another bite. She started out of the room, but he motioned toward her.

"Kendra, wait," he said.

She stopped in the doorway as he pointed at the empty glass of milk.

"How about seconds?" he asked, his mouth full, a milk moustache clinging to his lip.

She smiled and pointed at the glass.

"More cold milk," she said.

The glass filled with milk again.

"Thanks," he replied, picking up the glass.

"Now, get some sleep, okay? I'll be downstairs if you need anything."

He nodded, picking up the last Pop Tart again.

———

KENDRA SPENT THE MORNING AND PART OF THE AFTERNOON ON THE phone, talking with locals about warehouse space, banks about financing options, and discussed distribution strategies with boutiques and clothing stores interested in Toni's dresses.

She did her best to focus all her attention on Toni's business plan, but her thoughts kept wandering upstairs to Shade Fletcher. The heat flushed her face at the thought of him. She'd never felt this way before.

Dammit, she didn't have time to feel this way! Even if she did, she was leaving soon. And hookups weren't her thing. Especially the way she already felt about the guy.

If she slept with him, she might volunteer to be his love slave. Of course, she could always write a tell-all: *I Slept with The Green Man.* She grinned. It would be much more interesting than this business plan.

Kendra set aside her ThinkPad and rose from the couch, her long legs stiff. She walked around the room, stretching her arms and legs when she heard creaking on the stairs. She started down the hallway when Fletcher appeared, dressed in shorts and his torn shirt hanging open. He staggered a bit, head down, steps uneven.

"Fletcher, what in God's name are you doing?"

She moved toward him and grabbed hold of his arms. He tried to step around her, but he was too weak. His knees buckled and he sank. She caught him, easing him down onto the stairs until he was leaning against the wall.

"Thought I'd get back—to my place now."

Kendra smiled at him and shook her head. "You're not going anywhere, mister. At least not today."

His glacial eyes sparked a cold flame, but he was too exhausted to protest.

"I'm...not used to this," he said in a tired voice.

"What?" she asked, dropping down on her haunches beside him. "Not used to taking orders or not used to being cared for?" She shook her head. "Neither one will kill you, you know."

He flashed her an indignant look and looked away.

"I get it. It's the being taken care of part you're not so good with. Well, Fletcher, sometimes you've got to trust people. We don't always suck."

His gaze met hers this time and he stared at her a moment. "What about you?" he asked. "Do you trust me?"

She leaned against the opposite wall in the hallway. "Complicated question," she said, brushing hair out of her eyes. "If you'd asked me that question yesterday, I'd have said no. Today...after watching you get between those shadow people and their weapons—for me, I'd say yes."

The corners of his mouth lifted into almost a smile.

"What about you, Fletcher?" she asked, arms across her stomach. "Do you trust me?"

He looked at her a moment then nodded. "More than you'll ever know."

His words sent a chill and a rush of emotion through her. What was behind those words? He was deadly serious, not even a blink of those ice blue eyes. He didn't know anything about her but he'd known Gem. Maybe that's all he needed to know?

"Because of Gem?" she asked.

He shook his head. "Not exactly. How can I not trust a woman who saves my life after I punked her front yard?"

Kendra laughed, remembering the hot pink yard she'd woken up to and that sexy smirk on Fletcher's tanned face when he admitted he'd done the deed.

"Did that paint glow in the dark?" she asked.

He burst out with a belly laugh, holding his side as he nodded. "It was a thing of beauty from the street that night. You could see it a mile away."

Kendra couldn't hold in her laugh, imagining how her glow-in-the-dark, hot pink yard must have looked from the road.

"Okay, it was funny," she said, sitting up. "But I wasn't going to tell you that."

He nodded, glancing down at the floor. "Figured as much."

"Why'd you really do it?" Kendra asked. "Because I called the cops on your party? Looking back, your Eidolon guests weren't much of a party. Sorry about that."

He waved her off. "That was my initial reason, but when I saw you through the window that night..." He bowed his head again, running his hand down his calf and bare foot. "I—I wanted to get your attention."

He looked up as she started to speak but the intenseness of his expression shook the words right out of her head. Her chest tightened.

He wanted to get *her* attention.

"Because you were a pervert, peeping through my windows?" she asked with a grin and poked him in the shoulder.

"Pervert?" His eyebrows pressed into a hard line above his eyes. "I was a voyeur...and your drapes were open—"

She pressed her hand to his mouth. "Lighten up, Fletcher," she said in a quiet voice. "It was a joke."

Those warm, soft lips pressed against her palm, kissing, sipping, and her arm drooped. He took hold of her arm, running his fingers down its length as he kissed the top of her hand.

She gasped.

"By the way," he said with hurried breaths. "Can you cook red meat?"

"Why?" she asked, drawing in a quick breath. "Why would you ask me that—now?"

"Because," he said, kissing down her arm. "I invited a couple of vampires to dinner." His face was against her neck now, nuzzling, sipping her neck with soft kisses with his hot mouth.

Kendra moaned and turned her head to smash her lips against his in a hard kiss. She opened her mouth to him, her tongue against his for a moment. Then she pulled back.

"Wait, what'd you say?" she asked.

He pulled her toward him again, his mouth against hers, kissing her lips and down her neck again.

"Vampires," he said between kisses. "Your house for dinner. Tomorrow night. They love steak. Rare."

Oh. Of course. Vampires. At her house for dinner tomorrow night. Steak. How silly of her to expect they'd be vegans.

12

Kendra pulled away from him, eyes wide, mouth open. "Vampires? Are you high?"

Shade sighed. Okay, so maybe that hadn't been the best way to tell her that vampires were part of the magical world. Or coming to dinner.

He held out his hand, trying to calm her down, but she jumped up from the steps and retreated into the family room. She began pacing the wooden floor, arms folded against her chest. The boards creaked with her constant motion.

"It's only two," he said, trying to keep the annoyance out of his voice. "It's not like I invited the whole North American tribe."

Her hands flew to her hips as she whirled around, those brown eyes sizzling. He held back a grin. She was so sexy when she got mad, the heat radiating.

"No, of course not. Only a couple. How much could they eat? Hey, it's a small neighborhood. We'll have a barbeque, invite the neighbors. Won't they wonder why there aren't more steaks on the grill? Or why we're asking all these questions about their blood types?"

Shade bristled. "Not all vampires are B-movie predators, Martin.

They're a good bunch of people. Will help you sometimes when no one else even offers."

The memory of the garden burned through him, when Sebille and every magical creature within range wanted to throw him to the Eidolon. Only Gabriel and Lenora offered their unconditional support.

She shook her finger at him. "I saw Dawn to Dusk and Interview with a Vampire, so don't tell me they aren't predators! I still have nightmares about Kirsten Dunst. That little girl was terrifying!" She glared at him. "And don't you dare tell me they all sparkle. I will hurt you."

He tried not to laugh, but it bubbled up as he leaned against the wall, his knees feeling shaky.

"Give 'em a break, okay? They helped me out of a jam and they're willing to stand with me against the Eidolon. Gabriel and Lenora think very highly of your garden and they want to preserve the magical balance. And you."

At last, she calmed down, crossing her arms again, her frightened eyes narrowing now with that quiet anger she'd shown about her hot pink lawn. He felt some of the tension drain. Glad that was out of the way.

"Okay, they can come to dinner," she said and laid a hand against her throat. "But I'm wearing a turtleneck, got it?"

He chuckled. "Don't you think that might be a bit insulting to our guests?"

"Our guests?" she sputtered. "First of all, you're a guest, too and second of all, I consider it pretty insulting to make your hostess one of the undead. Undead is not how I wanted to spend my summer, Shade Fletcher...although, this is Indiana. No one would notice—at least for a while. When husbands and friends started disappearing..."

He held up a hand, still smiling but feeling tired again. "Martin, I wish you'd meet them first. They're good people."

"I don't know how to cook a steak," said Kendra in an exasperated voice, her features sharpening with anxiety.

He walked toward her and before he'd even thought it through, he slid his arms around her shoulders and pulled her against him.

"I'll grill the steaks. You cook the rest of the meal. Lenora's bringing the wine."

He was surprised to feel her trembling. He held her out at arm's length and studied her face a moment. "You really are scared, aren't you?"

She sighed then nodded, looking away. "I'm not used to all this magic stuff. First, shadow creatures nearly slit my throat and now, I have to entertain vampires." Her gaze flicked toward him, the anger returning. "You're used to pixies and vampires and werewolves and God knows what else. These things are part of childhood horror stories to me."

He shook his head. "No werewolves. Too unpredictable. Besides... I'm allergic to dogs."

She laughed. "Really?"

He nodded. "I much prefer werecats."

"Why?" she asked, clutching his arms.

"Werecats hate humans. Most of the time, they stay far away. And when they do go near humans, it's to claw up their furniture and pee on their rugs."

"You're making that up," she said, the smile brightening her face.

He let go of her to hold up his right hand. "The Moon's own truth, Martin. I swear it."

She laid her hand against the side of his face, brushing a lock of hair out of his eyes as she moved toward the kitchen.

"I won't let any harm come to you, Martin," he said, following her. "That, I promise you."

He sat down hard in a wooden chair beside the window, gazing out at the handfuls of butterflies flitting through Kendra's garden. Many of those butterflies were faeries, but he wouldn't tell her that yet. They swam through the air in sparkling gold trails that caught the sun's shimmer.

"Coffee?" she asked as she opened the cabinet and held out a red bag of coffee. "It's Seattle's Best. Cinnabon."

He frowned. "What's that?"

"You've never had Cinnabon?"

He shook his head. Sounded like something he'd like.

"Let me introduce you to a little swirl of heaven, Fletcher," she said with a smile and held out her hands, palms up. "Much better than those Pop Tarts of yours." She stared at her hands a moment. "Two Cinnabon's on a plate. Hot. Extra cream cheese icing."

The strong smell of cinnamon wafted through the room as two gooey cinnamon rolls materialized in her hands on a bright white plate. She carried the plate over to the table and set it down, rich scent of cinnamon and warm cream cheese filling the room. Then she returned to the kitchen to make coffee.

"What, no instant coffee, too?"

She turned around and winked at him and he felt that wink burn through his veins. "Not even magic's better than fresh brewed."

In a minute or two, the coffee maker squinched steaming coffee into a glass carafe. She filled two red coffee cups and set them on the table. She set Gem's cow-shaped creamer and crescent moon sugar bowl on top of two small red plates, grabbed two forks, and plopped all of it down on the table.

"Dig in," said Kendra, reaching for a plate and one of the huge rolls. She plopped one on her plate and licked the cream cheese icing off her fingers with a delicious smile on her face.

His blood boiled watching her. And he wanted to kiss that icing off her lips.

"Go on," she urged, "before they get cold."

His stomach felt a little queasy, but he slid one of the rolls onto the other small plate with a fork. He cut into it. She watched him as he lifted the big bite to his mouth. She snickered at him.

"You've got icing on your nose," she said and hurried into the kitchen for some paper towels. "Here," she said, handing him one.

He wiped away the icing as he chewed, the pastry warm and saturated with cinnamon.

"Where do you get these cinnamon things?" he asked. "Besides conjuring them up from thin air."

"At the mall," she said, taking another bite, the cream cheese icing clinging to her upper lip.

God, he wanted to taste that icing on her lips.

Okay, so this Cinnabon thing was much better than a Pop Tart. Without her little gift, he'd never have another one though. He was the Green Man. The mall wasn't his thing.

They ate in silence until finally he'd finished his Cinnabon, as she called it, and drank his coffee. He slid his plate away from the table's edge and rose unsteadily from the chair.

"I think I'm well enough to go home now. Thanks for everything, Martin."

She stood up, scrubbing her hands with the dry paper towel.

"No way, Fletcher. One more night to make sure that lung's okay and the fever's gone."

"It's not necessary," he said, waving her off as he walked toward the back door.

Kendra stepped in front of it, arms splayed, feet apart, ready to fend him off from the door.

"I'm not letting you leave, Fletcher."

"Why?" he demanded, stepping forward until his feet were touching hers, her nose an inch from his throat.

"Because," she said, her voice soft as she looked into his eyes. "What if more of those things are lying in wait for you in the woods behind your place? With your reflexes slowed, they could kill you in your sleep. They wouldn't need to be in shadow form."

The cold logic cut through him. She was right.

He had no idea how many Eidolon got through that night. The fact that they'd nearly killed Kendra meant they could attack and kill him easily, too. No shadow form needed. No telling how many remained out there, lying in wait for him.

"Could they materialize somewhere else and travel here?" she asked.

He shook his head. "No, they can only through in close proximity to me. It's how the obsidian gates work in my realm."

She frowned. "Obsidian gates?"

He nodded. "Katorin obsidian is highly prized for its prismatic focus of magic. The temple gates were created to find others through the veil that had similar magics and transport my people to them. Magic ebbs and flows with the cycles of the moon. When the moon is new and dark, the magical tide is low. So, crossing the veil doesn't cause ripples in magic or time. And crossing is easier."

"So, the ebony moon is low tide for magic?" Kendra replied. "Makes it easier to cross and less likely someone will notice?"

"Exactly," he said with a deep nod.

There was also safety in numbers, especially since Kendra could protect both of them with her magic. Until he learned to focus his abilities.

A warding spell! If he taught her how, she could help him set one around his place. The dull ache in his back still throbbed with each breath. He was better but not one hundred percent yet. He didn't have the strength or the concentration to teach her how to ward anything right now—or contribute his part of the magic to create a protection spell.

Maybe one more night wouldn't hurt? Besides, he'd risk it to spend one more night with Kendra.

He nodded finally. "Okay, you win," he said. "I'll stay tonight." He reached out and cupped her chin. "And tonight, I'll give you your first lesson."

Her eyes widened and she licked her lips, her body tensing as she leaned toward him.

"My first lesson in what?"

"Magic," he said.

"Oh. Right. Honestly though, there's not much to it," she said with a shrug.

His mood darkened a little. Dammit, she had a point. All she had to do was think of something and it materialized. What did he have left to teach her? He was the one who couldn't focus his magic into anything useful.

"Good point." He reached out and ran his fingers through her soft, raspberry-scented hair. "Maybe you can give *me* my first lesson then? Without your tempering flame, my magic has no focus."

Kendra frowned as she slid past him, wandering toward the family room, a pensive look in those warm brown eyes. He followed her, old pecan-wood floors creaking.

"But how can I give you focus, Fletcher? I'm willing to try, of course, but I don't know what to do."

"I'm not exactly sure yet," said Shade with a sigh. "But I know someone I can ask. Tonight...when the moon rises."

He moved over to the yellow couch in front of the window and sat down, feeling tired. Laying his head back, he stared at the ceiling with its crown molding nestled around a light fixture that looked like six ivory candles perched on a metal ring suspended in the air.

"Who will you ask, Fletcher?" Kendra asked, walking into the kitchen.

He heard dishes clinking in the sink. The rush of water from the faucet filled the room, followed by more dish clinking. In a moment, she returned and sat beside him on the couch. She stared at him expectantly a moment.

"Fletcher?" she said. "Who you planning to ask?"

"Rhiannon," he said, lifting his head.

He stared into Kendra's animated brown eyes, admiring that touch of innocence that sometimes appeared when she let down her guard.

She frowned, cocking her head. "Who's that?"

"Goddess of the moon."

He flinched. Once his lover.

Long ago, he'd lost his heart to her, given it freely, all of it. At first, she'd loved her Green Man. She loved his otherworldliness, his mystery, his love of the forest, and the wilding that raged inside him. But those attractions soon became annoyances until she grew to despise them. And him. Rhiannon loved him in her own way, but the moment she'd laid gaze on Pwyll, there was no other.

In an instant, it was over between them.

For a long time, he'd carried a torch for her, a flicker of hope. And he'd swallow that pain and seek her help if it meant an end to the Eidolon domination in his world. He'd lived a long time as an outcast in both realms.

Rhiannon still saw him as an outcast. She carried her own darkness inside, that sharp-edged slant of her own truth that stung and cut deep, denying reality, denying how much he'd loved her once, and denying the depth of his sacrifice to save his world.

Despite her milky skin, golden hair, and the fastest white horse the world had ever seen, she was still more darkness than light. The night ruled her and she preferred it that way, loving the moonglow and the stars and the delicate softness of the world under that indigo blanket.

There had never been a place for him under the moon's glow. It had already controlled him for centuries. And he tired of living half a life. Always alone.

"So, now, I've got to entertain a moon goddess, too?" Kendra clicked her tongue at him. "I swear, Fletcher, before this summer is over, you're going to drive me completely insane."

He cast an uneasy glance at her. "I hope we live long enough for the trip."

"So, what exactly do moon goddesses eat?" she asked, rising from the couch to pace again.

She did that a lot.

He chuckled, leaning back on the couch to relieve the ache in his back. "Relax. She's a vegan."

Kendra rolled her eyes. "Terrific. I'll serve her as the appetizer to the vampires. Or is a moon goddess best served cold—to werewolves? Sorry, werecats." She groaned. "Where's Emeril when I need him?"

He grinned, imagining Rhiannon and Lenora facing off. Not a bad image, he realized, laying a hand against his chin. Add Kendra to the mix and he might pull up a chair for that one.

Kendra muttered to herself about side dishes and what kind of salad dressing vampires ate as she rushed into the kitchen and pored through the kitchen cabinets.

His money was on Martin in that fight, he decided. Nobody had ever made him feel quite the way she made him feel. Comfortable. Normal. And he barely knew the woman. He knew he had to be careful though. If this kept up, she'd have his heart in her hands before summer's end. Before long, he'd be willingly handing it over to her.

"Kendra, come sit down. Why are you worried? You conjured cinnamon rolls right out of the air. You could ask for their dinner preferences when they arrive and snap it into existence."

Her head popped up above the sink, dark hair in her eyes as she smiled at him.

"You're right," she said, smiling, those eyes sizzling with sunlight. "I'll worry about that tomorrow then."

He patted the cushion beside him and motioned her over.

She hesitated, her eyes widening, but when he motioned at her a second time, she shuffled out of the kitchen and sat down beside him.

"Tell me about your world," she said, her gaze filling with wonder.

He gritted his teeth, remembering the devastation, so many Katorin villages burning, the great cities of their land still under a shadowy siege.

They came at first light. When Airell's streets were rain-soaked from the long night and pale grey clouds reflected in the puddles from the first rays of dawn, Carvahl's army scaled the walls.

He'd fled with his siblings into a swell of Katorin soldiers and citizens, flooding into the streets as his mother led them to the edge of town. To the scryve's cottage. He and his family had been preparing for this moment for a long while. Despite the terror of this sudden attack, they knew where to run.

Hekalie, an Eidolon scryve and his grandmother, knew what to do, too.

His father's mother had been sworn to the grim task of using her magic to cross the veil into the human world, sending through one Katorin with the magic.

He remembered Hekalie whispering in his ear that morning, her tall, slim body rheumy and slow, dark hair in wild ringlets around her long, aging face. Sky blue eyes so bright with magic. She looked like a thin, gnarled tree in full leaves, her movements stiff as she gathered up her tools and placed them around her obsidian scrying ball.

The black, mirrored ball reflected back the terrified faces of his four siblings, all with their warm brown hair, dark eyes, and summer tanned faces. And the taut desperation in his mother's face, eyes filled with tears, knowing she had to say goodbye to her first born.

A lump rose in his throat and he swallowed it hard. She knew she may never see him again.

"Find it," his mother had insisted, kissing him on the cheek, stroking his hair. "You're our last hope, Shade. Bring home the tempering flame before everything is lost."

So, Hekalie, with the strongest Eidolon magic he'd ever seen, conjured up shadowy forces that swirled and danced around him, wrapping him tight in smoky fibers as they carried him through the sphere. Through darkness amid his own shouts of fear to a strange, wild place filled with superstitious humans and other magical beings like him.

He sought them out, huddled with them, shared meals, and lodging. He'd been barely seventeen at the time, aging so slowly in this backward place. The years fled past as the only ability he could rely on flourished: the greening. All that time lost, when he should have searched for the tempering. But he'd spent it learning to survive and honing the abilities he could summon.

What would he go back to now? What would be left of Katori after all this time?

The hand against his face reached through his thoughts and into his soul with such comfort that he gasped. He spiraled back to Kendra's living room, staring into those patient brown eyes. Katorin brown eyes, he realized, but those flecks of fiery gold were from the Celts. Looking into Kendra's eyes brought him home, even if it was only a moment or two.

"It must have been horrible," she said in a quiet voice.

"What?" he asked.

"Whatever happened there. Whatever sent you out of your world and into ours."

He nodded, unable to tell her about the bodies in the streets, the cobblestones running with blood, and the buzzing darkness that had descended like locusts on Airell. Chaining it to the night. Enslaving his people. The place he was born, the only home he'd ever known.

"You know what's the most horrible?" he asked, laying his hand against hers.

Her brow furrowed, her mouth pursing as she shook her head.

He held out his other hand into a fist and shook it in the air. "Within my hands, I hold the power to defeat the Eidolon, to take back our cities, and release the prisoners from their dungeons." He gritted his teeth, his fist shaking. "But I can't use the power. It's there, but I can't even call it up. Why?" He squeezed his eyes shut, feeling defeated as he let his hand fall to his side. "Why?"

Her hand was on his shoulder, her warm body against his, her breath steady and brushing against his neck.

"Maybe you were the strength needed to keep it safe—until you could use it. Without that, the power may have perished."

He looked up at her, into those Katorin brown eyes. She meant that. Was that true? Was he meant to carry it to safety only to bring it back again when it could be used against the Eidolon? He had stayed alive by his own wits and his own hand all these centuries. He'd survived countless ebony moons. Even when the others fell, he'd escaped by mere threads. Maybe Kendra was right?

"Maybe," he said in a quiet voice. "I'd never even considered that."

"You should, Fletcher," she said. "Don't hate yourself for surviving. You had as much right to live as anyone else. If anyone can do something to help your people, my money's on you."

He smiled, reaching up to caress her face. "You have the most amazing Katorin eyes," he said, staring at her.

"Katorin?" she said in raspy voice.

He nodded. "Like my mother's people. I look more Eidolon than Katorin—like my father."

Kendra's eyes narrowed. "Aren't the Eidolon the bad guys? Aren't they the ones you're fighting against?"

"Yes, most of them. They're the ones I'm fighting, but not all Eidolon are evil."

She looked puzzled now, setting back against the cushions to study him a moment, not quite sure what to believe now.

"My father risked his life to bring news of the impending invasion to Katori. For that and the crime he committed, they branded him a traitor and locked him away in the oblivis because of it. He believes the Eidolon and Katorins can help each other, but the majority of Eidolons believe otherwise."

"I'm sorry about your father," she said, her voice sympathetic now. "What is this oblivis that you talk about?"

Shade felt the muscles in his jaw tighten and his stomach twist into a knot, the guilt raw in his chest.

"It's a world of total, constant darkness. And silence. They've locked him in a cell deep under the Eidolon capital. Once a day, the prisoners are blinded when the great hatch is thrown open and food is dropped down. Otherwise, he sits alone with not even a candle for company."

"Fletcher—that's horrible." Her hand was on his shoulder again, caressing, squeezing.

"It's my fault he's there. And unless I defeat the Eidolon, especially Carvahl, the man who put him there, my father will die."

"What crime did he commit?" she asked.

He turned to face her, swallowing hard but unable to dislodge the lump rising in his throat. "He helped a capital criminal of Eidolon escape."

"What criminal?" Kendra asked, wide-eyed.

He sighed, running his hand through his hair.

"Me."

"What?" Her face was a mixture of shock and surprise. "I didn't know painting someone's lawn hot pink was such a crime in Eidolon."

He laughed. "In my world, there's a price on my head. I'm to be shot on sight because the magic I carry is so dangerous to the

Eidolon. That was before they began systematically killing any Katorin with the tempering magic. They've killed them all now."

Her face went pale and Shade felt guilty for telling her that, but she needed to understand how important she was to his cause, how dangerous she was to the Eidolon.

"Killed them all?" she said in a thin voice.

"Yes, hunted them all down in Katori. But they missed one line."

She was quiet, her brown eyes still wide and fearful as she waited for him to continue.

"That one line slipped through a scryve's orb long before my mother was born. Came here to escape the politics and responsibilities of her station in Katori. She had no idea that her actions would be Katori's last hope of survival."

"Who was she?"

"Aeryn O'Riley ni Katori. Your great grandmother, Kendra. You have the bloodline and you've shown the magic. If we can combine our gifts into one power, Katori will survive."

"That's a heavy story, Fletcher," she said, her gaze falling to the hardwood floor.

"I know you know nothing about my world and have no reason to care what happens to it, but what happens there is a dry run for your world. Their movements are insidious and they cover their tracks well."

She was silent and he watched the indecision wash over her face. He couldn't blame her. He wondered how he might have reacted had she shown up on his doorstep with a wild story and asking for his help in a conflict he didn't understand. He stared into her reflective brown eyes that so boldly displayed her emotions. For those eyes, he'd have agreed to anything.

He took her hand in his, squeezing it.

"Kendra—you're my last hope."

She bowed her head, wincing at his words, but he understood. It wasn't an easy thing to ask, but without her, he stood no chance at all.

"That's clear to me now," she said in a soft voice and met his gaze. "Gem told me wonderful stories about great grandmother Aeryn, about her love of the old country and her refusal to ever leave it. Gem said it had been hard to leave her for America, but she'd done it, knowing she may never see her again. And she didn't. Aeryn died before my mom was even born."

Kendra let go of his hand and rose from the sofa. She walked over to the bay window that looked out on backyard garden. She kept her back to him.

"I think I've always known there was something a little different about my mom's family, especially Gem. My mother seemed embarrassed of it, but as a kid, I'd loved her ways. As an adult, too. She never saw the darkness in anything, the most optimistic person I ever knew."

Shade nodded. "She was always a bright light in my darkness, too, Kendra. And so very fearless."

She turned around, nodding, those soulful eyes misted with tears. "Even on her deathbed, with the whole family clustered at her side, she spun yarns about a place she was headed. A place of crystalline skies and flower-drenched meadows. A place she'd seen in her dreams since she was a kid. She told us not to cry but to wish her well. That she was happy and ready to travel. At last, ready to travel."

Kendra's voice quivered, her eyes filling with tears.

"Then she closed her eyes, took three deep breaths, and smiled as the fourth one never came."

Shade struggled to rise from the couch, feeling a little unsteady. He was moved by her story and he wished he'd known Gem longer, spent more time with her, but he suspected that everyone who met Emmaline Martin felt that way. He stood in front of Kendra, laying his hands against her shoulders.

"That place," he said, smiling, "It's from a Katorin poem. Wrap me in silk and lay me under crystalline skies. In flower-drenched meadows and perfumed fields where no one really dies."

Her face turned pale, her mouth falling open as she stared at him. "I've searched for that poem since I was a little kid, but no one's ever heard of it."

Shade nodded. He knew that poem well, as did all Katorin children.

"The author is Gisai Celawn ni Katori. The poem's called Final Summer's Journey. She's describing Katori in summer, where she wants to be buried."

Kendra wiped away the tears that slid down her cheek and pulled in a breath.

"Katori has been with me my whole life through Gem and I never knew it. But I recognize it in your words and hers. But why didn't Gem help you? Or my mother. Why did you have to wait for me?"

"Through Gem, I found you," he said, his hands still against her arms.

She watched him through tears, struggling with something. The tension was obvious in the clutch of her jaw, the wrinkling of her brow.

"At first, I thought she could help me," he continued, "but as soon as I met her, I felt her light fading from this plane. And knew she couldn't help me."

"She had cancer," said Kendra, sniffling. "She didn't even try to fight it. Wouldn't have chemo or anything. She said it was time to go." Her voice cracked and she pulled in another breath. "I was so angry at her for that."

The ache burned through Shade's chest as more tears slid down her face. He couldn't watch her cry any longer and pulled her into his arms, trying to ease her pain.

"Loving people is hard," he said. "And it usually hurts at some point or another. But think what you'd be missing if you'd never known her."

He felt Kendra nod against his shoulder, her arms tight around him. After a moment or two, she let him go and wiped away her tears. She walked back to the bay window a moment, casting one last look at the garden before she turned around.

"I wouldn't trade those memories for anything," she said, offering him a smile. "And I won't let the place that Gem loved be destroyed. I can't deny this strange connection I feel to you. I don't understand it but it haunts me." She lifted her chin a little, standing straighter now. "I'll stand with you, Fletcher. To the very end."

He couldn't stop the grin that spilled across his face or the thumping of his heart against his rib cage. His knees felt shaky as he moved toward her by the window. She meant more to him at that moment than any woman he'd ever known, including Rhiannon. He burned for her. And her courage took his breath away.

That's when the floor rushed up to meet him.

13

It took Kendra a few tries, but she managed to get Fletcher back onto the couch. She couldn't lift him, but she called up a little magic and got him stretched out on the couch. He lay on his stomach, his face turned toward the window. Out cold.

She shook her head, watching him breathe. Typical male bravado.

Thought he was his old self again, underplaying the severity of that knife wound. He could have died. That thought terrified her. She knew almost nothing about these shadowy creatures that nearly killed him. And her.

Getting a green patchwork quilt out of Gem's hall closet, she covered him up. He was shivering. She plopped down in the blue wingback chair that sat beside the yellow loveseat and watched Fletcher sleep, fearing he would stop breathing.

But her brain reeled from everything he'd told her about his homeland, about the place where she apparently came from, too, she realized. Katori. Crystalline skies. Flower-drenched meadows. It sounded wonderful, but with the Eidolon invasion, it was probably more fairytale now. She wondered if Fletcher had ever seen Katori the way that Gem had described it.

But she'd agreed to help him. No, stand with him.

Those had been her exact words. She had no idea what that meant, but she wouldn't let anything happen to him. She was so incredibly attracted to Shade Fletcher. Once she got past his devilish exterior, she was surprised to uncover a serious, vulnerable man. Even more surprising was the way he'd already reached out to her, laying bare his desperation and fears. He was complex and tiring but determined to save his people.

And her, too.

On the new moon or ebony moon as Fletcher called it, the Eidolon would come through in overwhelming numbers. Somehow, they had to stop them.

Together.

IT WAS DARK WHEN FLETCHER AWOKE WITH A GROAN, LIFTING HIS HEAD from the couch, his eyes wide with surprise.

"What happened?" he demanded in a groggy voice.

"You passed out," Kendra said, looking over her tablet computer at him.

"I did?" He sat up, his dark hair tousled, one side sticking out above his ear.

So sexy with that bed head look and that long, lanky body that she craved to explore.

"You've slept at least three hours." She set her tablet on the walnut end table beside her and leaned toward him. "Hungry?"

"I could eat," he said in a clipped voice.

"Name it, Fletcher," she said with a smile. "I'll put my magic to good use."

"Lasagna," he said. "And garlic bread."

"Salad?" she asked.

He nodded. "Italian."

Kendra rose from the chair and walked into the kitchen. She turned on the light, the corners of the rooms pooling with shadows.

The sun had dropped past the horizon, pulling thick trails of pink and gold clouds behind it. The soft fragrance of lilacs filtered through the screen. She'd opened the window to cool off house but hadn't expected the scent of lilacs. It was well past lilac season, but in Gem's garden, everything bloomed when it chose.

The flutter of moonglow drifted past her window, casting out any thoughts of lasagna. She gasped and rushed to the window, expecting fireflies, but the sight took her breath.

Beside the lilac bush was...she leaned closer...it was a faerie!

She had hair the color of lilacs, her teardrop eyes deepest amethyst, her gown like pressed sunlight as it drifted around her in layers. And her wings—like smoke! She stood as tall as a five-year-old and was as delicate as porcelain.

"Fletcher!" she called out in a high-pitched whisper, motioning him toward the window. "Fletcher, quick!"

"What is it?" he asked, his voice sounding thin.

She heard his unsteady footsteps across the wood floor until he was beside her, leaning a little.

"Do you see her?" she asked, whispering as she pointed at the willowy figure who leaned out to smell the lilacs.

He chuckled. "They're returning to Gem's garden. She's one of the Fey."

Kendra was mesmerized by the fragile woman as she took to the air like an angel and crossed the garden toward the spirals of melon vine sparkling in the twilight. In the air, little orbs floated and danced like motes of stardust.

She huddled closer to Fletcher, gasping as a unicorn stepped out from underneath the Japanese maple. On the other side of the garden, beside the herbs, small faeries with wings of blue and pink and purple flitted like butterflies among the dogwood blossoms.

The air was electric with magic and flowers, the scents of roses and lilacs mingling with a spicy hint of rosemary and basil. She glanced up at Fletcher and he was grinning, watching her.

"It's the most wonderous thing I've ever seen," said Kendra, turning back to the window.

"Me too," said Fletcher, his warm breath against her neck.

She closed her eyes a moment, inhaling his sultry cedar scent. She wanted to feel his touch again, taste those warm lips again. What would it feel like to wake up in his arms? He leaned over and kissed the side of her face.

"It's time I called for Rhiannon. She'll tell us what must be done."

He walked with unsteady steps toward the back door and Kendra rushed after him.

"Fletcher, wait—I'm coming, too."

His eyes widened a moment, but he seemed pleased as he opened the back door and motioned her out.

She hesitated.

"Will I frighten them away?" she asked.

She didn't want to chase the magical creatures away. She'd love to walk among them, with them.

He laughed, the sound like warm maple syrup. "Frighten them? Kendra, you're one of them."

Was she? That statement gave her chills.

His words rattled over and over through her brain. Technically, that was true, but she felt like an ugly stepchild by comparison. How could she consider herself one with these glittering, shiny creatures that took her breath when she watched them? She did have some sort of magic within her and no matter how many times she denied it, it rushed back to her every time she summoned something out of thin air.

"Am I really one of them?" she said in a breathy voice, staring into his hypnotic ice blue eyes.

He held his hand out toward the garden. "Time to find out."

She nodded and gingerly stepped past him onto the patio, past the white plastic chairs, past the faded wooden chaise lounges and the black charcoal grill. A hint of old charcoal clung to the air as she walked toward the pergola where pale pink English roses wound around purple wisteria.

A radiant woman appeared, startling her.

She was slender, golden tresses trailing down her back and

tumbling over her shoulders. Her skin was luminous as she stood beneath a cascade of roses. Her dress sparkled pure gossamer, her eyes Ireland green. Even before Kendra heard Fletcher behind her, she knew the woman under the pergola was Rhiannon.

She looked past Kendra as Fletcher walked across the patio toward her, his eyes alight. His gaze fixed on this woman's face and Kendra felt small and invisible as the woman turned to him, a brilliant smile on her oval face. Rhiannon was total perfection, her pristine complexion smoother than the finest airbrushed makeup ad. It made her feel funny inside as she watched Fletcher interact with Rhiannon.

Who was she kidding? She felt jealous of this woman. Correction, this goddess. She was all light and perfection in a way that Kendra (and most human woman) could never compete.

"I expected to beg for your appearance, Rhi," he said, walking slowly underneath the pergola toward her.

Kendra felt movement beside her and glanced to her left. Three tiny faeries fluttered next to her, grinning, and tugging playfully at her hair. One landed on her shoulder. Her hair was the color of ripe raspberries and her eyes the color of fresh mown grass. The air smelled soft with honeysuckles.

"The garden is so lovely again. Thank you."

"You're very welcome," she said, reaching out with her pinky to touch the little faerie's outstretched hand. "Thank you for sharing it with me."

The faeries hovered together a moment then waved as they darted across the garden toward the pergola. They knelt on the rosebuds above Rhiannon, the moon goddess, chins resting against the petals.

"On the contrary, Shade," said Rhiannon in a rich alto voice, her head in a slight bow, looking up at him with a demure expression. "I've felt the shadows on the earth. I know why you've called me here and I admire you for swallowing an old hurt to do so."

He shrugged, his jaw line sharpening.

"I need some answers," he said finally. He glanced over at Kendra for a moment. "Kendra Martin is of the only surviving line of Katorins with the tempering."

Rhiannon's gaze bore through Kendra and she felt frightened, fearing some sort of challenge. She turned her gaze back to Shade and nodded.

"Yes, I see its flame. Go on."

Shade glanced at his feet a moment, as if trying to gather the words.

"You know my heritage, Rhi—better than anyone except my parents."

She nodded.

"I'm filled with their darkness but cannot summon it without tempering."

"The Eidolon," Rhiannon said, her voice hard. "Their threat comes very soon. It's in the air, vibrating in the land, rippling through the seas. They amass even now to destroy you." She studied him a moment and a softness filled her eyes, turning them watery. "I underestimated your importance, Shade. I never looked past the greening, my Green Man."

"Many don't," he said with a sigh. "The wilding is strong in me. Can you teach Kendra and me how to harness it? You see everything in the night, Rhi. You understand darkness."

"'Tis simple but it will be the hardest thing you ever do."

Kendra stepped forward until she was standing beside him. She bowed. "Rhiannon, I'm Kendra."

"Good evening," said the moon goddess, her gaze unblinking.

"Tell me what to do," said Shade, "give me some hope, Rhi, that we can beat them back to Eidolon."

Rhiannon encompassed him with her gaze. "You must act as one. It's that simple."

"But how?" Kendra asked, holding out her hands.

A faint smile rose on her pale pink lips.

"Very few people can act together as one," she said, raising her hand into the air. "Think of the bow and arrow. The sun and moon.

One goal. One pushes the other along toward it. One supports the other to reach it. It's like a—"

"Marriage?" said Kendra, staring at Shade.

She held back a laugh. He was turning pale.

"Yes, exactly. Shade, you summon your wilding and Kendra supports it with her tempering before the magic shatters. The more you practice, the more you learn of each other, and the more attuned you become. When you know the other's soul, you'll find that balance you must have to face the Eidolon army. And if you can drive them back in projection, Shade, you can face them in the flesh. For the last time."

A deep sigh rattled up from his chest. In his eyes, she saw that flicker of hope fade. And then he was pulling back, drawing himself away again. Kendra reached out a laid her hand against his face.

"Fletcher, look at me," she said in an urgent voice.

It took him a moment or two to recover. He drew his gaze toward her, looking defeated.

"What is it?" she asked, studying his eyes, studying the mask he'd thrown between him and the world.

"It'll never work," he said in a sad voice.

"Why?" she asked.

"Shade has a problem with letting people in," said Rhiannon, walking toward them on the patio's edge.

Kendra frowned, shaking her head as Rhiannon approached.

"Tell her, Shade," said Rhiannon, staring at him, her gaze hard now. "Tell her why you left me."

"You said she left you," said Kendra, hands on her hips.

Fletcher ran his hand over the back of his neck. "She did leave me," he said, staring at the ground. "But truth be told...I probably drove her away."

Pain touched those bright green eyes, a ripple of shadow across her otherwise perfect face.

It was true. She hadn't rejected him. It was the other way around.

"Why?" Kendra asked, her voice softening, her hands falling to her sides. "I can see the hurt in her eyes. She loved you."

His head snapped up and he stared into Rhiannon's eyes. Kendra felt another stab of jealousy watching the long moment of silence between them, a moment she was outside looking into. For an instant, his face mirrored Rhiannon's tension and pain, but it faded behind his mask again.

"I couldn't be with you, not like you wanted of me, Rhi. I tried. All those long months I tried to be but..." His voice trailed off into a sigh.

Rhiannon smiled at him, laying a hand against his shoulder. "You let me go before I dismissed you, isn't that it, Shade? You pushed me away before I could hurt you."

He nodded. Kendra's eyes turned misty, seeing some past hurt in his eyes. "It's true."

"Your past wounds you, Shade," said Rhiannon, stepping back from him. "And until you put that behind you, you'll never be one with anything." Her gaze fell onto Kendra and she squirmed against those scrutinizing eyes. "Or anyone."

Kendra reached out and ran her hand across his shoulders. "This is your chance to heal those wounds, Fletcher," she said.

He turned to stare at her a moment, the hint of lightness returning to those arctic blue eyes. A hint of hope.

"How?" he asked.

"You've been running so long," she said, cupping his face in her hands, his days old beard so silky soft against her fingers. "Now's your chance to face it. Head on. With all that power inside you."

"Listen to her," said Rhiannon, turning away. "She's very wise for a new magic. I think I understand why you left me now, Shade."

"Why?" he asked.

Rhiannon turned, the gossamer folds of her dress settling like veils around her. She glanced at Kendra.

"Isn't it obvious?" Rhiannon winked at her. "Or at least it will be. Soon."

Fletcher took a step toward Rhiannon. "Will you stand with us on the ebony moon?"

Rhiannon stepped under the pergola again. She stood there

among the tiny faeries and the gleaming orbs and her image haunted Kendra. The moon goddess shook her head.

"'Tis not my fight, Shade. Only mine to observe, no matter how much it hurts. Be as one and the Eidolon will fail, but be warned—they are among us now. Only a handful but they plot against you, seeking to use your magic against you."

Kendra's stomach fell when Rhiannon pointed to the empty pedestals throughout the garden. She knew instantly. Her gazing balls!

"Fletcher," she cried, grabbing hold of his arm as she pointed. "They're gone! All of them now. I forgot to bring them inside."

Gem's gazing balls. Anger burned through her.

Her grandmother loved those glass reflection balls, had cherished them, placing them in reverent locations throughout her garden. Kendra had only wanted to feel her presence when she'd put out the gazing balls.

Now they were gone. Lost forever.

Fletcher's face was taut, his teeth gritted as he rushed past a unicorn to stand beside one of the empty stone pedestals. He shook his head, looking unnerved.

"Why are they missing?" he said. "I don't understand it."

"You're Eidolon, Fletcher," said Rhiannon. "Think. What use would they have for these trinkets?"

He paced around the pedestal a few moments, head down, arms crossed.

"What reflects can absorb, Shade. I'll see you soon."

Rhiannon faded into the air like an apparition. Like she'd been an illusion, a trick of the light.

Kendra rushed across the garden toward Fletcher, who was still deep in thought.

"What did she mean by that?" Fletcher said, mostly to himself as he continued to pace.

Kendra started to reply, but the two dark figures standing on her patio startled her.

She tugged on Fletcher's sleeve as she studied the sandy-haired man dressed in jeans and a white, long-sleeved shirt. Beside him stood a woman with bronzed skin and a stylish blonde bob angled at her chin. She wore black pants and a pale pink pin-striped blouse and carried a large bottle of wine.

Kendra tugged on his sleeve again. "Uh, Fletcher..."

"Absorbs...what does that mean?" he continued to mutter.

Kendra pulled hard on his sleeve until he looked up at her.

"What?" he snapped.

She pointed at the patio. "I think the vampires showed up early for dinner."

A grin spilled across Fletcher's face as he hurried across the garden, still a little unsteady. He extended his hand to the man.

"Gabriel, I'm so glad you're here." He turned and kissed the woman on the cheek. "Good evening, Lenora. Thanks for coming."

Kendra stood between the delphiniums and the dahlias, feeling awkward and a little apprehensive. Vampires. Seriously?

She fought down the urge to lay her hand against her throat and watched Fletcher talk to them like old friends. Unaffected, the Fey creatures darted around their heads, waving and chattering.

She felt someone beside her and turned. A tall, willowy dark-haired woman dressed in a loose poet's blouse the color of lilacs and a white short skirt stood beside the sunflowers raising their faces to the starry sky. Her skin had a lavender cast to it, her ears curved into delicate points.

"Don't fear them," she said, offering a smile as he laid her hand against the sunny gold petals. "They're from an honorable clan, respecting life force and magic. They've been allies to the elvish a long time." She lifted her hand toward the sky and pointed at a bright star in the western sky. "They follow the sunset, but beyond that is the elven star. To see that star is to see all magic. Do you see it?"

Kendra grinned as she nodded and pointed at the brilliant star gleaming almost blue in the night sky.

"I see it there. It's blue, isn't it?"

The elven woman nodded. "I knew you would see it." She bowed to Kendra. "It will guide you on the ebony moon. You and Shade won't be alone. My elven clan will stand with you against the shadows."

Kendra felt her eyes mist. She reached out and hugged the elven woman.

"Thank you," she said, unable to rein in her emotions.

The elven woman nodded and slipped away toward the unicorns that nickered and pawed at the stepping stones.

"Kendra," Fletcher called, motioning her onto the patio.

Fighting back images of black capes, bats, Transylvania, and bad B movies, Kendra approached the vampires. When she was within five feet of them, the man stepped toward her with his hand extended. They looked more like movie stars than vampires, tall and coiffed. Perfect features. Bright smiles.

And teeth. Lots of teeth. It unnerved her.

"I'm Gabriel Duchene," he said, smiling at her.

She shook his hand. "Kendra Martin," she replied. "Nice to meet you."

"This is Lenora Hamilton," he said, gesturing at the tall but petite, bronze-skinned blonde.

Her eyes were a warm mahogany brown. She had a sweet expression, almost doll-like as she held out her hand.

"Hi, Lenora. Glad to meet you."

"You, too," she said and held out the bottle of wine. "We brought the wine. Hope you like Bordeaux."

"Yes, thank you," said Kendra, accepting the bottle. Her mouth fell open when she read the label: Chateau Margaux. 1900.

"Chateau Margaux? From 1900?"

Her father loved wine and bought many an expensive bottle to share over special occasions. She'd tasted a few Margaux's, but a 1900? He'd have a coronary over this one. She couldn't wait to brag about it when she spoke to him again.

"I loved that year in France." Lenora exchanged a knowing look with Gabriel and then turned to Kendra. "We *are* the undead, you know. Gives us the chance to collect things. And create some pretty amazing wine cellars."

Vampires with fine taste. She liked them already.

"This wine is beyond amazing. Thank you so much."

Gabriel motioned at the garden. "Thank you for resurrecting Gem's garden."

Her eyes widened. "You knew my grandmother?"

Lenora smiled. "Everyone knew Gem. She was a gem and we loved her."

Kendra couldn't stop the grin from touching her face.

"What would you like for supper?" she asked.

"Is there a menu?" Gabriel asked, a serious expression on his face.

He looked a little like Matt Damon, his features more chiseled, his body a bit taller and leaner. Lenora favored Halle Berry with Diahann Carroll's poise.

Fletcher poked his thumb at Kendra. "She can make anything you imagine. Trust me."

Kendra nodded. "Tell me what you'd like, your favorite dish, anything."

A grin touched Gabriel's face and Kendra saw a hint of his fangs. It jolted her a little, but she focused her attention on his eyes.

"Steak Diane. Haven't had it done right in years," he said.

"What's the secret?" she asked.

He pressed thumb and forefinger together. "A hint of the finest ground mustard, a solid cabernet, flavorful mushrooms, and cooked just right."

Kendra nodded, taking in his description until she could picture it. She turned to Lenora. "What's your pleasure?"

She offered a shy smile. "A flaky cut of salmon Provencal with heirloom tomatoes and the finest balsamic vinegar. And surprise us with dessert." She hesitated a moment. "Can you really do this? We don't want to impose."

"No, please—it's fine." She held out her hands. "We'll need wine glasses." Four glasses appeared in her hands.

Gabriel stared at her a moment then at Fletcher. "You weren't kidding, were you?"

Fletcher nodding, looking almost proud. "Not at all." He

motioned them toward the wooden table with the white plastic chairs. "Let's sit down."

Kendra set the glasses on the table. "This old thing is all wrong. I see polished teak. A rectangle. Set with fine china and silverware. And loveseats on both sides. A country French theme. With strings of blue lights overhead."

The patio transformed into an outdoor dining room. The teak wood table was draped with yellow and blue fabrics. The gold-edged china sat on top of gold charger plates, soft butter yellow napkins folded as fleur-de-lis. The loveseats were a pale blue toile. Blue lights flickered above the table like stars. Perfect.

Fletcher sat down on one of the loveseats while Lenora and Gabriel sat across from him. Kendra set the wine on the table.

"Pour while I serve," she said in a soft voice to Fletcher.

He smiled. "Wine opener?"

She held out her hand and one appeared.

"Thank you," he said, winking at her as he took the opener. "By the way, I'll have what Gabriel's having."

AFTER THE STEAK DIANE, SALMON PROVENCAL, AND THE CHATEAU Margaux, she conjured peach melba. Four scoops of vanilla bean ice cream topped with a poached peach and fresh raspberry sauce in silver dishes. She set them in front of each person as Fletcher poured coffee for everyone.

"Kendra," Lenora replied, closing her eyes a moment. "This is so divinely Victorian!"

Kendra shrugged. It was one of her mom's favorite desserts, so that's why she chose to serve it.

"Victorian?" Kendra replied.

Lenora nodded as leaned back on the blue toile loveseat. "Oh, yes. Peach Melba was a dish created for Victorian opera star, Nellie Melba. I saw her perform in 1893 at Covent Gardens." She clapped her hands together. "Pagliacci. As Nedda. It was divine." She picked up her spoon and poked the peach half covering the ice cream and drenched in raspberry sauce. "Like this dessert. A little ball of heaven."

"That reminds me," said Fletcher, gazing from Lenora to Gabriel. "Kendra says there are gazing balls missing all over the neighborhood," said Fletcher.

"That's disturbing," said Gabriel, his brow furrowing.

"Rhiannon said what reflects can absorb," said Fletcher, sliding his spoon into his ice cream.

Sitting beside Fletcher, Kendra took a bite of the poached peach, sweet and syrupy with a tang of raspberries, the vanilla bean ice cream melding the flavors together.

"Sounds like the Eidolon are going to try and absorb your magic with them," said Kendra.

Fletcher turned around to stare at her a moment. She set down her spoon.

"That makes sense but why?" he asked.

"What could they do with the captured magic?" Kendra replied.

Lenora poured herself another cup of coffee. "Open the veil wider, I suppose. Let more of them come through?"

Fletcher sucked in a quick breath, the fear rising in his eyes. "You're right. Use my magic against me to amplify and open the veil wider. But how do we stop it?"

"They've taken several by now," said Kendra. "Including Gem's and those belonged to her grandmother. Oh, God, Fletcher. They're Katorin."

Fletcher hung his head. "And infused with Katorin magic. To use against me on the ebony moon. What are they creating with those things?"

She rose from the loveseat, thinking about the string of orbs that the Eidolon probably had already stolen from this neighborhood. And with Gem's Katorin gazing balls, they were all probably lit with magic now. Together, like a string of pearls. Why a string? A circle. No beginning, no end.

"A circuit," she said. "Fletcher, it's a circuit."

Fletcher's mouth fell open. "That's it—a circuit! A floodgate. This is bad. We've got to find it and short it out."

"Otherwise, your magic will be completely turned around on you," said Gabriel, nodding as he rose from the loveseat. "Like pointing a mirror at a caster."

"Exactly!" Fletcher was on his feet now, too. "How long until the next ebony moon?"

Gabriel studied the sky a moment and the pale crescent moon low on the horizon. "Two weeks, I'd guess. Sorry, left my phone behind."

"Three weeks and three days," Lenora replied, her phone in her hand.

Gabriel turned to Fletcher, a dire look on his face. "That gives you three weeks and three days to find and break this Katorin circuit, Shade." He motioned to Kendra. "Between the two of you, you have the ability to accomplish it."

Lenora set down her coffee cup and got to her feet. She motioned to the table of dirty dishes.

"Need any help cleaning up, Kendra?"

Kendra grinned. "Thank you but no." She turned toward the table. "Back the way you were."

The old table appeared with its faded plastic chairs and worn wooden chaise loungers beside it. Everything else disappeared.

"All done," she said to Lenora.

"My kind of clean up," said Lenora with a smile. She reached out and hugged Kendra. "Take care. We'll see you soon. You're not alone in this. Remember that."

"Thank you," said Kendra. "That means a lot."

Gabriel shook her hand. "Kendra, it was a pleasure. And Shade, I'll talk with you in a few days," said Gabriel

Gabriel and Lenora walked into the garden toward the gate.

"Looking forward to it," Fletcher called to them.

"Bye, Lenora. Bye, Gabriel," Kendra said, waving at them.

The two vampires faded into the garden's shadowy edges.

Fletcher started toward the garden, but Kendra grabbed his arm.

"Where do you think you're going?" she asked.

"To look for gazing balls," he said.

She shook her head. "No way. Tomorrow. Tonight, you need to rest."

"I'm fine," he said, eyes haggard, eyelids drooping.

He ignored her, taking a few steps past her into the garden but stopped. She saw the heaviness in each step until he stopped and his shoulders sagged.

"I hate it when you're right," he said with a sigh.

He turned around and walked onto the patio again, headed for the back door.

"Get used to it, Fletcher," she said with a smile and laid a hand against his back. "Since I'm half this team now."

She caught the hint of a smile on his face. "What did I get myself into?" he said in a tired voice, heading toward the hallway and the stairs.

Something wonderful, Kendra thought.

Something she hadn't felt in a long time. She wasn't quite sure yet but something else had blossomed besides this garden.

14

Kendra did her best to concentrate on Toni Ambrose's business plan, but her mind was anywhere but work. Fletcher had gone home this morning, leaving her alone with her laptop and a stack of papers. She stared at them, spread in piles across the coffee table, on the couch, and stacked at her bare feet. A cobalt coffee cup ringed a paper towel on the white marble top as she slid the cup away from the edge. She leaned back and spread-out color photographs of Toni's dresses, each one as delicate as the faeries that strolled her garden.

One dress stood out and Kendra couldn't help but stare at it. It looked exactly like the moon goddess' dress. Thin wisps of white gossamer, the sheer fabric beneath those layers sparkling across cap sleeves, bodice, and skirt. It was identical.

How could that be?

She studied the other photos and an eerie chill brushed her skin. That sheer lavender poet's blouse and short skirt—worn by the elven woman—appeared in the last photograph. Modeled by a gangly girl who was fifteen at best.

Had she somehow conjured up the dresses and accidentally

changed the photographs with her magic? Or were these dresses really designed by Toni?

Kendra folded her arms against her pink camisole. Two of the outfits she'd seen last night, but the others in the photographs had that same ethereal quality, like the lavender dress she'd seen in Toni's window. All of her clothes had this...Kendra struggled for a word... this Fey quality to them.

Even if she had conjured these two photos by accident, the rest of Toni's designs matched their style, their otherworldliness.

And it was more than a coincidence. Like this entire trip to Indiana...from the moment she'd entered the house.

She rose from the couch. She had some questions to ask Toni. Either the entire magical world shopped at Toni's store or she was somehow part of it.

Kendra hurried upstairs, laying the two photographs on the top step. She changed out of her navy sweatpants, slipping into tan shorts and sandals. After sliding off the navy scrunchie, she fluffed her hair with a little water and picked it out. She grabbed the photos, slung her purse over her pink camisole, and headed outside to the car.

As she pulled out of the driveway, Maddie waved at her. She wore a yellow T-shirt and jeans as she watered her petunias along the walkway to her house. The bright-faced purple, pink, and white petunias circled a concrete bird bath and empty pedestal where her green gazing ball had been.

Kendra drove around the country road's curve, looking at the houses, checking for the gazing balls that once dotted the roadside. Every last one of them was gone.

Empty pedestals stood by several houses, including the Littleton woman's double-wide where small ceramic squirrels and deer stood silent watch over empty spots where gazing balls had been. She'd had five in all among her hollyhocks, hydrangeas, and red rose bushes. She'd counted them one day, amazed by how vividly they'd reflected the flowers and their colors.

All five were missing.

It made the hairs on the back of her neck stand up, wondering why Fletcher's shadow people would take such mundane objects. Could they really create something deadly with such wonderful little globes? With Gem's Katorin globes, they'd probably harnessed whatever strange magic had lurked within the shiny spheres. Her cheeks burned at the thought, knowing that four of Gem's prized, hand-blown globes were among the missing.

Somehow, she'd get them back. Hopefully, not in pieces.

The country road curved into a main road that shot straight into downtown Chauncey. In five minutes, she was driving around the tiny downtown square where Main Street crossed Third Street. She pulled the rental car right in front of Toni's store and checked her watch.

Eleven nineteen. Not quite lunchtime.

She locked the silver Volkswagen Jetta, purse on her shoulder, photos in hand, and walked toward the door. That same diaphanous lavender dress—so faerie-like that it made her gasp—hung in the picture window, two other silky, gossamer gowns on either side: one mint green and the other a pastel print of some sort. Like brushed strokes of watercolors on fog. She squinted. Or strange symbols—she couldn't tell.

When Kendra stepped inside, she walked past the parlor-like fitting area with its purple Victorian settee and swan fainting couch (which she hadn't noticed the first time). On both sides of the room stood two bamboo changing rooms, a mirror between them. The spicy scent of floral potpourri hung in the air as she walked toward an old walnut desk where an antique gilt cash register stood. Toni leaned against the desk, her dark hair in a shiny bob that hugged the gentle curves of her face. And flawless complexion. She set her jaw. One that might befit a moon goddess.

"Kendra!" Toni called out, smiling as she hurried out from behind the counter to greet her.

Kendra hugged her school friend, noticing the silk, butter yellow skirt that hugged her body, a delicate yellow and lavender flowered camisole underneath a sheer white blouse. A hint of sparkle clung to the silk blouse as if it had been spun from moonlight. Just otherworldly enough to startle Kendra.

Toni stared at her a moment, a flicker of surprise in her deep blue eyes. Eyes that hinted of amethyst, Kendra realized.

"Shopping or planning today?" Toni asked, motioning her toward the settee.

Kendra followed. "A little of both, I suppose," said Kendra, sitting down on an ivory fainting couch, the single walnut arm shaped like a swan.

Toni sat down on the settee, hands folded in her lap as she studied Kendra.

"Still thinking about that lavender dress, aren't you?"

Kendra nodded. "Sure am. Haven't been able to put it out of my mind. It has this magic about it..."

She watched Toni's eyes intently, but her expression didn't change. Still that sweet smile she remembered. Toni was a good friend, there for her when high school heartbreaks had been too much. At the top of her buddy chat list through college when she'd been in New York and Kendra had been in Maryland. They'd drifted apart since college, but sitting here now, she saw those same things that had made them friends. But did she connect with Kendra in another way? Through the wild magical world that peeked through the thin, frayed edges of this one. Was it a world Toni was part of, too —like Fletcher? And Gem?

"The fabric is made especially for me."

"Really?" Kendra reached out and touched the sleeve of Toni's blouse. "This fabric?"

"Yes, this silk organza is very delicate and doesn't really exist anywhere else but my work."

"Where do you obtain these fabrics? Thailand? Malaysia?"

Toni shrugged. "The dupioni and habotai are mainly Asian," she replied, laying a hand against her skirt. "The special pieces—these unique silk organzas and gauzes—we make right here in Indiana," she replied.

Kendra frowned. "You didn't tell me about the weaving of special fabrics," she replied, fumbling a small pad of paper and a pen out of her purse. She scribbled down notes about the special fabrics and the imports. "I'll need to include that in the plan. You'll need a facility for creating fabrics, too—otherwise, that could bottleneck your entire production schedule."

Toni held up her hand. "No, you won't need to plan for that, Kendra."

Kendra looked up from the pad of paper. "No?"

"I already deal with a supplier for those fabrics," Toni said, her smile not wavering.

"But you said *we* make the fabric," said Kendra, dropping her pen into her purse.

"We do," she said, motioning toward the nearest wooden rack of dresses. "But not in house, is what I should have said. The fabric supplier makes it to my specifications."

Kendra nodded and picked up her pen again, running a line through the in-house fabric production on her list. She put the paper and pen back in her purse and held out the photographs to Toni.

"Are these your favorites?" Toni asked, looking at the two outfits in the photos.

Kendra nodded. "Especially this one," she said, pointing at the dress. "It's fit for a moon goddess, wouldn't you say?"

The smile faded for only an instant, but it was enough for Kendra to realize Toni's fabrics were conjured not woven.

"Sure," said Toni, glancing from the photograph to Kendra as she nodded. "Fit for a goddess."

"Like Rhiannon."

"Rhiannon?" Toni asked.

Kendra nodded. "It's amazing. I saw this exact same dress on Rhiannon, the moon goddess. Last night, as a matter of fact. Like it was made for her. And this." Kendra handed her the other photograph. "Worn by an elven woman I met."

Toni motioned her up from the couch. "Let's go in the back room," she said and walked past the back desk and the doorway beyond it.

Kendra gathered the photos and her purse, following. Toni led her to an office, each wall painted a different pastel color. A simple maple desk sat in one corner, a green desk chair behind it and two lavender chairs in front of the desk. A small bookshelf stood against the wall, a picture of Victorian faeries flitting through a dark window hung above it in a modern black frame.

On the top shelf was a white coffee maker, the glass carafe full of hot water. Books and magazines filled the shelves, a Boston fern perched on a wooden plant stand, draping its ruffled leaves over onto the bookshelf. The room smelled like stale brewed tea and that spicy potpourri scent. Toni sat down in one of the lavender chairs, silent for several moments.

"Am I right?" Kendra asked, leaning against the back of the other chair. "Or do you have a shop between the worlds?"

Toni looked up at her, a touch of sadness in her eyes. "I had no idea you'd figure it out so quickly. Especially since you'd never noticed it in high school."

"That you have a gift, Toni?" She smiled and sat down in the other chair, taking hold of her hands. "It's an incredible thing and where it comes from isn't important. But why you brought me here is. Was it really to do this business plan?"

Toni nodded. "It was at first. I needed some help with the mundane portions of the business: shipping, distribution, things I didn't know about it. But the other things—the fabrics, the designs— they have to be kept secret. It's where my magic lies—the moonglow fabrics, the inner sparkle of the threadwork. I weave the fabrics myself, no facilities needed but the night sky."

"Your work is amazing, Toni," said Kendra, imagining Toni working by moonlight to create these one-of-a-kind faerie fabrics.

"That's why I wanted you, Kendra. I knew you could handle all of this, but honestly...I didn't know we—uh, traveled in the same circles at night."

Kendra chuckled. "Neither did I. Not until last night anyway. When I met Rhiannon."

"I designed that dress for her."

"It's amazing," said Kendra. "For a moon goddess." She studied Toni's face and it had lost some of its brightness. She hadn't told her everything.

She reached toward the shelf and handed her a dress box. "Here," she said. "A gift for you. Please take it."

Kendra took the box, staring at her a moment. "It's that lavender dress, isn't it?"

Toni nodded. "It's styled for you with clean lines, plunging neck line, and those diaphanous layers," she said. "In case you encounter the moon goddess again. Don't want you looking like twins and angering her."

Kendra reached over and hugged her. "Thank you," she said. "Really...I'd be honored to wear one of your dresses."

"Might turn a head or two," she said with a wink.

Fletcher. And tonight, was the perfect occasion to wear it. Something different for him instead of all that magical perfection in her garden. She smiled. Might even give him something to think about—like taking it off her later.

"Toni, you said *at first*." She couldn't help but ask. She had to understand Toni's place in all of this magical chaos. "What did you mean by that?"

"You know there's more," said Toni, sighing as she brushed her dark hair behind her right ear. "The ripple in the magic. Everyone felt it—even me. For two days, it clouded my fabrics, turning them indigos and charcoals."

Kendra shuddered, recalling the dark moon when the Eidolon attacked Fletcher, nearly splitting his head in two with an axe.

"The Eidolon," said Kendra.

Toni's eyes widened and she bit her lip, nodding. "The shadow people from some distant realm. They've begun to poison our magic, Kendra. Every month, my fabrics spoil if the moon is new. And it's getting worse." She reached out and took hold of Kendra's hand, gripping it. "But they say the Green Man can stop them. His line touches the Fey from that distant realm. And he needs another with the tempering to stop them. That's why you're here. It's Gem's line,

Kendra—it's you. I thought that if you returned to the house, that the magic would appear again and—"

"It has," she said, squeezing Toni's hand. "I've met this Green Man and tonight, we train for the next ebony moon."

"The shadows are building," said Toni, her voice hushed with a fear that echoed through her in cold waves. "We'll lose everything if they get through, Kendra. Everything."

Kendra nodded. "I know. I feel it, too, now."

"That's why you're here. That's why I called you. To save my business...to save it all."

Sighing, Kendra slumped back in the chair, letting go of Toni's hand. She liked it better when it was only a business plan.

When she wasn't saving the world.

15

That evening, Kendra walked across the field, dressed in Toni's gossamer lavender creation that wrapped itself around her body like it had been made for her. And it had —with magic. She hurried around the pond and past the sleeping swans on the bank. To Fletcher's front door for the first time.

He'd invited her over for supper and training. The house she'd described as dark and foreboding from her patio looked softer and almost vulnerable when she stood in front of it.

Soft glimmers of blue lights hung at all the eaves of the house, around the doors and windows. A strange faerie light she'd never seen before. It must be some sort of protective magic against the Eidolon. He must have asked Rhiannon or one of the Fey for a protective spell of some kind. She hoped it worked—and lasted.

The musty scent of algae and pond water tinged the air, the cool scent of the surrounding forest smelling crisp and clean as she knocked on the front door. That axe was propped against the front door, right where he'd left it the night that the Eidolon came through. She felt a profound sense of loneliness as she knocked again.

In a moment or two, the door opened and he greeted her with a smile. Barefoot, he wore short, navy nylon running shorts and a pale green camp shirt that hugged his lanky body—and that leanly muscled chest. His long dark bangs looked combed for once, those icy blue eyes smoldering like pilot lights. He looked more rested, like he'd gotten some sleep.

"Hey, Kendra," he said. "Glad you stopped by."

Stopped by? She frowned at him. His life was in danger, his world hanging by a thread, depending on him to master the wilding, and he was glad she stopped by? At least, he was calling her Kendra now instead of Martin, like she was his shortstop or something.

"You invited me over, remember? Dinner and training?"

"Oh, yeah—so I did."

Fletcher in his best noncommittal tone. He didn't make a move to open the door wider. He stood in the opening, watching her with those wild blue eyes.

"God," he said with a hiss. "That dress...is...stunning."

She grinned. So, he had noticed it. After the *stopped by* comment, she wasn't sure if he'd even noticed that she was a woman.

"Were you planning to keep me on the porch all night?" she asked, hands on her hips.

His gaze fell to the floor. "Uh, listen...before you come in, I need to explain something to you." His hand was on the door, keeping it flush against his body so she couldn't see inside.

"Explain away," she replied, studying the strange look on his face.

What was going on? This was strange even for Fletcher. He seemed...nervous?

He stuttered a moment or two. "The greening...you know about that, right?"

Kendra grabbed hold of the door and pushed it open. "So, your place is a bit messy. I get it. I can deal with it. Let me in, Fletcher." She pressed passed him but stopped when she saw the forest unfold throughout the house.

An entire forest. Inside his house. A forest.

The cool air smelled of rain and newly tilled soil. Rooms that might have been family room and dining room were filled with oak trees, fiddlehead ferns, and river birch. Leaves and moss carpeted the floors, a small stream running past...she squinted...moss-covered furniture and tables. It was all open, no walls left, the roof open to the sky.

A fire crackled in the fireplace, vines draping over kitchen counters. Birds fluttered through the treetops, singing songs only heard deep in the forest. The soft scent of pine and wildflowers wafted down the narrow hallway, opening into two other rooms—clearings, she realized. One was his bedroom. A bed of vines and wildflowers beneath the boughs of a white pine tree, moonlight shining overhead. Cardinals chirped from tree branches and water tumbled over rocks where his dresser stood, covered in moss and vines.

"Fletcher..." She turned to him, enchanted. "This...is incredible."

"You like it?" he said, surprise on his face as he closed the door behind her.

She nodded. "I love it! It's the most amazing thing I've ever seen."

The corners of his mouth quirked as he laid a hand against her cheek, moving closer. "I should have never doubted it."

"Doubted what?"

His body was almost against hers now and she stared into those pale blue eyes that began to warm like a crisp spring sky.

"You. You've liked everything I've shown you, enjoyed even the smallest magical wonder I've pointed out. And you stood with me when Carvahl tried to cleave my skull. And punctured my lung."

She shivered as he ran his fingers through her hair, his touch so gentle and feather soft.

"I've never allowed a soul beyond my door stop anywhere in the world. Ever. Because of...this."

He looked so humbled. So, vulnerable with an almost boyish innocence, something she wasn't used to seeing in Shade Fletcher.

"Not in all the centuries since I arrived in your world. You're the very first one to share my secrets, Kendra."

God, she wanted him. With every breath and every emotion.

She pushed against his lean body, sliding her mouth over his and he kissed back. Frantically. Wildly. He wrapped her in his arms. And pressed his body hard against hers, his tongue exploring her mouth, his hands sliding past those lavender gossamer dress layers and under her bra.

She enfolded him in her arms, kissing him harder, urgently, his body taut and fiery against hers as he slow-walked her down the hallway. Across the thick, cool carpet of moss. Her heart raced.

Into his bedroom.

She tugged at the buttons on his shirt, trying to unbutton them. Desperate to feel his hot bare skin against hers. But they wouldn't slide through the button holes.

She tugged hard until the buttons popped off in all directions.

His shirt fell away from his shoulders.

His kisses were anxious, frenetic now, his breath ragged and huffing against her mouth, his hands stroking, pleasuring.

A few more steps and her dress joined his shirt as the foot of his bed was against her calves.

She kicked off her sandals as he laid her on the bed of moss and wildflowers and unfastened her bra, sliding it away as she tugged down his running shorts. His hands glided over her bare breasts, cupping them as he crawled onto the bed beside her, skin so hot, his mouth covering hers in deep, frantic kisses. Sliding up to her neck now, his other hand on her hips, delving past the lavender cotton bikinis that he slid down her thighs.

She shuddered, gasping, arching her back to his touch between her legs.

"Dance with me, Kendra," he whispered in her ear, his hands exploring her curves, caressing, stroking.

"Fletcher," she whispered.

"It's Shade," he said, his hot breath against her ear as her thighs parted at his touch.

He slid on top of her. The weight of his body made her ache with need as she felt his hardness and the need that burned through him. She opened her legs to him, wanting him inside her.

"Make love to me, Shade Fletcher," she whispered against his ear. "I've never wanted anyone like I've wanted you."

His hips moved against hers, his fingers stroking her breasts. She gasped when she felt him enter her and she rocked her hips at his frantic strokes. Wrapping her legs around him, she pulled him closer, deeper, her body moving against him at first and then with his thrusts as he pushed harder against her.

His breath was ragged, husky against her neck as he sipped her throat and breasts then her mouth as a fiery wave of ecstasy trembled through her. She shuddered against him, overcome by the intensity of the climax that surged through her as his dark magic entwined with her tempering.

And it became explosive.

She felt the rush and swell of magics ebbing and flowing through her like electric current. Like fireworks. Until it exploded through her body in waves that made her gasp.

His frantic rhythm continued and she moved against him, with him, his passion, and the Eidolon magic rushing through her until she felt the first shudder roll through him. She held him tighter in her arms, thighs wrapped around his legs as she felt him approach the edge, thrusting, trembling, until she felt him shudder against her as her own passion flooded through her again in quivering waves.

Slicked in sweat, he collapsed against her, still inside her, his breath heaving so hot against her hair. She wrapped herself around him, not wanting him to move, not wanting anything to shift.

For a long time, they lay entwined until at last he rolled off her to lie on his back. She laid her head on his chest, entwining him with her body as she listened to the steady chirp of cardinals so crisp against the burble of the water across the rocks, scent of wildflowers cool against Shade's warm cedary scent.

Before long, someone softly called her name, gently shaking her shoulder.

"Kendra?" the patient voice called and she realized she'd been asleep.

Her eyes rolled open and he was leaning over her, smiling, tucking a white daisy behind her ear.

"Fle—Shade," she said, reaching up to caress his face.

"Hungry?" he asked with a relaxed smile.

She nodded, stretching as she sat up, naked in the bed of moss and wildflowers. A pale blue sheet draped across her and she tucked it under her arms as she leaned against the wooden headboard draped in vines.

Dressed only in those tight running shorts, Shade rose from the bed and disappeared into the hallway. He was gone twenty minutes or more, but Kendra listened to the trickle of water and call of birds until he appeared with a wooden tray. He set it on the bed. It looked like a bowl of fettuccine, still steaming hot from a pan. The gooey parmesan cheese clung to the thick noodles, scent of garlic divine. Two pieces of garlic bread were tucked on the edge of the bowl, two forks and two plates beside it. Kendra wrapped the sheet around her body and crawled toward it.

"I can't call up your heart's desire," he said with a smirk. "Best I can do is fettuccine alfredo."

"You did cook for me," Kendra said with a grin, picking up a hot piece of garlic bread. She bit into it, tasting the butter and garlic and something a little tangy that she couldn't place. "How about some wine?" she asked and held out her hand.

"Sure," he said, watching her through those wild pale blue eyes. The icy cast was gone, thawed she realized as she ran her hand down his arm.

Kendra extended her hand. "A nice bottle of chardonnay."

Nothing happened.

Shade stared at her a moment, frowning as he sat down beside her on the bed and picked up his fork. He watched her as he took a bite.

"A nice bottle of chardonnay," she repeated, holding out her hand.

The cardinal's call echoed through the room and suddenly the water running over the rocks sounded so loud.

"Chardonnay," she said again. "A bottle. Napa Valley. Chilled."

Nothing appeared in her hand. Her eyes were wide as she stared at Shade who had set down his fork.

"What's happening?" she asked.

He shook his head. "I don't know. Where's the magic?"

She studied him a moment, wondering if he'd somehow taken her magic when they made love.

"Have you somehow absorbed it?" she asked.

"Don't think that's possible," he said.

"Try it," she said, poking his shoulder. "You try to summon the wine."

"A bottle of chardonnay," he said in a half-hearted voice and held out his hand.

Nothing.

Kendra shook her head, feeling frightened now. "How could it suddenly disappear like this?"

"Finish your food," he said, picking up his fork. "When you're done, we'll get dressed and go back to the garden. I've got a bad feeling about your magic."

"Like what?" she asked, staring at him, the slice of garlic bread still in her hand.

"We'll know soon enough," he said, waving her off as he took a bite of hot fettuccine dripping with melted parmesan.

"No, Fle—Shade, tell me now!" She rose on her knees to stare at him. "What's your theory?"

He sighed, setting the fork back on his plate. "I don't think your magic extends past Gem's house, Kendra—past the garden. If that's the case, we may have a problem."

She sank back against the headboard. He was right. If her magic extended no further than the garden, how would she stand with Shade in Katori? Or here—at his house or the pond?

"What if you're right?" Kendra asked, staring at him.

His jaw tightened and he glanced down at his hands a moment before he met her gaze.

"We'll deal with that after we test your tempering." He offered her a reassuring smile and that surprised her. "Don't panic. Let's eat and go out by the pond to test out our combined magics."

"You're right," said Kendra, picking up her garlic bread and taking another bite.

There was no reason to think the worst. After all, this strange magic of summoning anything wasn't the tempering magic that Shade needed to stop the Eidolon.

He picked up his plate and set it in his lap as he ate in silence. Kendra felt ravenous and plopped some fettuccine alfredo onto her plate. She swirled noodles around her fork, devouring them and both pieces of garlic bread. When she'd scraped up the last drop of sauce, she set her plate back on the tray. She put on her new lavender dress while Shade finished eating.

He sat back and admired her in the dress a moment, those arctic blue eyes sparking. Finally, he rose from the bed and slid open the moss-covered door to his closet. He pulled out a navy V-neck T-shirt that hugged his beautiful slender body and showed a peek of that smooth, leanly muscled chest. He slid his feet into some beaten up dark leather loafers as Kendra found her sandals.

"Ready?" he asked and she nodded, following him down the hallway and out the front door.

"What are these blue lights?" Kendra asked, pointing to the hazy light against his window.

"Protection wards," he answered. "Rhiannon asked one of Sebille's people to set them."

She followed him to the edge of the pond where he turned to face her. He stared out at the dark water a moment then turned his gaze back to her.

"Kendra, I'll be honest. I have no idea what I'm doing. I've always tamped down this Eidolon energy, not letting it rise to the surface because I knew I had no control over it."

She felt her stomach twist at the thought. But she'd felt its power when he made love to her, felt it flowing from his body into hers with such force that even now, it made her face flush.

"If I call it forward, maybe your magic can direct it?"

"That makes sense...I think," she replied. She hoped that she'd know how to do that. But she had no idea what could happen if she didn't direct it properly.

He stood there staring into the murky water a long time. Finally, he ran his hand through his hair and those long bangs and finally turned his gaze toward her.

"Eidolon magic—at least the kind I've inherited—isn't subtle like the shadows that come through the veil. It's a dark, angry power, all shadows, fire, and force. When I let it free, you'll need to steer it toward the pond until it dissipates."

He looked nervous, unsure of himself, an expression she wasn't used to seeing on him.

"What if I can't?" she asked in a quiet voice, folding her arms against her chest.

"Don't worry, it will fade quickly. I can't release much. I confess, this thing inside my body terrifies me."

"Why?" Kendra asked, stepping toward him. "Are you afraid you can't stop it?"

He sighed, shaking his head. "I'm afraid it will control me. And I'm afraid that I'll like the power I hold."

Power was intoxicating. He had good reason to fear it. She stood taller, watching his movements.

"Okay, Shade—whenever you're ready."

With a nod, he turned away from the pond and stared into the open field. For a long time, he stood there motionless, the warm evening breeze carrying a hint of lilacs from her garden.

Finally, he lifted his arms and with gritted teeth, he closed his eyes, shaking as he called forth something dark and malevolent that crouched in the field.

It turned its shadowy form toward her. With a screech, it shot forward. Right at her.

16

E very nerve and muscle screamed as the shadowy ball of energy rushed at her. Kendra's body seized up, her brain screaming at her to run.

"Try to direct it!"

Shade's voice cut through her flight response.

She set herself, holding out her hands to ward it off, but then she remembered this was about focusing the magic. Shade's magic.

She straightened and held her palm up, focusing on the writhing ball of darkness careening toward her face. She thrust up her other hand to protect her face.

The ball of energy grazed her palms, sending a wave of hot pain across her skin as she pushed back at the energy, managing to hold it away from her face. Her arm muscles trembled from the effort. Grinding her teeth together, arms quivering, she held the ball of dark energy in mid-air. And began to push it backward.

After a few painful moments, the dark force slid a few inches away from her face. It still hovered there, pushing harder as she felt her resolve weakening.

Shade called out to her in a muffled voice, saying something she couldn't understand.

The buzz of magic in her ears was too strong.

She drew in a sharp breath and concentrated on moving this dark thing away from her, but it hovered close despite her best efforts.

In frustration and fury, she pressed as hard as she could against the shadowy thing. Flinging it ten feet away.

The dark ball of magic crackled and hit the ground, rolling away. It skittered into the dark field.

In moments, it exploded into sparks and flames, disappearing into the growing darkness.

"Sorry, Shade," she replied and dropped down in the grass.

Feeling defeated.

He moved beside her, a hand on her shoulder. "It's all right. Did you direct it at all?"

Direct it? She shook her head. She hadn't even tried. She'd been more worried about it hitting her face. She did her best to keep the magic at bay and hadn't even tried to send it anywhere. Only away from her face.

"No," she moaned, surprised at how defeated she sounded. "I wanted it away from my face. It frightened me."

He sat down beside her, crossing his legs, elbows propped on his knees as he stared out at the pond and the sleeping swans on the bank.

"I know," he said in a kind voice. "Eidolon magic is pretty terrifying. Still startles me and it's always inside me. We'll try it again. This time though, try to push past the fear. The Eidolon feed on fear, so expect to face that."

"I'll do my best," she said and stood up, brushing away the dust and grass from her shorts.

He rose from the grass and leaned forward, kissing her lips. That kiss sent a burst of heat roiling through her body like the blast of a car heater in August. And she wanted more.

He faced the field again, eyes closed, head tilted down.

After nearly a minute, his arms trembled as he lifted his hand. Dark energies shot from his outstretched fingers and skittered into the empty field.

She watched the energy twitch and writhe, the ball of energy tumbling through the grass.

Direct it, he'd said. *Did that meant calling it?*

She set herself, muscles taut as she angled her right hand toward the writhing darkness and summoned it toward her.

The energy spun in a wild dance like a tumbleweed across the field, turning like it had wheels, and surged across the field toward her.

She was ready this time.

Extending her hand toward the dark energy, she felt its hum rattle through her bones. The ball of shadow shot forward like a basketball, the static charge crackling as it neared her face.

Heat rose and her cheeks flushed like opening a hot oven. Fighting the urge to shove away the magic, she focused on directing it.

It lurched forward a foot then rolled backward. She poked at it again.

Two more times it rolled back toward the field, but she kept it in front of her, focusing on the pond. Trying to direct the dark energy away from her.

No, not away. Toward something.

The energy burned her hand and she gasped, grabbing it, ducking as the energy rushed past her again.

"Sorry," she said, clutching her throbbing hand as the energy pulsed across the field and landed near Shade's house.

"It's okay," said Shade, moving toward her. "Let me see your hand."

"It's all right," she muttered as he turned her palm over to see the redness coloring it. "It's only a first-degree burn—like a sunburn."

"That's enough," said Shade, wincing.

"It scared me again."

Shade nodded, not saying a word, but she saw the concern in his eyes. She wasn't sure whether he was concerned about her well-being or the fact that she couldn't redirect his wilding. Either way, he kept quiet, watching her struggle against the pain in her hand. His eyes looked a little sad.

"How's the hand?" he asked in such a gentle voice that surprised her.

She shrugged. "Let's try again," she said.

His eyes narrowed. "You sure?"

"Of course. I've never done this before and neither have you. Two tries mean nothing. Let's keep going."

"When it gets too much, we're stopping, Kendra," he said, a firmness in his voice now. "I'm not going to let this magic harm you."

She smiled. She liked his concern. Clenching her toes against her sandals, she watched Shade struggle to call up more of that strange dark energy coursing inside him. And set herself for more of those dark spheres flying toward her.

LONG PAST MOONRISE, A SMALL, DISTANT MOON HUNG IN THE DARK night—the full moon beginning to wane. Cicadas scritched and crickets chirred in the warm, muggy darkness. They'd been casting the two magics for a couple of hours. Kendra worked beside Shade, trying to juggle the dark energy orbs. And hadn't made much progress.

Across the field, her garden gleamed with life and magic and she longed to sit and watch it all unfold. But here in Shade's front yard, in the smoky night, she still struggled to focus his wild, unpredictable magic. With magic she'd never used before tonight.

It seemed impossible.

At last, she sent the dark, writhing orb into the tall weeds. Exhausted and aching, she sat down in the grass. Shade trotted over to her, eyes wide. He dropped down beside her and slid his arm around her shoulders as she huffed for breath.

"You okay?" he asked, eyes wide and filled with worry.

She nodded, enjoying that concerned look that was all for her.

"Fine, Fletcher—Shade."

He pulled her into his arms, holding her close. His face was soft despite his unshaven jaw. Even now, it surprised her. His stubble wasn't like men's scratchy beards in this world. It was soft, silky against her face and it still surprised her. He gazed up at the starry sky.

"That's enough for tonight."

"This is much better," she said with a smile, tilting her face up to kiss his lips. He covered her mouth in a deep kiss then settled back in the grass with her beside him.

"I don't think we're doing it right," he said.

She snuggled into him. "Practice makes perfect."

She felt him laugh, a deep rumble in his chest. "No, the magic. Maybe our focus is wrong?"

"In what way?" she asked.

He summoned the energy and she directed it. It made sense.

He shrugged, his arms tightening around her. "I don't know...I feel like you're doing all the work. And in the end, this is my fight."

"If it's your fight, shouldn't your magic direct these spheres at your targets? Shouldn't my magic be sharpening yours somehow?"

"Exactly," he said. "Rhiannon said we had to work as one."

Kendra poked him in the ribs. "Already covered that one tonight."

He chuckled, his hands sliding over her breasts, slipping underneath the gossamer folds of her dress, caressing. She ran her hands underneath his shirt, exploring the well-defined muscles of his chest.

"Wait a minute," he said, sliding his hands back. He held up his right hand, palm toward her. "Mirror my hand," he said.

"What?"

She let him go and he scrambled onto his knees in front of her. He held up his right hand again.

"Lay your hand against mine," he said. "Like a mirror."

She hesitated a moment but laid her palm against his. He moved his hand in a clockwise circle in the air and Kendra kept hers and against his as he moved.

"Do you see?"

"See what, Shade?"

"It's a mirror," he said, grinning as he moved his hand in a counter-clockwise motion and she followed his movements, her palm still pressed against his.

Kendra shook her head, not quite following him. She understood what mirroring meant but not what he was trying to say about it.

"Guide my hand," he said, pressing his palm against hers.

She moved her hand in a clockwise circle, pushing against his to move it along with her circle. Excitement burned through her face. If she guided his magic with hers, giving him her ability to focus his magic, then he could direct it at the Eidolon.

When she'd made a few revolutions, he was grinning. "Now, do you get it?" he asked. "You reflect your magic onto me and that allows me to focus mine."

She nodded. Sort of like the gazing balls reflecting back the image of the garden. It enhanced the garden.

"I cast my magic on you and that allows you to focus your magic."

He threw his arms around her, holding so close that she felt his heart beat against her chest. She wrapped her arms around him and leaned her mouth up to find his. His kisses were intense as she felt the tension drain from him.

"Ready to try again?" he asked.

She nodded, letting him go.

He walked toward the pond again and this time, she followed, standing beside him as he closed his eyes, fist clenched, and called up the Eidolon magic within him.

The moment he lapsed into concentration, Kendra turned her focus on him, summoning the tempering flame within her and concentrated on casting it onto him.

He stared at the tall stand of weeds to his right.

His muscles corded as he struggled with whatever energies warred inside him. The wilding as he'd called it. She fought against the urge to let go of all the magic and concentrated on his hands, on those strong, squared fingers.

He nodded toward the tall weeds again.

"There," he said, his hands beginning to shake. "I'll try to cast the energy orb into the weeds."

At last, the writhing darkness rose from his hand, balled up, and hummed with fire.

Kendra turned her focus to him. And cast her tempering flame until a red haze hung around him.

"Trying...to focus on—the weeds." He gritted his teeth, face taut, hands shaking.

She cast more tempering magic onto him as the stubborn orb scuttled around in a circle. She laid her hands on his shoulders, picturing the Queen Anne's lace and horse grass.

"Keep trying, Shade," she urged, feeling the rush of magic flow from her into him.

In an instant, the orb careened into the weeds with a whine and exploded in a haze of red sparks.

His eyes snapped open. "That's it! But I have to be sure. Again."

She nodded and waited for him to find the energy to summon more Eidolon magic. When a small orb flickered in front of him, nearly touching his outstretched hand, he turned his body toward the pond.

"Casting toward the pond," he said.

Kendra kept her hand on Shade's shoulder, struggling to keep the magic flowing.

Clenching his teeth, he held out his hand and cast the orb aloft. It sailed into the middle of the pond. A direct hit.

"We did it!" he cried, grinning.

He whirled around and lifted her into the air, dancing her around in a circle, in his arms.

"It worked, Shade—it really worked!"

They had to work as one in order for him to focus his magic. Touching him sent enough magic coursing through him to focus the magic and pinpoint his target.

He threw his head back, laughing as he turned around and around, Kendra still in his arms.

"I can stand against them, Kendra! After all this time. At last, Carvahl's troops will be turned back!"

He turned circle after circle until he was so dizzy that he fell to his knees, chest heaving. She held onto him as he sank onto his back in the tall grass. She laid against his chest, brushing that dark hair out of his face and those wild blue eyes.

"Look up there, Kendra," he said, pointing. "It's a new sky. A new hope for Katori and a chance to end the Eidolon reign forever."

She rolled onto her side and laid her head against his chest as she watched the stars spill across the sky like sugar. It had to be around midnight. The moon was almost full. Her heart clenched.

In two weeks, the ebony moon would rise in darkness and the Eidolon would come through with a massive army.

"What happens if we defeat the Eidolon on the ebony moon?"

"When we defeat Carvahl's troops here, you and I must strike when the Eidolon are weakest."

A heaviness sat on her chest at the thought. "Which means?"

"It means," he said, holding her close, his hand stroking her hair. "We must follow them back through. To Katori."

"To do what? Take on their entire army in the flesh? You and me?"

He shook his head. "No, I have to take down Carvahl, the man responsible for everything. With Carvahl dead, his Eidolon army will collapse into its warring factions. That's why I so desperately need your tempering focus, Kendra. Facing Carvahl will be difficult, even with him in a weakened state from crossing the veil. I'll need your focus for Carvahl. Here and in Katori."

"Are you sure that killing Carvahl will end this, Shade?" she asked.

She felt his body stiffen, his shoulders tightening.

"Carvahl must enter Airell, the captured remains of the Katorin capital, in order to cross through to your world. That brings him out of his fortress where I could never touch him."

"Why must he go to the enemy's capital?" Kendra asked.

He propped himself up on one elbow, studying her, trying to look unaffected, but she felt his tension, heard it tighten his voice. She watched the worry flicker in his eyes, probably worried sick about his family. How long had it been since he'd seen his mother, talked to his siblings? She swallowed hard. His father?

"It's the point where the veil is thinnest. Crossable. And one of the last Eidolon scryve women who lives there can still open the veil—and the obsidian gates. They can't hide their abilities." He pointed to his face. "These light blue eyes give them away."

Kendra frowned. "Why don't these women refuse to open the gates and stop all of this?"

"What good would it do? Carvahl would find and coerce the most vulnerable of them."

"What does Carvahl hold over this particular scryve in Airell?" Kendra asked, trying to imagine this old woman with Shade's clear blue eyes huddled over some dark mirror that would part a veil.

He sighed, bowing his head. "My father—her son."

"Shade...she's your grandmother?"

He nodded. "She has no choice, Kendra. I don't blame her. Scrying the mirrors is all she knows and she only wants my father's release."

Scrying the mirrors. Mirrors parted the veil...what about that word stuck in her throat?

The missing gazing balls...they were mirrored glass. Why? Why mirrors?

"Shade, your scryves use mirrors to open the veils, correct?"

"Yes, the shiny surface helps them direct their magic," he said. "And so does Katorin obsidian."

A cold fear balled up in the pit of her stomach and she felt sick. Suddenly, she understood why the Eidolon shadow people had stolen the gazing balls.

"The gazing balls," she said, sitting up, her heart racing.

"What about them?" Shade asked and sat up beside her.

"Dozens of them have been stolen, taken out of yards all around here, right?"

He nodded, his brow furrowing as he listened and waited for her point.

"What if the Eidolon were using those gazing balls to open a much wider gate than we thought? Much larger than anything used before? If they create enough reflection on this side, the opening in your veil could accommodate a massive Eidolon force. Large enough to overrun us within minutes of the ebony moon's rise."

She watched the comprehension spread across his face, the color draining from his cheeks as he dropped his head in his hands.

"By Rhiannon, you're right, Kendra. Why hadn't I paid better attention? Some of Carvahl's troops slipped through. They're the ones gathering the gazing balls. They're creating a circuit somewhere, readying it to throw open the flood gates." He looked up at her, a sick look on his face. "They're also going to use those orbs to confuse our focus, Kendra. Use the mirror effect to throw off any precision we might develop with your tempering magic. To bounce it off target."

He was quiet now, his shoulders hunched in a mixture of defeat and anger. She knew his anger was at himself. He'd dismissed the missing orbs as not important and all along, the Eidolon had been using them against him. She gave him a moment to think about the situation as she watched the night shimmer around her, comfortable and lazy in its summer warmth.

"Shade?" she called finally, tugging on his shoulder.

"What?" he answered, sounding defeated.

"Between now and the ebony moon, we've got to hunt down those gazing balls, find them before Carvahl uses them against us."

"But how?" he asked, running his fingers through his long, dark bangs. "They could be anywhere."

She shook her head. "No, not anywhere."

He squinted at her. "Why do you say that?"

"They have to be close in order to reflect whatever it's reflecting, right? In order to stop you from using your magic, it has to be close enough to you to reflect something. And they couldn't have taken them a long distance. They'd need to assemble them all quickly when they come through—otherwise, you'll destroy their troops."

The light returned to his eyes as he nodded, a thousand thoughts rushing past his eyes.

"Kendra, you're right again. They'd have to be close by or they couldn't complete any kind of circuit quickly. But where?" His voice trailed off and he was lost in thought again.

It was a valid question, with too many possible answers.

"Why don't we try and get the Fey to help us?"

He chuckled. "Sebille? Helping us?"

"Why not?" Kendra replied. "If those flood gates open, they'll affect her, too."

"I'll put it to her like that. Maybe she'll agree to help track down the gazing balls?" He reached out and laid his hand against her face, stroking it with his long fingers. "I've never met anyone as smart as you, Kendra."

She'd never met anyone like Shade Fletcher, on so many levels. He faced his troubles head on whenever possible and she admired that for him.

"And I've never met anyone quite as crazy as you. Shade."

"I strive to be the best in my field," he said, the corners of his mouth lifting. "The one between our houses."

She ran her fingers through his hair, gazing into his luminous eyes and that sexy mouth, wanting to make love to him all over again.

"I have someone who might get the Fey to help us. I'll ask for her help and you talk to Sebille. If we can send out the smallest of the Fey to search for the missing globes, then we stand a better chance of finding them and dismantling this—this circuit."

He nodded. "I'll talk to Gabriel. Explain what we're looking for... see if he can help."

She glanced across the field at the faerie lights floating around her garden, knowing things would get even stranger in a couple of weeks when the moon was dark in the sky. The garden was a crossroads for every magical creature residing within the human world. If she spread the word about the gazing balls, maybe some of them would remember seeing the mirrored globes. Even the tiniest of these magical creatures may have seen where the globes had been taken. It was probably somewhere they weren't likely to look. But they'd better start looking under every rock and every leaf.

Shade's life might depend on it.

"Should we start looking?" Kendra asked, staring into his eyes, but his hands were pulling her back against him.

He shook his head. "Not tonight. Not with you in my arms and all this moonlight."

"But Shade, if the globes—"

He laid his fingers against her lips. "We'll have better luck looking for the gazing balls in daylight. With the sun reflecting off them."

She hated to lie here doing nothing, but she'd make the best of it. She smiled. In his arms.

17

S hade stayed with Kendra until the moon slid from the sky. When the world began to lighten, he walked her home, kissing her good morning. She tested her magic at the door and easily summoned two cups of coffee. With her in his arms, they sat together on the wooden chaise, sipping coffee, and watching the unicorns prance under the Japanese maple. When her eyes began to close, he half-carried her to the door and she kissed him good morning again, disappearing inside for some sleep.

Kendra Martin was dangerous, he realized as he walked across the dewy field, the air corn-sweet and sultry. As much as he'd strained against it, he was in love with her.

He wanted to shout it up to her window and through the garden, but he didn't know what the next ebony moon would bring. That dark moon would soon rise and all hell would break loose. And he didn't know if he'd survive it.

But now that he and Kendra had learned how to combine their magics as one, he felt confident about facing Carvahl. For the first time since he'd passed through the veil.

Until the ebony moon rose again, he and Kendra would be inseparable, practicing each night until the veil parted. But the gazing balls still worried him. Was there a massive gate waiting to open? One that would overrun this world with Eidolon shadow soldiers?

His chest ached at the thought. He had to find those missing orbs before the veil parted again.

And what happened beyond the new moon? If he defeated Carvahl in Katori, where would that leave him and Kendra?

He had to return to his homeland. To help rebuild his cities—and his life. He had to tell her that, make her understand that his life was in Katori and not here. He'd been away too long.

His breath caught in his throat. Would telling her that be the end of their relationship? Would he lose her forever?

When he reached his porch, he checked for the pale wash of blue light that signaled the active Fey protection wards. The lights still held. No more stranded Eidolon would sneak inside with those Fey wards still lit.

He hurried inside and dropped down on the moss-covered chair in his living room, yellow maple leaves drifting around him. Gnarled oak trunks shadowed the corners of the room as he slid out the obsidian slab from underneath a vine-draped end table and summoned his mother. Contacting her now was so risky, but she had to hear the news. She had to hear the words—the news that she'd waited a lifetime to hear.

He had to risk it. She had to know.

It took him several tries to summon her image through the veil and the layers of obsidian. Her dark hair was piled in loose curls around her face. She looked tired and worried. Thinner than she had the last time he'd spoken to her.

"Shade!" Her face burned with fear as she reached out to him. He could almost feel her touch through the obsidian. "They're coming for you! You've got to flee again."

"No, Mother. Not this time. The time for running has ended."

Her face turned pale. "What? You're staying to face them? Shade, you can't. They'll kill you—like they've killed everyone with the wilding. You can't stay."

He couldn't contain his grin. "I can. The woman with the

tempering magic... she's the most wonderful woman I've ever met. I—I can't explain it, but it's more than an attraction."

"Shade, your life's in danger."

Her face was stern, frightened, and he could almost hear her telling him to think of himself and his people, not some woman.

"We've focused the wilding, Mother! With Kendra beside me, we can finally stand against Carvahl. Once and for all."

With Kendra beside him, he could do anything.

For several moments, she couldn't speak. She stared at him through a haze of tears as if she hadn't heard everything he'd said.

"Did you hear me, Mother?" he replied. "I've focused the wilding! It can be done. We can save Katori."

The tears threaded her cheeks. "You're sure?" she asked finally. "Really, truly certain, Shade?"

He nodded. "Finally, we can end this. I can face Carvahl in the flesh now and destroy him."

"What about Braeden?" she asked and Shade could see her trembling as she pressed her hands together. She hadn't seen his father since Shade went through the veil at seventeen.

"Father will soon see the light of day, Mother. You have my word."

She closed her eyes and bowed her head as more tears dripped down her face. His chest ached to see her cry like that. He reached out to her, forgetting for a moment about the veil and the great distance between them.

"Don't cry, Mother."

In a few moments, she looked up at him, smiling. "And finally, my son will come home."

He choked up. How long had it been since his exile from Katori? He'd been away so long. To finally go home was more than he'd ever dared hope for, more than he could even think about right now.

"I've dreamed of crystalline skies and flower-drenched meadows," he said.

She smiled at his mention of that poem, but her face turned pale, fear hovering in her eyes.

"Come home alive, Shade—not in a shroud."

"Don't worry. This is our time—Katori's time to finally rise."

She nodded. "How will you defeat Carvahl?"

"He'll be weakened when the new moon sets. I will face him in daylight with Kendra beside me and let his arrogance take him."

His mother frowned, shaking her head. "His arrogance? I don't understand."

Shade dug his nails into the moss-covered armrest, the thought of Carvahl's condescension infuriating. "He says my Katorin heritage poisons the Eidolon magic I carry. Because of that, he thinks my magics can never be mastered, never used against him. He'll learn otherwise."

"Don't get yourself killed, Shade. I couldn't bear it and neither could your sisters."

He bristled at her omission of his younger brother, Jaxon to that list.

"Jaxon might be pleased by that turn of events."

Anger lit her brown eyes. "Never let me hear you say that again about your brother. Jaxon has his own views about what happened here, but he's still your brother, and he loves you."

Shade snorted, holding back the caustic laugh that burned in his throat.

Jaxon had called him the vilest of names the night Shade slipped through the veil. Coward was the highest one on the list. It hadn't been Shade's idea or choice to flee from Carvahl. Braeden, his father, had demanded it and his mother made the arrangements without Shade's consent. He was still a kid himself then.

He remembered that night vividly as he'd packed a small satchel, his sisters crying and clinging to him. He'd hid his face as he packed only necessities, not wanting them to see his own tears. He'd expected to be gone from home only a month or two—not more than a decade.

He remembered Jaxon standing sullen and angry in the doorway of Shade's bedroom, muttering taunts and insults about him running away. All the while, his anxious parents had waited at the front door, two horses saddled. One for him and one for his father. The whole family would have to flee Airell the moment that Shade went through the veil.

It was a treasonous act by his father, an Eidolon.

Shade had hugged each of his sisters, then his mother. When he'd faced Jaxon, his younger brother's brown eyes were ice cold. Shade remembered reaching out, laying his hand on Jaxon's shoulder.

"It has to be this way," he'd said in a quiet voice. "I'm sorry. Take care of them. They'll look to you soon."

Jaxon shrugged off his touch, anger burning past his cold indifference as Shade pressed past him. He was halfway to the front door when Jaxon shouted his name.

Shade remembered turning around, expecting a last moment concession from his brother, maybe even a hug. But when he saw Jaxon's face, he saw the rage as Jaxon spat out the word, *coward* again. It was the last thing Jaxon said to him as Shade thrust open the front door and rushed outside behind his father.

"You and I both know he thinks me a coward, Mother. That I ran. To save myself."

"Jaxon has had a lot of time to reflect on that night, Shade. He's grown up a lot since then. He's had to."

He'd had years, in fact. Time moved so much slower in his realm than it did here. Years on Katori were centuries here, much like the Fey. The veil allowed his people to move through those centuries at will. His grandmother had hidden his entry point from her mirrors by using obsidian that night, allowing its layers to reflect back at the mirror. So, Carvahl couldn't find him and the others through her scrying. It took that monster centuries to track him and the others by their magic— through the obsidian gates. Kept him and the others alive for a long time.

If only it had kept them safe, too.

Shade bowed his head, letting the memories fade. "I hope you're right, Mother. Please get word to Hekalie that I'll need safe passage into Airell. For me and Kendra. The first sunrise after the ebony moon. It's crucial that we come through immediately after the moon sets."

His mother frowned, biting her lip. "How will you get a human through the veil?"

"She's the great granddaughter of Aeryn O'Riley ni Katori."

"Aeryn?" She gasped, her eyes wide. "Shade, are you sure?"

"Yes, why?" He frowned, tensing as he studied her worried expression. That look had always meant trouble.

"Aeryn married one of the Fey, a black-haired weaver, distant cousin to Sebille."

"Is that a problem?" Shade asked, watching for any subtle change in her eyes, her expression.

"I'm not sure," said his mother, not quite meeting his gaze.

That was trouble—he was certain. Nevertheless, whatever troubled her would stay in the background for now. She wouldn't mention yet.

"The Fey magic combined with her Katorin lineage should be enough to cross the veil. But I'll consult with Hekalie."

He saw past her comments about getting Kendra through the veil. She was concerned about Kendra's relation to Aeryn. But why? He looked forward to asking her in person.

If he survived this fight against Carvahl on the human side of the veil.

"Hopefully, the next time you talk to me, it will be in person, Mother."

She reached out with both hands and pressed them against the obsidian as if touching his face.

"A moment I've looked forward to for so long, Shade," she said. "I hope I will see you soon." She waved at him as the obsidian went dark.

He sat staring at the obsidian slab for a long time, the yellow leaves drifting past, the chirping of birds soothing.

What about Aeryn ni Katori had troubled his mother? Had there been something dark surrounding Aeryn? Something that she feared Kendra might carry back to Katori again?

He wandered into his kitchen and grabbed a cold Bell's Oberon beer from the fridge, his thoughts racing past Carvahl and Sebille's wait-and-see attitude.

Back to Kendra.

Warmth spread through him despite the cold beer as he walked into his bedroom. He stared at the moss-strewn bed, smell of wildflowers infusing the room. Warmed with sunlight and traces of the raspberry scent of her hair, lilac fragrance of her skin. He smiled at the memory of her skin scorching his body as he made love her. He loved how the life—the passion—burned in her warm brown eyes.

He sat down on the bed and took a long pull off his beer, his body humming with magic despite the weariness that clung to him. He'd given himself to her last night, left everything bare to her touch, her exploration. He'd told her his greatest fears and his dreams, but he'd left one wish out.

The one that placed her beside him forever.

He wanted more than only days that they'd share and he couldn't find a way to tell her that. Somehow, he'd find a way before the ebony moon. But she had to know that his life was in Katori—the thing he feared telling her most.

After kicking off his shoes, he unbuttoned his shirt and draped it on the arm of the chair beside his bed. Down to dark blue running shorts, he settled back against the headboard, beer in hand, and his thoughts racing. Sunlight streamed through the skylights above his bed, casting warm rays of light through the white pines and cedars, illuminating the fallen yellow leaves turning gold against the footpath that led to the bathroom.

Here, in Kendra's world, his greening was magnified. Anywhere he lived turned into a forest like this inside. In Katori, at least his Katorin magic would be in balance again. Where he could control it. But he was a long way from returning to Katori though.

So much to do and prepare. So much to overcome.

He whispered a prayer to the worlds, to the forces here and beyond this realm. And asked for justice. Nothing more.

Before the week was over, he'd return to Kendra's garden and call for Sebille and the others. He'd tell them about the missing gazing balls, Kendra's theory, and his suspicions.

He smiled and took another long drink of beer, knowing he'd be with Kendra again tonight. His eyelids drooped, sleep fighting to quiet his thoughts. He set the beer bottle on the nightstand and stretched out on the bed of moss and wildflowers. Unfolding the quilt at the foot of the bed, he pulled it across him. He closed his eyes, thinking about the day when he could show Kendra the places where he grew up, the city that would rise from the dead, and the family he hadn't seen for centuries in her time.

SHADE AWOKE TO KNOCKING ON HIS DOOR. HE ROLLED OVER, SLIDING off the quilt, and sat up.

The light had fled from his windows, silvery plum of twilight bruising the blue sky, shadowing the world. He sighed. Setting the stage for the Eidolon's return. The full moon was gone. Tonight's moon waned fast, shrinking from the sky as the Eidolon army approached. He hoped he hadn't spoken prematurely about returning home.

The knock echoed through the house again as he got to his feet, hair pressed into unnatural waves and swirls, bangs in his eyes, as he walked into the hallway. He ran his fingers through his hair, trying to coax it into place as he opened the door a crack.

Kendra stood there, wearing a white tank top (no bra) and a short navy skirt, long, tanned legs curving into white slip-on tennis shoes. She peered through the crack, smiling playfully at him.

"It's after eight o'clock," she replied, hands on her hips. "Thought you were coming over for supper."

That smooth skin, thick dark hair, and those firm little breasts made him ache to touch her.

"Sorry, I overslept," he said, a hand against his head, trying to hide his bed hair.

Her gaze traveled over him, her pupils widening, that smile

unshakable. She leaned against the door frame as he opened the door a little wider.

"Should I give you some time?" she asked, laying the side of her face against the door frame, watching him.

She reached out with her forefinger and traced a line down his bare chest.

He sucked in a breath. "Alone?" he asked.

She shook her head and nudged the door open. She eased her arms around his neck, those firm breasts and long legs pressed against him. She brushed her lips across his, sipping, nibbling his bottom lip.

"Not quite what I had in mind," she said and thrust her mouth over his in a long, deep kiss, her tongue against his as she explored his mouth.

He pulled her inside the house, lifting her into his arms as he closed the door. Her hands slid across his chest, down his back in desperate strokes, caressing—hungering.

He carried her into the bedroom and laid her on the bed under him, entwining his fingers in hers as he lifted her arms over her head and smashed his mouth to hers in a hungry kiss. Her body arched at his frantic pace, her hips moving in response.

She moaned as he let go of her hands and slid up her tank top, stroking her breasts. He ran his hand down her flat belly to the hem of that short navy skirt that had ridden halfway up her thighs. His blood rushed as he pushed the hem up farther to reveal thin blue bikinis underneath. He slid them off her hips and down those long legs. Her legs parted to him and he explored the length of her body.

She slid down his running shorts, pulling him onto the bed.

"I'm falling hard for you, Kendra," he whispered in her ear as he rolled on top of her.

"Love me," she said to him as his hips met hers.

"More than you know," he said.

Her eyes closed, body arching, hips moving with him as he entered her.

18

Days rushed past as Shade and Kendra spent their evenings working in tandem to summon and focus his wilding. And afterward, exhausted, they fell into his bed until morning lit the quiet Indiana countryside. With Kendra beside him, he could call up his Eidolon magic with little effort now and with her focus, he could direct the dark fire with accuracy.

Would it be enough? He would know soon.

The ebony moon rose around six AM this morning. Tonight, the new moon's darkness would blend with the night and the veil between his world and the human world would part again. Tonight, the Eidolon would pour through the veil. They had to kill him or risk him and Kendra returning to Katori. To fight them face-to-face for the first time since he'd come through to her world.

But despite an exhaustive search, they failed to find even one of the stolen gazing balls. He had no choice now but to face whatever the Eidolon had planned for those mirrored globes.

And him.

He and Kendra ate supper on her patio by the light of the garden and the fading sun. She wore faded jeans, holes in both knees, a white tank under a sheer orange blouse. He'd put on cargo shorts, loafers, and a green T-shirt, his axe propped beside Kendra's hoe at the back door.

Already, the faerie orbs glistened throughout the garden. More would appear as night fell and the Watchers began to appear. He sighed. Eidolon shadows would follow as they stalked him, intending to destroy him.

His shoulders ached, muscles burning, and his gut felt tight at the impending battle. He dreaded the night and the fight to come. He'd waited for this moment for centuries but now, the thought of it gouged at his gut.

Tonight, Kendra made lasagna at her place...by hand not by magic. She'd covered the patio table in Emmaline's familiar red tablecloth, white plates glistening against the lasagna's melted mozzarella, bright red tomato sauce, and green spinach. A wicker basket sat in the center of the table, filled with parsley flecked garlic bread slices. The scent of garlic was warm and comforting.

He took another piece of garlic bread and set it on his plate. He picked up the glass of merlot beside his plate and sipped it, studying Kendra's distance. She seemed quiet and a little distracted, picking at her food. She'd only half-listened when he talked about Katori and what awaited him there after he and she crossed the veil at first light.

"Kendra, what's the matter?" he asked finally, setting down his wine glass.

She glanced up at him as she took a sip of merlot. Her gaze fell to the glass she cradled in her hand, staring into it as if she saw the future. A bleak one.

"All of this is ending tonight, isn't it?" she asked, at last, looking him in the eye.

"Ending?" He frowned. "What do you mean?"

She motioned toward the garden. "The garden, the faeries, the lights..." She stared at him now, uncertainty in her eyes. "You and me."

She expected him to leave her tonight.

"It doesn't have to end, Kendra," he said softly. "Why do you say that?"

Her gaze fell to the glass again, watching the garnet red liquid swirl around the glass and hug the sides as it splashed around.

"Toni's business plan was mostly pretense," she said. "To get me here—because of the Eidolon. She told me that what I've already done is more than enough to finish the project."

Shade's eyes widened. "Your client knows about the Eidolon?"

She glanced up at him. "Yes. Toni Ambrose."

He nodded, knowing Toni from her frequent visits to Gem's garden when Emmaline got really ill. The dresses she'd made for Rhiannon. Toni was Fey and her dresses were legendary among magical circles. He had no idea she'd brought Kendra here to help him, but he'd make a point of thanking her when he commissioned a new dress for Kendra. As a surprise.

"She's very talented, but I'm impressed that she'd bring you here. I'll have to thank her for her exceptional taste."

Kendra didn't crack a smile. "I'm serious, Shade. When we face these shadows, we return to your world to finish the fight, correct?"

He nodded, his brow furrowing, not understanding her concern. Or what was upsetting her. Beyond the evident *do or die trying* part. Wasn't it obvious that he loved her? "Yes. At first light. To face Carvahl and his army."

He felt her burning stare on him and he met her gaze.

"What happens after that?" she asked, pain in her voice.

"After we defeat Carvahl," he said, "the Katorins will retake Airell. Then Gwydon. Then Sulahn. Until Katori is free of Eidolon rule."

"And what about you?"

"Me?" he asked, laying a hand against his chest.

"Yes, Shade...what happens to you?" Her face looked pinched, as if waiting for him to say something that she dreaded.

He smiled, trying to reassure her. "I'll free my father from the oblivis and retake my family's home in Airell where I'll live out my..."

He let his voice trail off at the pained look in her eyes, understanding, at last, what was bothering her now.

"I'll never see you again, will I?" she said in a deathly quiet voice, her unblinking gaze boring through his chest.

Already, he felt her distance as she pulled back from him.

"Why wouldn't you see me again, Kendra?" he asked, shaking his head.

He slid his chair closer and took hold of her hand, but she pulled it away.

"*This* is my world, Shade," she snapped, voice quivering. "This is where *I* belong. I thought you belonged here, too. You've lived most of your life here."

Shade winced. She wouldn't leave her world for his and until now, he hadn't realized that he'd ever ask that of her. But she was right. After he retook Airell, he would take back his family home and return to Katori for good. He sighed. And Kendra would return to her world but not even to this house, this place. No, she'd go back to Baltimore, where she'd lived before Shade even knew her.

And no amount of persuasion would sway her or him.

He'd been exiled from his world for centuries. To ask him to give up that return now was cruel, yet even as he felt that pain and anger, he knew he was exiling himself from this woman that he loved so deeply.

It was a gut punch.

He bowed his head, understanding her pain. Sharing it.

"I've been exiled for so long, Kendra. To ask me not to go home now would be...wrong."

She nodded, her eyes filling with tears. "I know. That's why I'd never ask it."

"What if we lived part of the time in each world?" he offered.

At last, the hint of a smile brightened her face. "You'd do that?"

"I would if it kept us together," he said, picking up his wine glass for a long sip. "Besides, I know what it feels like to miss your home. For me to ask you to give up yours would be just as wrong."

She slid her hand onto his, squeezing, but he rose to his feet, drawing her up from her chair and into his arms.

"Kendra, there is something else I need to tell you." He laid his face against her hair, inhaling that sun-washed scent of raspberry.

She stiffened. "What?" she asked, the dread returning to her voice, trying to take a step back from him.

He held her tight. "I think I love you," he said. "And it's making me crazy."

She pulled away from him, her eyes wide, lips pursed. "Oh, God, Shade...did I hear you right?"

His eyes narrowed. "Didn't I say the words? The big three? The ones all you women say we never say first. I didn't tell you have a brain tumor. I said I love you, Kendra."

She chuckled, laying her hand to her mouth, and that made him angrier.

He crossed his arms against his chest, looking away, but her hands were cupping his face, her lips brushing his in a teasing kiss.

"I wanted to hear you say it again," she said with a laugh and his mood softened. "Before I said that I love you, Shade Fletcher."

He swallowed hard. It was the first time a woman had said those words back to him and meant them. She nibbled at his lips and he let go of his anger, pulling her into his arms again, his mouth covering hers.

"How sweet," said a mocking voice from the pergola.

Sebille.

Shade scowled and gazed toward the garden. He'd recognized her voice by its unwavering condescension. He let his lips linger against Kendra's one last time before he turned around to face the faerie queen.

"Sebille," he said with a smirk. "Right on time, I see."

She nodded her head ever so slightly at him. She wore a blue, sleeveless gown that paled against the darkening summer sky. The air smelled warm with roses and garlic as Sebille walked along the pergola as if it were a red carpet, her entourage of Fey behind her, as she called softly to her magical charges.

With fluid grace, the faerie queen held out her arms to the garden as unicorns, gnomes, and elven folk stepped out from the flowers and trees, gathering at the edge of the pergola. They carried rakes and hoes and picks. Even satyrs and centaurs trotted out into the garden to stand behind Sebille, tails twitching and hooves tapping against the ground, bows and quivers strung across their muscular backs.

More and more elvenkind arrived, the tall, waifish creatures milling around each other, whispering in soft voices. Except for their height and pointed ears, the elvenkind's silvery skin and delicate features were indistinguishable from the Fey.

A flock of griffins descended from the deep blue sky to circle and land at the edge of Kendra's patio, their great eagle heads and clear gold eyes so strange against their lion bodies. With talons and hind claws, the griffins looked formidable and he was grateful they would stand with him, rather than against him.

He wondered what creatures would join the Eidolon as they passed through the veil. The veil would part within twenty feet of Shade, drawn to his presence. He knew the forces in this garden were not all the magic in this world.

Some of the other races would side with the Eidolon. He was certain of it.

He regretted that the Eidolon would come through the veil near his house and far from this garden and Kendra's strange Fey gift. With other humans around, he risked their lives if he'd didn't keep this battle confined to his property and the woods surrounding it. No, he'd let the humans in this sleepy country road believe it was a wild party like all the other ebony moons when he'd battled the Eidolon.

Delicate chimes rolled through the garden as a procession of the Fey strode along the pergola. Sebille delighted in their approach. Some rode atop badgers and silver foxes, golden cords and painted ribbons trailing while others soared on the backs of cardinals and flew like glowing butterflies beside them.

The elvenkind were as tall as Shade with their elegant, sculpted looks and large, haunting eyes the color of emeralds, sapphires, and amethysts. Without those delicate gossamer wings at their backs. The air tanged with myrrh and sandalwood as lantern light flickered through the quiet garden, its inhabitants looking as awed as he felt by the Fey's arrival.

Shade grinned. The Eidolon would regret this night.

As the last rays of sunlight surged from the orange sun hanging low on the horizon, the garden path lit with an ethereal glow.

The golden hour, one of the most magical hours in this world.

Rhiannon stepped out from the rays of golden light to stand beside Sebille. She was radiant with her golden hair and pale indigo gown the color of twilight. It hugged her body in waves of gauzy silk. Two glowing white orbs hung from a short chain around her throat.

Rhiannon smiled at him, waving and he nodded toward her.

"I cannot interfere, Shade, but I've come to lend my support."

"Thank you," he called to her.

As the sun slipped toward dusk, more and more magical creatures amassed in the garden. When the golden hour washed over the flowers and faeries, the warm golden cast gave the world a fragileness that took Shade's breath away. For a short while, it reminded him of Katori, what she'd been before Eidolon greed blotted out everything that mattered.

Almost everything. Now, he had a chance to wash away the corruption and free his people.

When the sun dissipated into a pink and gold sea of clouds, the light faded quickly to grey as twilight descended. As the world darkened, a black haze rose on the horizon, blotting out the cloud banks.

Everyone looked up.

Shade felt Kendra's arms tighten around his waist and he drew her closer.

"What is that?" she whispered. "The Eidolon?"

Shade shook his head as he watched the darkness draw closer to the garden. When the shrill chatter of bats was audible, he grinned.

The North American vampire tribe approached.

"It's Gabriel's people, Kendra," he said in a soft voice.

All around him the tiny bats darted and fluttered, until one by one, they perched on the eaves of houses, on the edges of the pergola, anywhere they could hang. Their little rounded ears shifted in constant motion against bright brown eyes and little foxlike snouts.

One by one, the tiny bats somersaulted off the rooftop and the pergola, landing in human form. Some vampires dressed formal in anything from tuxedos to leather armor, others dressed in ragged street clothes. Many wore sunglasses and carried tire irons, chains, even broadswords and katanas. Young, old, middle-aged, they gathered on the patio and in the grass, some tall, others short.

Gabriel stepped onto the patio and extended his hand to Shade. He wore faded, torn jeans and a black Chainsmokers T-shirt, a katana sheathed at his side, black wayfarer Ray-Bans hanging from his collar.

Lenora stood behind him, dressed in thigh-high black boots, a jean skirt, and a burgundy lace lingerie top. A heavy chain hung as a belt around her waist, black leather fingerless gloves on each hand, a Louisville slugger in her left hand. Her eyes were ringed with smoke, a line of plum blush outlining her bronzed cheekbones, her lips the color of bruised cherries. Kendra nodded at her.

"We're ready, Kendra, Shade," said Lenora, smiling as she slid on her sunglasses—tortoiseshell Ray-Bans.

Kendra reached out and squeezed Lenora's hand. "Thank you," she said.

Shade stepped forward to shake Gabriel's hands.

"Thanks for coming, Gabriel," he said, giving the sandy-haired vampire's hand a brisk shake.

"Glad to help. I think we all have equal stake in this problem, Shade." He clapped Shade on the back, smiling. "Besides, the Green Man is one of our own legends that we've got to protect."

Shade laughed. "Everybody has a story," he said.

"True," said Gabriel with a smirk. "Yours is a little crazier than most."

Shade felt Kendra rubbing his arm as she stepped beside him.

"So true, Gabriel," she said, offering her hand to him.

He reached out and hugged her, kissing her on the cheek. "Good to see you, Kendra. Ready to fight the good fight?"

She shrugged. "I'll do my best."

"We still haven't found those missing gazing balls, Gabriel."

Gabriel's smile faded and he spoke in a low voice to Lenora.

"Is that true?" Lenora asked. "You still haven't found them?"

Shade nodded. They'd turned over every stone and every yard but turned up nothing. It didn't make much sense. The gazing balls had to be here somewhere, ready to use when the veil parted again tonight. Beneath the darkness of the new moon.

He kept shifting his nervous gaze toward the pond, expecting any moment to see the Watcher orbs dance across the water, reflecting their dangerous lights back at them.

Gabriel propped his hands on his hips as he walked along the patio, deep in thought. "Could they have been carried through the veil?"

The Watchers would slip through the veil tonight in record numbers, but one thing Shade knew for certain: those gazing balls hadn't been carried through the veil. They were here...somewhere close. Waiting for the Eidolon to use globes against him.

"No, the veil has been closed since the last new moon," said Shade. "If they plan to flood this world with Carvahl's army, the gazing balls have to be on this side. But where?"

"Where would an Eidolon hide a bunch of brightly colored glass?" Lenora asked, gazing around the darkening landscape.

She seemed to be thinking aloud, pacing behind Gabriel with her head bowed.

"They could be anywhere," said Shade. "Deep in the woods. Up in the trees. In one of these houses. Hidden somewhere no one would ever look."

Until it was too late to stop the Eidolon from pouring through the veil.

Finally, Gabriel stopped pacing. He stared at Shade a moment then cast his gaze into the haze of twilight. "It's too late to worry about them now. All we can do is move ahead and defeat the Watchers as they come through the veil."

Shade nodded. "You're right. We have to focus on the transformed shadows as the Watchers pour through the veil. Destroy them and keep destroying them until the sun rises. It's what we have to do."

Gabriel pulled Shade to the edge of the patio. His eyes were steely, a touch of fear in them which surprised Shade. "All the tribes support you in this fight, Shade, but some of the clans have rebelled," he said in a low voice. "They've sided with the Eidolon and plan to defend their return to this world. Just so you know."

A rush of fear hit Shade at the thought of fighting vampires and the Eidolon. He nodded. "I expected that."

"And for every ten elvenkind and Fey standing here, there will be two of their kind against this fight. How many will fight with the Eidolon, I don't know. Lenora and I asked some of the sisters of the cauldron to pass the word among their ilk. No word."

Shade sighed, casting a gaze at the horizon. True night wasn't yet on them. It would come sooner than he hoped.

Sebille moved along the pergola again, back toward the patio, faeries, elvenkind, and gnomes in her wake as other magical creatures gathered. Even the vampires huddled together with the satyrs and centaurs near the pergola until Sebille walked onto the patio and turned to face the crowd of magical beings packed into the garden.

When Shade returned to the patio, Kendra leaned against him, her mouth against his ear.

"Can my neighbors see all of this?" she asked.

He chuckled. "Only if they have a hint of magical lineage in their veins. They may see some of the faerie lights but that's about it."

"Not even the vampires?"

"Only if they want to be seen."

"Good," she replied. "I didn't want my cell phone to blow up with frantic calls and texts."

He waved her off, smirking. "Wouldn't they call the police on this wild party?"

Kendra blushed and he laughed, sliding an arm around her shoulders.

"Best thing that ever happened to me," he said, pulling her into a hug and a quick kiss.

"Everyone, your attention," Sebille called out, hand raised, her clear alto voice silencing the whispers and murmurs until the only sound Shade heard was the flutter of sparrows' wings through the garden.

"When twilight deepens, lights then shadows will come through to our world to be met with their consorts. All are intent upon destroying those who could stop them. The Eidolon. And our own kind who may stand with them. These shadows are projections of the Eidolon from a distant place. Their mission is to destroy our Green Man, Shade of Katori. And Kendra, our Fey cousin."

High-pitched twitters and whispers touched the stillness again until Sebille lifted her hand to silence them.

"We could do nothing, of course," Sebille continued, casting a wary gaze at Shade. "We could watch as Shade and Kendra die by their hand and go about our business as if nothing happened. But the Eidolon attack will not stop with the Green Man. The Eidolon seek to enslave this world, too. They will flood our world with their kind, destroying it unless we stand with Shade now. As one force. And destroy their light and shadow forms. But you may have to take up arms against your own kind. I regret this inevitability."

Gabriel stepped beside Sebille.

"The North American tribe has begun to arrive, Sebille," he said, pointing up at the sky as another flock of bats swooped toward the garden. "We will battle the Eidolon at yours and Shade's side."

Sebille smiled, looking pleased by Gabriel's declaration.

"Thank you, Gabriel. Your assistance is appreciated." She turned her gaze back to the collection of magical creatures crammed into the garden. "Knowing you may face brothers and sisters, cousins as well as the Eidolon, I ask all of you to stand with us."

For several minutes, the garden buzzed with voices as the magical creatures debated their involvement.

"You have my support, too, my Queen," came a voice from the garden gate.

Kendra turned to stare and a smile rolled across her face as she grabbed Shade's arm, shaking it. A dark-haired woman in an ocean blue dress stood at the garden gate, slowly lifting the handle to enter the garden.

"Shade, it's Toni Ambrose!"

Kendra hurried off the patio and rushed to the gate, opening it, and allowing Toni to enter. She hugged Toni, gripping her hand a moment.

The faerie queen turned toward the gate, an annoyed look on the woman's face. Shade resisted an urge to roll his eyes. Sebille's drama had been spoiled, upstaged by the little dressmaker. The queen of faerie had to delve deeper to regain her stage.

"Toni, dear, how good of you stand with us," said Sebille, her polite smile a little flat. "Your healing talents will be of great help."

Toni glanced at Kendra who drew her onto the patio as she faced Sebille.

"My Queen, I feel responsible for Kendra Martin's presence here, so I felt the least I could do was join her in the fight."

"And it is gratefully accepted," said Sebille in a deep bow.

Shade shook his head, knowing that bow was born of mock graciousness, but it eased Toni Ambrose's apprehension.

"Sebille," said Shade, stepping toward her as he left Kendra and Toni on the patio. "A word in private, please."

She nodded a moment then held out her arm to him and he approached. Sebille tucked her arm in his.

"Walk with me a moment, Green Man," she said and leaned against him as they walked toward the herbs and boxwood hedges.

"Sebille," he said in a quiet voice. "I thank you for your assistance tonight. Without your help—"

"No need for speeches, Shade. Your debt is all that I require."

He cast a nervous look at her, his brows furrowing.

She laughed in that crystal voice. "I'm joking, Shade. You will owe me nothing after this night. Perhaps a favor someday, but if we never meet again, our slates are clean."

He nodded, feeling a little uncertain, but he had little choice with the ebony moon bearing down on him. His life was in her hands.

"What about the Fey and other creatures who side with the Eidolon? Are you prepared to battle your own kind?"

Sebille was quiet a long time, a shadow of sadness on her perfect face. "Like my Nevar?"

A lump rose in Shade's throat. The king of faerie had sided with the Eidolon? Sebille would battle her own husband this night. He watched the tears fill her vivid lavender eyes and he dropped to his knees before her and pressed her hand to his face.

"I have no words," he said, his voice tight. "You're giving more than I have a right to ask tonight, Lady Sebille."

Her fingers stroked his dark hair. "I regret this night deeply, Green Man. And I've cursed your name countless times. But to side with the Eidolon is wrong. It will destroy our magical sanctuaries and break our barrier between humans. Nevar knows what he risks tonight." She sighed, the sound like wind chimes. "What will be, will be, Shade. We all must choose and fault no one but ourselves for that choice."

He kissed her hand and she smiled, wiping away those dangerous tears that had entrapped many a human. But she shed them from her heart tonight.

"Rise, Shade and stand with us."

Shade rose to his full six-foot-two height and stared into Sebille's eyes a moment. She meant what she'd said and he thought more of this Fey queen than he'd ever thought possible.

"Thank you, Sebille," he whispered and leaned forward, kissing her on the cheek.

She smiled, laying a hand to the spot as he turned toward the patio.

"Listen everyone to your final instructions," Sebille called and the garden quieted again. "Shade of Katori will tell you what to do. Go with strength." She motioned toward Shade and folded her hands against her stomach.

He turned to face the sea of silent, nervous magical creatures.

"Across the field from this garden is where they will come through." He glanced up at the darkening sky. Almost true night. They had to hurry. "The first sign of them will be Watcher lights over the pond. Destroy them at all costs. If they gain a foothold, their lights will fade to shadows and their attacks will be stronger. Hidden. Deadly. For now, they are only projections."

"How do they gain solid form?" Gabriel asked from behind.

Shade sighed. He didn't turn to face the vampire. "They gain solid form by killing me and taking the heart of my magic."

"Shade!"

Kendra's voice pierced the quiet and he felt her hands on his arm. He didn't turn, not wanting to show weakness in front of the magical creatures expecting only strength from him.

"With that core in their hands," he continued. "They'll have the rare magic I carry. A magic that will allow them to come through the veil in solid form. As I came through centuries before to keep that magic from them."

Murmurs and conversations erupted in the garden as he glanced at Sebille then Rhiannon who stood by the gate. A hint of sadness shadowed their faces.

"Until a crescent moon shines in this sky again, the night will bring Eidolon attacks. But tonight is different. I'm the last of my kind to carry this magic and all of Eidolon will project through the veil tonight. This will exhaust Carvahl, their leader. By morning, he'll be extremely weak if we hold back the tide. At first light, when no more Eidolon can pass through the veil, Kendra and I will go through to Katori and face Carvahl in the flesh. If I defeat him, it's over. If not..."

He gritted his teeth, his eyes narrowing as he gazed out at the pond. If he failed, all was lost. When he finally looked out at the solemn faces again, he knew no more words were needed. He cast a look across the field at his white ranch house that looked dark and shadowed. Already, the trees had blended into the darkness.

True night was close. It was time.

"To say thank you seems horribly inadequate, but I thank all of you for standing with us." He glanced up at the sky again. Cold white stars poked through the darkening fabric. "It's time."

Shade turned to cast an uneasy glance at Kendra as he crossed the patio to pick up his axe. She was beside him, now, picking up her hoe. She gripped his arms.

"I'm so scared for you," she said in a half-whisper.

His jaw tightened, the muscles in his cheek twitching as he fought to swallow the lump in his throat. He could lose her tonight and the thought of that made him crazy. All the other times he'd face the Eidolon, he hadn't cared if he lived or died, but tonight, more than anything, he wanted to live. He wanted to be there when she woke up and had her coffee, when she went to bed at night. And for everything in between.

He sighed. He wanted to be there when she needed him —wanted him.

Thrusting his arms around her, he pulled her hard against him. His frantic kiss smashed against her mouth, desperate to feel her against his body and the thrum of her heart against his chest. For only a moment. He pulled in a hurried breath and let her go.

"I need you," he said in a ragged voice.

She laid her hand against his face. "I'm not going anywhere," she said as she slid her hand into his. "Ready?"

He nodded. "Let's go," he said and hurried across the patio, Kendra at his side.

He opened the garden gate and rushed out of the garden. Behind him, magical creatures poured out of the gate, soared into the air, and trotted along behind him. Toward the pond and the vacant field.

19

I ndiana's summer heat clung to the night like dryer lint, the air sweating with moisture as Kendra stood beside Shade, clutching her hoe. Freshly cut grass tanged the air, mixing with the nearby grain factory's corn-sweet smell. Gabriel stood on the other side of Shade. They were a good twenty feet or so away from the pond.

The vampire's hand rested against the katana at his side, sunglasses covering his eyes. Lenora was beside him, a hand on one hip, Louisville slugger dangling beside her thigh-high boots. The Fey and the elvenkind clustered in the woods at the edge of the field as the vampires ringed the pond. Sebille stood with her people, Toni beside her. They took up positions halfway between the pond and Kendra's garden.

The night was deadly quiet, fatally calm when the first pale yellow Watcher orbs appeared over the pond.

Shade sucked in a quick breath, swallowed hard, and then lifted his axe.

Kendra was terrified for him, his words in the garden still echoing in her head. *They would kill him to take some magical core.*

He ran toward the pond, swinging at the orbs with his axe.

Gabriel rushed ahead, Lenora beside him, Louisville slugger leaning against her left shoulder.

Kendra ran through the tall weeds toward the pond, swinging her hoe at the lights that flowed through the air in a river of light now.

Globes of light choked the air, exploding into sparks that stung when they scraped across her skin.

She winced as she smashed a nearby string of orbs and the sparks burned her arms.

The air shifted on the other side of the pond and she glanced toward the disturbance.

Bats fluttered down from the dark sky, emerging as vampires. Dressed in grey clothing, they carried swords and axes, their pale faces illuminated by the massing Eidolon orbs.

One of them pointed across the pond and Kendra turned.

They pointed at Shade who had his back to the water, smashing orbs by the dozens.

She rushed through the haze of orbs and grabbed Shade's sleeve. When he looked at her, she pointed. He turned to look, eyes wide. He stiffened, his axe balanced in both hands now.

The vampires moved around the pond, heading toward Shade as Kendra's heart pounded into her throat. Her mouth went dry as she raised her hoe.

A shadow surged past her and she turned her head. Gabriel was beside her now, stepping in front of Shade, katana raised.

"Part of the Paris clan," said Gabriel with a sneer as Lenora appeared beside him. "There's Solange and Marcel, Lucien, Geri. Their elder forbid them to come here tonight. Said their clan would remain neutral."

Lenora glared at them, turning her baseball bat in little circles at her side. "So did the Vienna and Berlin clans, yet there's August and Henrik. Even Derica and Jaeger decided to show their ignorance." She clucked her tongue, shaking her head. "Fools. Let's send them home in style, Gabriel," she said, flashing him a smile as she lifted her baseball bat.

Gabriel grinned, nodding. "Shade, you keep up the Watcher fight with the Fey while we keep our own kind busy."

"Thanks, Gabriel," he said and turned back to the Watchers.

Gabriel and Lenora surged across the grass toward the other vampires as the swarm rounded the pond. A swell of the North American tribe was on the renegades, swords and chains flashing beneath the gentle hover of Watcher lights.

Kendra moved closer to Shade, guarding him as she destroyed more orbs.

When she looked up again, another stream of bats filled the air to join the renegade vampires and the fear gripped her again. As more of Gabriel's forces met the other vampires, the force left to face the Eidolon shrank.

And the bulk of the Eidolon forces hadn't even come through the veil yet.

Something felt wrong, as if they were acting and reacting like the Eidolon had expected.

No, orchestrated.

Magical flashes erupted like blue lightning from the faeries and elvenkind as they rushed at the orbs, some swinging rakes, and others wielding axes. Griffins dived toward the renegade vampires, helping Gabriel's tribe as more and more opposing vampires arrived.

Through a haze of smoke, six vampires emerged, swords raised, eyes blood red, mouths gaping. They'd slipped free of Gabriel's forces and headed toward Shade.

"Shade, look out!" Kendra shouted as the vampires rushed toward him.

He turned to her and held out his hand and she knew immediately what he sought.

She grabbed his hand, calling up the tempering flame he'd need to aim the dark fire within him.

Watcher orbs burned across her flesh, but she blotted out the pain, concentrating only on the pressure of Shade's hand against hers.

She felt the writhe of invisible flame between their palms and she let go as the vampires were an arm's reach from Shade.

He lobbed a black fire orb at the vampires as she swung her hoe, catching the closest vampire in the head.

The ruddy-haired vampire turned, fangs bared as he grabbed her by the shoulders, but the black fire ignited, catching all six vampires in its wake. Shade's arm was around her from behind, pulling her back from the explosion.

When the smoke cleared, six vampires had been incinerated.

Gabriel and Lenora stood on the other side of the thick smoke, their mouths open in shock.

"That's some magic, Shade," said Gabriel in a thin voice, looking a little shaken. "I see why the Eidolon want it."

Shade cupped Kendra's chin a moment. "I had some help."

Watcher lights flickered across Kendra's arm and she winced. Lifting her hoe, she swung it in a wide arc, striking down the gold orbs as Shade returned to destroying the new influx of Watchers swirling past.

The tiny lights floated past at an alarming rate and Kendra struggled with the others to destroy them before they changed into shadows.

Shade began to cast his magic now at the Watchers. She kept close, funneling her magic into him by gripping his arm or pressing her hand against his bare skin.

Beyond the pond's edge, more renegade vampires streamed across the dark skies. Griffins tore through them, knocking the new arrivals to the ground while Gabriel's tribe fought them. Satyrs and centaurs joined Gabriel's forces, surrounding the attacking vampires, and raining down silver-tipped arrows.

On the other side of the pond, the Fey, gnomes, and the elvenkind fought the Watchers. A herd of unicorns assisted, using the points of their horns to smash the Watcher lights.

The orbs were a deluge now, the night electric with their luminosity as Kendra struggled to keep up. Her hands and shoulders ached from swinging the hoe, but she pushed the pain aside, keeping watch on Shade.

She loved him. She wouldn't lose him now.

FOR HOURS, THE WATCHERS SPILLED FROM THE NIGHT SKY AND FLOATED across the pond toward Shade, intercepted by the Fey and Kendra who destroyed the orbs as quickly as they appeared. He kept casting writhing balls of shadow at them and the Watchers exploded. But as the night wore on, she feared everything might turn in a heartbeat in the Eidolon's favor.

Shade looked exhausted, his tired eyes narrowed, his features taut with concentration. Where were the gazing balls? Would the globes, linked by Gem's Katorin magic, cause the battle to turn against them? Any moment, Kendra expected the other shoe to drop.

Someone shouted and she looked up.

Across the field rode a huge procession of Fey that gleamed in the darkness. Riding pure white rabbits and soaring on the backs of sparrows, they approached beside a taller man who rode a dappled grey unicorn. His silver hair flowed, features smooth and pale, a crown of gold on his head.

"The king of faerie," someone called out.

Kendra moved beside Shade who still hammered away at the Watchers with his magic and the axe.

"Shade, is that really the king of faerie?" she asked, pointing toward the procession.

He winced and cast a mournful gaze toward the woods where many of the Fey fought the Watchers.

"Unfortunately, yes. It's Nevar—Sebille's husband. He opposes us and will fight with the Eidolon."

Sebille stepped out of the woods and stood with hands on her hips, her followers clustering behind her, continuing the battle against the Watchers.

"You dare to raise arms against your own kind!" Sebille called out to him. "Over shadows?"

He halted his dappled unicorn at the eastern edge of the pond as Sebille approached from the south. Sliding off his mount, he raised his hand to halt the others behind him.

"You dare to involve our world in theirs? Mortals." He spat on the ground.

"What you fail to see over and over, Nevar is that this war affects us, too."

Nevar crossed his arms, casting a gaze toward the fight swelling on the pond's northern side. "All of this for one human. It's disgusting, Sebille. You shame us by your participation. This help for the—the Green Man?"

The queen of faerie held her head high. "Shame us? I save us because you are too prideful to help a man you insist is merely human."

"He looks like them," said Nevar, glowering at her as he motioned toward Shade. "And I'll not help their likes."

Kendra swung her hoe in a wide arc, shattering a string of Watchers into a flurry of sparks. Her arms burned from Watcher marks, her muscles screaming from the constant swings, but she couldn't stop now. Not with Shade's life at stake.

"I appeal to you one last time, my husband," said Sebille as she took two steps toward him then stopped. "Humans aside, the Eidolon will swarm this land and destroy everything that we hold dear. Please...stand with us, not against us."

Nevar studied her a long time. Finally, he shook his head. "It's a human trick, Sebille. I cannot."

"So be it," said Sebille, the sadness evident in her voice as she turned away from her husband and faded into her followers.

Magic flowed in lightning-like flashes toward the pond, the battle against the Watchers renewed. Nevar made no move to join the renegade vampires. He watched the twinkling orbs appear over the pond, looking perplexed and undecided as he climbed back onto his dappled unicorn. The unicorn nickered and tossed its head, its tapered horn sparkling.

Shade cried out. She turned toward him as a sheaf of orbs swept over his body. The spheres' lazy pace accelerated, burning his arms and shoulders as he swung his axe.

She threw herself toward the orbs, crushing them into sparks beneath the hoe. Together, they brought down the orbs before they materialized into shadows.

"Thanks," he said, chest heaving as he bent over to catch his breath.

She tried to fend off the increasing numbers of orbs, but they were denser now, more behind them until the air was strangled with glimmering spheres. The vampires struggled against the renegades, their forces equal now, except for the satyrs and centaurs. Griffins flew over the pond to attack the expanding streams of orbs.

"How long 'til morning?" Shade asked, raising his axe to the new surge of Watchers.

Kendra glanced at her watch. Just after midnight. "A little over four hours."

His body wilted a moment, but he recovered, summoning that inner strength of his that had withstood so much already.

"We'll make it," she answered and nodded at him.

The corners of his mouth lifted a moment then fell as another flood of Watchers hit him. They felt like jellyfish stings, the pain lingering, but she shut out the pain and swung harder.

No matter how many they destroyed, hundreds more took their place. She wondered if Shade had ever seen this many Eidolon come through before. He was struggling now, axe swings and magic casting slower, breath huffing, shirt ringed with sweat.

When she looked up, four of the Fey and two elvenkind had gathered around Shade, supporting him. Some raised rakes and shovels while others lifted their hands to summon magic. He smiled.

"Thanks," he said to the magical creatures surrounding him.

One of the elvenkind nodded at him. "Rest a little, Green Man," he said in a quiet voice. "We shall take up the slack."

Shade nodded, but the orbs flowed faster than they could destroy them. So many orbs slipped through now, fading to shadow. Fear darkened Shade's eyes as more and more slipped past him.

"They're getting through!" he shouted to the Fey. "Be ready for their shadow forms. Tell the others."

One of the Fey women nodded and took to the air, stopping beside Sebille and then at other clusters of creatures, including the griffins darting overhead.

"They've built a gate with those gazing balls," Shade said, taking hold of Kendra's shoulders. "If only we'd stopped them."

He winced, his whole face contorted as he whirled around, axe raised. Three shadowy figures stood before him, more rising up from the ground.

The Eidolon.

"It's over, Shade," said one of the shadows. "You can't stop us now. We're too many. Surrender and we'll spare some of your friends."

Shade screamed in rage and swung the axe into the nearest shadow and it shattered. But for every one he destroyed three more sprung up around him.

"Kendra!" he shouted.

She turned as he held up a hand. She felt the dark fire burn in his hand and she focused on it, taming its wild movements, allowing him to hurl it into the massing shadows around him.

The explosion threw Shade and the Fey backward. They staggered to their feet, a little dazed but recovered quickly as more Watchers fell out of the sky and onto the ground, sprouting into shadows.

Soon, the orbs fell like hailstones, thumping against the ground and going dark, their shadows planted.

Kendra glanced around the pond. The Fey were locked in a battle against each other now, Nevar and Sebille facing off. The vampires were deadlocked in combat, leaving only a handful of others to destroy the Watchers.

In the flickers of light cast from the Fey's magic, Kendra saw something flash silver near the pond.

She swung her hoe again, catching a few more Watchers as shadows rushed at her. She slammed the hoe into them as a searing rush of fire tore down her arm.

Stifling a cry of pain, she turned to face an axe hanging in the air. An Eidolon shadow swung the axe at her.

She threw herself backward. "Shade!" she shouted.

The axe swung at her again.

Rolling out of the way, she thrust out the hoe.

Knocking away the axe.

She followed the thrust with a quick swing that cut right through the shadow, felling it. She grabbed the axe in her left hand and quickly handed it off to one of the elvenkind who helped her cut down more shadows.

When she turned again, another hailstorm of Watchers fell from the sky. She ducked. But another flash of silver caught her attention.

From the pond.

Where the floods of Watchers poured through now, more than she'd ever seen before.

Then she knew. The gate and the gazing balls were in the pond. The one place they hadn't looked!

She ran toward Shade, striking down shadows and orbs until she reached his side.

"The circuit!" she cried, struggling for breath. "I found it!"

The forlorn look on his face receded and he glanced toward her as he destroyed more shadows.

"Where?"

"The pond," she said and turned away, hoe raised. "Wish me luck!"

"Kendra, wait!" he shouted, but the hailstorm of Watchers forced him to engage them.

Shadows gathered around him, the elvenkind closing ranks to protect him as Eidolon voices rose.

"You've lost, Shade," a voice said with a hiss. "It's time to join your father in the oblivis—until it's time to cut out your heart."

Kendra felt her skin crawl at that familiar voice.

Shade fought this creature before. He'd nearly killed Shade that night with an axe. He was the one they would face in solid form in Katori. If Shade survived to make the journey.

"Carvahl," Shade said with a sneer, axe raised. "You're right on time."

Kendra dashed through the burning orbs until she reached the pond's western edge. Beneath the algae-green haze sparkled a luminous, mirror-like surface.

The gazing balls!

Several of the mirrored gazing balls were submerged in a ring below the water, gleaming with an eerie magical glow. From Gem's Katorin magic.

It made her heart hurt, but she had to destroy them. And break the circuit.

Taking a deep breath, she tossed down her hoe and dived into the water.

The water's chill startled her. She'd expected bath water from Indiana's hot summer temperatures, but the dark waters were icy against her skin.

Watcher lights drilled through the water toward her.

As she reached the pond's slimy bottom, her lungs burning, her fingers touched the first gazing ball. It glowed an eerie green despite its silver color.

Lights swam around her, slicing across her arms. She shut them out. And picked up a rock.

Aiming at a silver gazing ball, she smashed it with the fist-sized rock. The eerie green light flickered, but the ring held.

Pond water writhed with stinging Watcher lights as she struggled toward another gazing ball. Green.

That one might have been Maddie's, but Kendra raised the stone again and pounded it against the gazing ball twice until it shattered.

Struggling to breathe, she kicked up to the surface and gasped for air.

Watcher lights, agitated and flailing like ping-pong balls, careened into her head and toward her face.

She thrust her hand over her eyes to ward off the stinging blows and dived below surface again. And swung the rock at the other gazing balls.

Again, she surfaced, pulling in anxious breaths.

The nearby splash of water drew her attention. She looked up. Toni Ambrose swam toward her.

"Toni! What are you doing?"

"Helping you," Toni replied and pointed a finger at the haze of orbs pounding Kendra's head.

Toni lifted her hand and a bolt of blue energy struck the air above Kendra's head a. The Watcher orbs disintegrated. Toni reached out and laid her hand on Kendra's shoulder. She felt the rush of healing energy soothe the throbbing burns on her hands, arms, and neck. The exhaustion lightened.

"I'll keep the Watchers off you. Keep working on the gate."

Kendra grinned and took in a big breath before diving underneath the water again. She kicked hard against the chill until she'd reached the bottom.

At least a dozen more gazing balls remained in that large glowing ring.

She swung the rock at the nearest ball, hitting it until it broke into pieces. The glowing light shifted to gold and flooded back again as she moved to the next globe.

Above her, Toni's steady destruction of Watchers was a muffled crackle.

One by one, Kendra worked her way through the circle until only four globes remained.

After another deep breath of charged night air that smelled like sulfur, Kendra dived beneath the water again and smashed three more gazing balls. The green glow turned red, pulsing as she lifted the rock a final time.

Summoning as much strength as she had left, Kendra heaved the rock against the last gazing ball.

It broke in half and sprayed a shower of red sparks through the water.

For an instant, the world went dark.

She did it! She destroyed the gate!

She kicked back to the surface and found Toni weakening as she fought another huge cluster of Watchers.

Kendra grabbed Toni under her arms and dragged her out of the water, onto the pond's grassy bank. She grabbed her hoe and beat off the remaining Watchers until Toni sat up. She laid her hand against Kendra's arm and strength spiraled through her again.

"Save him, Kendra," said Toni, motioning her toward the swirling force of shadows surrounding Shade and his protectors. "With the gate gone, his enemies have nothing else to lose."

Through the tangle of battle, Kendra saw Sebille at Shade's shoulder, axe in hand, burns on her arms. Desperation touched the Fey queen's features.

"I'll be fine," said Toni, her hair curling into ringlets from the water. "Go."

Kendra pounded through the weeds toward Shade.

20

S hade backed away from the massing shadows, axe handle burning his blistered palms, muscles screaming from the hours of exertion.

And Carvahl still had the upper hand.

Dark fire roiled through him, fighting to explode from his hands, but Sebille was beside him and others he didn't want to harm. Without Kendra to tame the wilding long enough for him to aim it, he was powerless against Carvahl.

Would it all end here? He'd been so close.

"Hiding behind a woman's skirts," Carvahl said with a grating laugh, his shadowy shape brandishing an axe as he advanced on Shade. "That's so like you, Shade. But not even the Faerie queen can save you now. It's over."

Sebille held out her hand, a swirl of blue flame rising.

Carvahl's axe blade cut toward her.

Shade thrust out his axe, trying to block the blow. Missed.

Sebille gasped when the blade cut deep into her chest, black tarry blood flowing.

"Sebille...no!" Shade cried.

She pressed her delicate hand to the wound as she staggered.

Shade caught her. He grabbed her around the waist, holding her up as he backed away from the Eidolon, shielding her with his axe.

A scream of rage echoed across the pond.

Shade looked up.

In full gallop, a dappled unicorn charged around the pond toward the Eidolon. A flood of Fey rushed behind him.

Sebille glanced up, a thin smile on her face. "Nevar," she said, her eyelids fluttering as she sank against Shade's chest.

Shade kept backing away, putting himself between the Eidolon and Sebille, the axe holding Carvahl and the other shadows back.

To his left, more screams erupted as renegade vampires broke past the North American tribe, heading toward him.

Caught between vampires and Carvahl's troops. He'd been flanked.

His chest ached, knowing how little time he had left.

Had Kendra fallen near the pond?

His chest ached, his heart hammering against his rib cage as the rage burned white hot in him.

Was she lost to him? He may never know her fate.

Had he lost everything by missing that blow? Had Sebille paid the ultimate price for it?

Above him, something black tracked across the sky, casting shadows across the ground. The vampires' shouts drew closer.

Blood-red eyes burned. Pearly white fangs glinted.

Almost on top of him now.

He turned, axe swiveling around him, blocking shadow blows left and right, Sebille's blood spilling onto his T-shirt and cargo shorts.

Gabriel's clan chased behind the renegade vampires, Gabriel in the lead. But they'd never stop the renegades in time.

Shade blocked another blow. Pivoted. Blocked a low sweep of another axe.

Shadows massed around him, choking off the faint glow of magic. His heart dropped, a blade slicing across his forearm.

Too bad Gabriel and his clan wouldn't get to him in time.

"Thanks for all you did, Sebille," he said to the Fey queen as she sagged in his grasp. "Forgive me for not blocking that blow."

Another blade tore across his thigh. He turned, blocking the blade, another slicing across his calf.

The flash of black startled him. Right in front of him.

He raised the axe. Vampires were faster than he'd realized.

"Forgive me, Kendra and Katori—I've failed all of you this time," he said, turning the axe blade.

Knowing it was for the very last time.

He turned toward the nearest shadow, blocking the first renegade vampire that reached him first.

A line of women dressed in purple and black materialized between him and the Eidolon. Glowing with violet light.

One wore a wide-brimmed pointed hat and Shade grinned.

The Sisters of the Cauldron!

Always arriving late, according to Gabriel, but this time, their timing was perfect.

The renegade vampires halted, stopped by the magical light emanating from the coven. As Gabriel's tribe caught up to them.

Magic flashed as the witches broke ranks, hurtling spells at the renegade vampires.

The smell of ozone crackled through the heated air as Carvahl swung at Shade again.

Shade turned. Couldn't get his axe blade up in time to block the blow. He shielded Sebille, bracing himself for the killing blow.

Nevar stepped beside him, longsword in his pale Fey hands. Blocking the blow.

Slamming his axe upward, Shade knocked Carvahl's shadow backward, axe flying out of his hands. Shade stumbled back two steps and dropped to his knees.

Nevar eased Sebille out of Shade's grasp and into his arms, holding her against his side as he leveled the longsword at the shadows, swinging at the nearest one, bringing it down.

Shade scrabbled to his feet, axe raised as more shadows rushed at them.

The other Fey joined their king, thinning the shadows all around the circle that the witches had made around them.

Again, Shade raised his axe, slamming it into the wave of shadows bearing down on him.

But Carvahl was on him now, axe blade falling toward his face.

He blocked the blow, but Carvahl drew back the axe and swung again.

Something hit Carvahl from behind as his weapon rose, falling but missing its target. As the shadow pivoted, Shade saw Carvahl's attacker.

Kendra!

Baring his teeth, Shade lunged at Carvahl, allowing Kendra to slip through the thick circle of shadows. Into the coven's magical circle. His heart soared. To stand beside him.

When he felt her warm body against his, he lifted his right hand. Smiling, she laid her hand on top of his and her warmth took away the stabbing pain in his muscles. He gritted his teeth, concentrating on the dark fire writing within him. Drawing it up from deep inside and into his right hand.

His body shook as the dark fire roiled at his fingertips, struggling for release.

Like a gate opening, he felt Kendra's tempering magic wrap around him, clearing the way.

Dark fire exploded through his arms and fingers, but Kendra's tempering tamed the energy into a quivering ball in his hand.

Still shaking, he gripped the magic, turning. And heaved it at Carvahl moments before the axe blade careened toward him.

Kendra blocked the blow as the dark fire struck Carvahl. And blazed around the ring of shadows.

Shadowy forms caught fire, one after another, and then exploded until the world fell dark and silent.

His magic had destroyed the Eidolon shadows!

Exhausted, Shade sank to his knees, a laugh bubbling up.

"It's done," he said, grinning. He dropped the axe and raised his hands into the air. "It's done!"

The renegade vampires stared at him in confusion and slunk away as the witches chased them into the air as they turned into bats.

Gabriel dropped down beside him, Lenora at his side. He was battered and bloodied, his face bruised, jagged gashes torn across his chest, arms, and legs. By morning, it would all disappear.

He'd forgotten how much effort it took to kill a vampire. And a massive army of Eidolon.

"We did it," said Gabriel with a smile, ruffling Shade's hair.

"Thanks to you," said Shade, reaching out to grip Gabriel's hand a moment and then Lenora's hand.

"Glad to help," said Lenora. "And to kick some renegade vampire ass." She rubbed her right hand that she cradled against her chest. Her Louisville slugger was gone. "That felt good."

Shade glanced around for Kendra, but she threw herself against him, arms tight around him as her mouth found his. He smothered her with a deep, urgent kiss until they both struggled for breath. She laid her head against his shoulder.

"I thought I'd lost you," he said, closing his eyes as his voice shook.

"Looks like you're stuck with me," she said, nuzzling his neck.

He nudged Kendra and motioned toward Nevar who cradled Sebille near the pond. She lay limp in his arms as Toni pressed her hands against Sebille's wound. A faint blue glow encased Sebille's arm.

"I was wrong," Nevar lamented. "Never will I divide our people like this again. Or you and me."

Sebille's eyes opened to slits and she stared up at him, a faint smile on her face.

"I forgive you," she said as he buried his face in her hair, his shoulders heaving.

"Fear not, King Nevar," said Toni in a quiet voice. "The wound is deep, but she's going to survive. She'll need the court healer's skill to heal it completely. For now, I've stopped the bleeding."

Nevar lifted his face, the tears streaking down his pale face. He cupped Toni's chin in his hand. "I thank you."

He rose to his feet, lifting Sebille in his arms, and climbed onto the dappled grey unicorn.

"Good luck to you, Green Man. Sebille's faith in you was well-founded. Thank you for protecting her."

Shade nodded at him as Nevar turned the unicorn and galloped toward the garden, the Fey and elvenkind following the king of Faerie.

***

KENDRA WAS STILL BESIDE SHADE AS HE GOT TO HIS FEET, HER ARM around his waist. Gabriel and Lenora glanced up at the sky. It would be light soon.

Kendra felt dread burn in her stomach. At first light, she would cross through the veil with Shade to another battle—one as important than this one.

"We have to go now, Shade, Kendra." Gabriel hugged her and then Shade.

So did Lenora before the two of them took to the sky in bat form to escape the light. The griffins took flight behind the witches.

"Give them hell, Green Man!" the witches shouted as they took flight, brooms materializing.

The coven darted off through the dusky pre-dawn sky.

Soon, only Kendra and Shade stood beside the pond, the smell of ozone fading.

"What time is it?" Shade asked, walking stiffly toward his house, a little unsteady.

"Well after three—nearly four A.M.," said Kendra with a yawn as she dragged the hoe behind her.

"We'd better contact my mother. Make sure Hekalie will part the veil at first light."

He slid his arm around Kendra's waist and led her into the house. Once inside, he collapsed into a moss-covered chair in the forested living room. A pair of cardinals took flight from the cedar trees surrounding his chair. A small, vine-covered table stood beside the other chair.

Kendra started toward it, but Shade's arm slid around her waist, drawing her into his lap. He wrapped his arms around her, holding her close to his chest. God, he fit her like a glove.

"That's much better," he said with a smile, his face soft with beard shadow.

She kissed him then settled back against his shoulder as he picked up a dinner-plate-sized sheet of shiny black glass.

"What's that?"

"Katorin obsidian," he replied. "Hekalie uses it to scry. That's how I've stayed in contact with my family all these years. I've got to concentrate now."

He closed his eyes and laid his palms against the black stone, his eyes half-closed. Poor man was so exhausted.

"Let me help," said Kendra, laying her hands on top of his.

Almost immediately, a form took shape on the stone. A woman with worried eyes and dark hair.

His mother. It had to be.

"Shade! Oh, Shade, I've been out of my mind worrying about you!"

His eyes snapped open and he cast a puzzled glance at Kendra then turned back to the stone.

"Mother, it's over. We defeated Carvahl's forces. Have Hekalie stand ready to bring us through."

His mother looked past him and Kendra realized she was staring at her.

"Sorry," said Shade with a sheepish look. "Mother, this is Kendra Martin. The great granddaughter of Aeryn ni Katori." He paused a moment. "And the love of my life."

Kendra grinned and held him tighter.

"He is my heart," said Kendra to the woman. "My sun and my moon."

"Kendra," he said, motioning toward the obsidian. "This is Mallora ni Katori."

"I'm honored to meet you," said Kendra.

The woman's eyes filled with tears.

"Mother? What's the matter?" Shade asked.

His mother covered her eyes a moment, wiping away tears with a lavender handkerchief.

"Shade," she said, shaking her head. "This can never be."

Shade frowned as he looked at Kendra and then his mother. "What do you mean? I love her and she loves me."

Kendra winced. Why didn't his mother like her? "I know we come from two different worlds, but—"

"No, I don't doubt your love," said his mother. "It's your great grandmother, Kendra."

"What do you mean?" she asked.

"Aeryn had two daughters. Your grandmother." She paused, biting her lip. "And—my mother. I'm so sorry."

Kendra bowed her head as the horrible words bore through her chest.

"What are you saying?" Shade demanded as Kendra stood up, the tears filling her eyes.

"I'm saying that your grandmother and Kendra's grandmother were sisters, Shade. You and Kendra are cousins."

21

The first thin ray of light touched the clouds, leaving a red streak across the eastern sky as Kendra stood on the porch, arms crossed, eyes dry and burning as she waited. She didn't even know what she was waiting for anymore, except an end to this whole thing. She only wanted to get as far away from Indiana as possible now. As far away as her heartache would allow.

She couldn't have him. Couldn't be with him.

Tears burned her eyes again and she squeezed them closed. Couldn't touch him. He was her cousin.

He needed her tempering to destroy Carvahl, the Eidolon dictator and she would be there for him. She couldn't bear the thoughts of something happening to Shade any more than she could bear the pain of seeing him with someone else.

But she hated what came next—after the fight of Shade's life. When she returned to her world.

Without him.

The door behind her creaked open and his footsteps scuffed across the porch, the door closing. She felt his presence behind her, could almost feel his breath on her neck. She ached to put her arms around him, to feel the comforting heat of his body against hers, but she kept her arms crossed. She couldn't even bear to look at him.

It hurt too much.

"Hey," he said in a quiet, forlorn tone.

The porch boards shifted until he was standing beside her, looking up at the sky.

"Shade, I—I didn't—"

"I know," he said, his voice thin and tight. "It's too much. I can't even wrap my head around it yet."

Reaching behind her, she rubbed his calf a moment, trying not to look at his face. But she couldn't stop herself. She bit her lip to keep it from trembling and stole a look at him.

And felt herself melting all over again.

His beautiful face, those chiseled features, strong jaw—and those wild, arctic blue eyes. Glassy and narrowed as he concentrated on the horizon.

He laid his hands on her shoulders but pulled back again, hesitating, pain filling his eyes.

She closed her eyes, feeling so cold. The memory of his touch was so soft and so hot against her skin. God, she wanted to be in his arms, but she could only bow her head and nod.

He lowered his hands, shoving them into the pockets of tan trousers. He'd changed clothes. He wore what had to be a Katorin-styled tunic, snug against his lean torso and open at the neck. It looked like a poet's shirt in a soft olive green. Beside him, on the porch, set an old, battered brown knapsack.

"It won't be long until Hekalie calls us through," he said, changing the subject, that voice so steely and distant now. A voice that had once gushed about how much he loved her. "Here," he said, holding something out in his palm.

She reached for it, her fingers trailing across his soft hand as she picked up a black sphere the size of a plum. It was cold in her hand, shiny black with layers of shine through it. Obsidian she realized, like the large, flat piece he carried under his left arm.

"What's it for?" she asked.

"To help Hekalie focus when she parts the veil. The Eidolon would kill for that orb, so don't lose it. It's got lots of magic within its layers."

His voice was so distant now. It hurt so much.

She nodded and looked away as red fingers of light lengthened across the dark sky. The first rays of dawn. Holding the orb between her fingers, she studied its strange surface as it began to glow a soft mint green. Alarmed, her gaze darted to Shade. And he was fading.

"Shade!"

When she looked up, the world around her was dissolving into a wash of colors. She gripped the orb in her hand as everything around her churned into a whirlwind of darkness. It spun away into complete blackness then back again, the air rushing past until the scent of something sweet touched her. Abruptly, the world turned calm. And she was falling.

Someone caught her.

She looked up into Shade's intense blue eyes as he held her against his chest, his warmth all she'd ever wanted.

Her cousin. She winced. No...it wasn't true! It couldn't be!

"You okay?" he asked in a gruff voice, setting her down as if her skin was acid.

She nodded, unable to respond and turned away, the orb still clutched in her hand.

Candles. Hundreds. Guttered throughout the nearly dark room that smelled warm and sweet, almost like brown sugar.

Waxy white candles filled the room, strung across the tops of heavy, dark wood furniture that looked part Fey and part Mediterranean. They burned across a rough, unstained wooden workbench beneath a small window draped in purple silks. It was the only window in the room. Dripping white candles covered two long, narrow tables that stood on either side of the workbench. Several candles clustered on a clear glass plate in the center of a thick, round table in the middle of the square room.

She moved toward the table with four straight-backed chairs covered in shiny, dark green leather. A thin, purple satin cloth draped part of the table and a copper lamp hung above it, casting an oscillating circle of light across the scuffed tabletop.

Dark wood bookshelves the color of coffee beans lined three of the white walls surrounding her. The shelves were crammed full with heavy, leatherbound books in reds and greens and blues beside stacks of bowls, shiny metal boxes, and sparkling crystals in purples and yellows and blues.

She walked toward the shelves, the walnut-colored wooden floor creaking under her feet until she stepped onto a forest green wool rug. Above one of the tables hung a group of five realistic landscape paintings on unframed canvases. She didn't recognize the locations. The colors were off, yellow sky, indigo tree trunks, turquoise leaves. And three full moons hung in the sky: one black, one red, and one blue.

A scarecrow-like old woman with onyx hair and ice blue eyes stepped into the room from a doorway behind a brown curtain. She wore a long charcoal shift, a pale blue shawl draping her thin shoulders and face like a cowl.

"Shade! You're home—at long last!"

The woman rushed toward him.

He grinned, throwing his arms around her. "Gran, it's really you... after all this time."

"Let me look at you," she said and held him at arm's length. "You were only a boy when I sent you out of Airell and now, look at you. You're very much a man. So tall!"

"Gran," he said and glanced at Kendra. "I'd like you to meet Kendra Martin. Kendra, this is Hekalie, my grandmother."

Hekalie turned, a warm smile on her face, and took hold of Kendra's hands. "I feel it," she said, glancing at Shade then Kendra. "Your gift is very strong, Kendra. We are grateful to have found you. Without you, Carvahl and his army will destroy us."

"You're Eidolon," said Kendra, studying the old woman's face. It looked like sun-washed parchment, her blue eyes as piercing as Shade's.

"Yes," she said with a nod. "I carry a rare gift but nothing like

Shade's." Hekalie looked at Shade for several long moments then turned to Kendra with another searching gaze. "The eyes tell much, do they not?"

She watched the two of them and Kendra felt uncomfortable.

"Something is wrong between you?" Hekalie asked.

Shade's jaw tightened and he sighed, looking down at his feet. Kendra nodded, bowing her head. Hekalie laid her hand on Kendra's arm. "Whatever it is, it can be resolved. I promise you."

Kendra's eyes stung with moisture and she wiped at her eyes. "If only that was true," she said, crossing her arms and stepping back toward the bookcases.

The spines had strange letters on them, an alphabet she didn't recognize.

"Shade?" said Hekalie. "What is so wrong between you, two that no one can fix it?"

"Our grandmothers were sisters," said Shade, nearly spitting out the words.

The room fell silent and Kendra kept her back to Shade and his grandmother, not wanting to face them. She wanted to end this and return to Baltimore. Pretend this was all a bad dream or a book she'd read as a kid. Another one of those broken childhood dreams she'd get over like the rest of the world: with a lot of wine and years of therapy.

"Kendra?"

She turned around when Hekalie called her name. Hekalie stood beside Shade who had his hands in his pockets. He watched her with glassy eyes.

"Do you still have the orb?" Hekalie asked.

Kendra held out the obsidian sphere.

"Good," said Hekalie as she moved toward her. She closed Kendra's hand around the orb. "Use the orb to amplify your tempering. Carvahl had no idea anyone from your Katorin line still existed until a few hours ago. He's no doubt very weak and in great shock at his oversight."

"What do I do?" she asked.

Hekalie smiled, laying a hand against Kendra's cheek. "What you've done so far," she said, casting a glance at Shade. "Give balance and focus to Shade's wilding. Your ability to temper his magic allows him to use it. But remember, you must destroy Carvahl when he's weak. If he walks away from Airell, he will regain his strength and he will rebuild his army."

"I'll do my best," said Kendra.

Hekalie turned to Shade, reaching out her hand to him. He gripped it and she brought him close. Kendra stared into his eyes, seeing the apprehension mix with pain.

"You must go now. To the ruined temple where the old obsidian gate still stands."

She pulled the purple cloth off the table, revealing the other half. Made of obsidian. She stared into the polished, glassy stone as it glimmered with candlelight and an inner blue glow.

"I can see him even now, Shade," said Hekalie, staring into the obsidian. "He lies there alone, trying to regain enough strength to mount another attack and pass through the gate again."

She took Shade's hand by the wrist and pressed it into Kendra's left hand. Kendra couldn't help herself. She squeezed his hand. He bit his lip, eyes still glassy as he looked away.

"Let's go," said Shade, his voice strained.

"Lead the way," Kendra replied.

"Be careful and together," Hekalie called as Shade pulled her toward the brown curtain. Into a short, dark hallway. "And both of you—please...come back."

He rushed down the hallway toward another door and flung it open. She followed him outside into a misty dark haze that clung to the gently curved buildings that had a Scandinavian feel to the eaves and rafters. They looked empty and dark.

The sky had a deep yellow cast, trees with indigo trunks and turquoise leaves lined the cobblestone street. Hekalie's painting had been of this city, but it looked deserted. The house had a white wrought iron fence around it and dark stone steps leading to the deserted street. That curved in a circular arc, houses and buildings built with those dark grey stones clustered around it

The houses and buildings looked burned out, surfaces blackened and walls scorched. Abandoned. No smoke from chimneys. Not a single bird call or even the whisper of movement.

She glanced back at Hekalie's house. Small and squat, it was made of grey stone and had a steep, gabled roof that was as black as pitch. Its two windows and doorframe were framed in polished obsidian. Because of her scrying, Kendra wondered. Or was it for protection somehow? Masking? Two yellow stone urns stood on either side of a purple front door, lacy, royal blue flowers growing tall in the dry soil.

She hurried down the misty, dimly lit street beside Shade, noticing the empty, cobbled street's glossy jasper and agate stones gleaming in the mist as it wound past another cluster of abandoned houses. More of those indigo trees with pale turquoise foliage lined the streets, leaves clattering as they moved toward a large, forbidding dark stone building with four spires that stood alone at the end of another abandoned street.

This place had to be the temple that Hekalie mentioned. She swallowed a breath. It definitely looked like a villain's lair. Where they'd look for someone like this Carvahl who hated Shade and wanted him dead.

As they got closer, Kendra felt a tightness in her chest, the dread rising through her. Had this Eidolon sensed Shade's presence? The tightness was a thickening band and she struggled against it. Was Carvahl waiting to ambush Shade when he walked through those doors?

When she was four feet from the white, polished doors that look like marble, the temple's surface caught thin rays of sunlight through the mist. Some of the walls were smooth and frosty—like rose quartz. The rest looked like it had been bombed or burned. Its surface was blackened and scorched. A faint charred smell clung to the air as Shade walked up the stairs, Kendra behind him.

"You're just going to walk right inside?" she cried. "Right up the front steps where he's waiting for you?"

He pulled in a breath. "Yep. Sure am. Right in his ugly face."

Okay. Shade was going to grandstand his way into this fight and she had to be beside him to focus that angry, roiling dark magic inside him.

Shade's hand was like a vise against hers, but he let go when he reached the temple's marble double doors.

He grabbed the handles and threw open the doors.

"Carvahl!" he screamed and charged through the foyer, into the nave.

Half-moon benches sat throughout the long, narrow room, strewn with broken bits of that heavy dark wood. A few straight-backed chairs leaned against the wall beside a pile of wood that had once been pews or benches. A black dais stood in the center of the drafty temple with its vaulted, barrel ceiling.

The dais was a solid slab of obsidian. A tall, muscular man was curled up on it, bare-chested and wearing thin grey leggings and black boots. His face was smooth, hair dark like Shade's, eyes brown and glaring as he tried to sit up. A huge gash cut across his chest like a sash, bluish gold fluid dripping from the wound.

Fury and hatred burned across his face, but fear spread quickly. Until a smile curved across his face.

"Guards!" Carvahl shouted.

Kendra heard footfalls behind her on the cobblestones.

"The doors!" Shade shouted and lunged for the nearest door.

Kendra grabbed hold of the other one and together, they slammed them shut. Shade grabbed a straight-backed chair from against the wall and shoved it under the door handle. She rushed toward the wall and grabbed another chair, lodging it under the other door handle.

She and Shade were halfway to the dais, stepping over debris. As the neared Carvahl's prostrate form, the pounding on the door began.

The sound echoed in time with her heartbeat as Shade ascended the dais. He stood over the crumpled man who threw an arm over his face.

"It's over, Carvahl," said Shade and lifted his hand into the air.

She felt Shade summon the wilding. The magic thrummed through her body as she gripped the obsidian orb.

Behind her, the doors quivered, the pounding louder and more furious.

She kept her focus on Shade's wilding, forcing the writhing, expanding force into a dark, apple-sized orb in his hand.

Carvahl's eyes widened and he screamed, skittering backward as Shade drew back his arm.

The temple shook, an explosion ripping through the doors. The force threw her backward to the floor.

Shade turned as a dozen dark-haired Eidolon soldiers in onyx armor burst into the temple, swords raised.

He flung the orb at the squadron of soldiers and everything went dark, the temple shifting again.

Shouts and voices strangled. Light fixtures and rafters fell from the ceiling in a cloud of dust.

Kendra felt the hard stone floor beneath her, her palms flat against the dusty surface as she struggled to her feet. Shade lay on his side, struggling to free his leg from the rafter beam across his left leg.

The orb! Her heart pounded into her throat. It had fallen out of her hand.

She sifted through the dust, searching for the smooth obsidian orb.

Something scraped across the floor and she looked up.

Carvahl shuffled off the dais, grinning, dagger raised.

"Shade, look out!"

Shade's head snapped up.

Carvahl rose to his full height and ran at Shade who lay pinned against the floor.

"No!" Kendra shouted, climbing over rafters to reach Shade who lifted a bloodied hand.

The Eidolon commander rushed toward him as Kendra felt

Shade summon the wilding.

So much weaker now than his first attempt. And she didn't have the orb.

Kendra reached toward Shade, shutting out Carvahl, the bodies lying around her, and concentrated on the wilding as it expanded. She shoved all her strength against it, holding it down, back under Shade's control. Into an orb.

A dark image undulated in Shade's hand as Carvahl's dagger rose above Shade's head.

Kendra threw herself between Shade and the dagger as it fell. Bracing herself for the plunge of the blade.

But the explosive force of the wilding drove her backward against Shade. Something grazed her forearm then clattered to the floor.

And everything fell still, smoke roiling around them.

When the smoke cleared, a thick swath of grey powder coated the dais. Carvahl's dagger lay beside her, blood running down her arm.

"He's dead at last," Shade said, spitting on the floor. "You're hurt," he said, his blue eyes looking mournful.

She nodded. "My arm will heal."

But not her heart.

She stared at the dais and the grey powder coating the floor. And her heart sank, thumping faster as it rose into her throat.

Footprints pressed across the dusty powder. She swallowed a breath, tracking impressions across the ruined temple floor. Toward the back of it.

She felt a chill rush across her skin and a horrible feeling that this wasn't over.

"Shade..." she called in a wary tone and pointed.

He squinted at her. "What's the matter?"

"Look," she said in a hushed voice. "There are tracks in the dust."

His eyes darkened and his gaze followed them through the debris, past bodies until his face contorted.

The tracks stopped in the middle of the dais—a faint glow fading in its center. Now that the dais was empty, she saw that it was made of obsidian.

He turned his head toward her, looking devastated. "He—he escaped." Then fury burned in those wild, arctic blue eyes. "Dammit! Carvahl used my power to activate this old gate—and passed through the veil!"

Muffled voices rumbled near the doors and Kendra looked up as people climbed through the debris, cheering, and shouting Shade's name. Katorins, she realized and started to rise to her feet, but Shade grabbed her hand.

"Shade!" an older, brown-haired woman shouted.

Kendra recognized her from the images in obsidian.

The woman knelt on the floor and threw her arms around him, hugging him to her chest.

"Mother!" He wrapped her in his arms, holding her for a long time.

In a few moments, three young women with warm brown hair entered the devastated temple behind Shade's mother. They worked together, grabbing hold of the rafter trapping Shade's leg.

He winced, glancing up. A grin rolled across his face.

"Melise! Meriel! Seanna!" he cried, grabbing hold of the nearest young woman's arm.

Seanna had a long, cinnamon brown braid that hung over one shoulder. Melise had a headful of warm brown curls and Meriel had shorter, tomboyish hair that was a rich chocolate brown. Seanna leaned down to hug him, tears running down her face. The other two women put their arms around him.

Shade winced again from the pain as all three of the young women began lifting the wooden beam off his leg.

Only a heartbeat or two later, a solemn-faced young man walked up behind the women. He was a younger version of Shade with lighter brown hair and brown eyes like his mother. The young man took hold of the beam and helped the women move it off Shade.

As Shade struggled to his feet, he put his arms around his mother again. All of them talked at once now, surrounding Shade. Except the young man who hung back, looking sullen now.

Kendra held her hand against the gash on her arm as she

searched through the debris for the orb. After sifting through the debris for several minutes, she, at last, found it under a splintered board. She picked it up and slipped it into her jeans pocket.

"Kendra!"

Shade's voice cut through her and she heard his limping footsteps behind her. When she turned, he was standing behind her, his arm around one of the women's shoulders. Hekalie and Shade's mother stood beside him. His mother wore a green dress with a cream mantle, her chocolate brown hair swept back from her face. She reached out and took Kendra's hands in hers.

She worked hard to force a faint smile onto her face.

"Kendra, this is my mother, Mallora ni Katori."

"Thank you," said Mallora and nodded toward Shade. "For bringing him home alive. The Eidolon are finished here."

"You're welcome," said Kendra, pressing her lips together to keep them from trembling when she looked at Shade's face. He was home. Back where he belonged, his exile only a memory now. And when she crossed the veil, she'd only be a memory to him, too.

But he hadn't told them about Carvahl's escape yet. Didn't they realize that this wasn't over yet. That monster had escaped through the veil—somewhere into her world, somewhere in time.

"What about the dais?" she asked Shade in a quiet voice.

"Tomorrow," he said in a half-whisper, pain in his eyes. "Today, driving the Eidolon out of Airell is enough."

He stared at her a long time, his eyes looking haunted. Was it longing she saw there? For her? Or regret—that he'd loved her once. He glanced at her arm then reached out and caressed her forearm. His soothing touch made her eyes well with tears.

"That needs to be looked at," he said, his gaze flicking from the wound to her eyes.

She shoved back her grief and forced a smile onto her lips. It was so hard to stare into his intense blue gaze and not fall into his arms. It was the one place she yearned to be—and the one place she could no longer reach. The man she loved was her damned cousin!

"I'm fine." She looked past Shade at Hekalie. "Whenever you're ready, I'd like to go home."

His eyes widened. "But Kendra, I thought that we could—I mean, I could..."

His voice trailed off in frustration, his gaze falling to the temple floor

"I should go," she said.

There was no reason to prolong the most painful goodbye of her life. Shade Fletcher was lost to her now. Staying only made it hurt worse.

"This way, Kendra," said Hekalie, looking puzzled. "Back to my study."

Kendra took a deep breath, summoning her last bit of courage. She took one last look at him, memorizing the curve of his chin, the intense light blue of his eyes, the sizzling memory of his lips against hers.

"Goodbye, Shade Fletcher."

He swallowed hard. His eyes misted, mouth pressed flat. "Kendra...I—"

She brushed past him, her bottom lip trembling, the tears streaking down her face as she hurried out of the temple, Hekalie behind her.

Once out on the cobblestones, she broke into a run, Hekalie calling after her. She didn't want to see any more of this place. This world she would never be a part of—his world. He was forever lost to her. Her Green Man.

When she reached Hekalie's house, she sank down on the steps by the yellow urn and covered her face, the sobs trembling through her.

"Kendra, what is it?" Hekalie asked, dropping down beside her. She slid an arm around Kendra's shoulder.

"I love him so much," she said, her voice breaking.

"I could tell that from the moment I met you," said Hekalie. "But why are you so upset? It's over. He's free now."

She looked up at Hekalie. "It's not over," she said. "Carvahl escaped through the gate."

Hekalie's eyes grew wide. "What? Are you certain?"

She nodded. "He was badly injured, trying to stab Shade. And then Shade hit him with his wilding. When the smoke cleared, there were footprints in the dust. They disappeared on the obsidian dais."

Hekalie moaned, wringing her hands together. "Oh, no—this can't be true! It can't! Shade was supposed to face him on the ebony moon with the tempering magic—here, in the temple for the last time."

Kendra shook her head. "Shade said he would break the news to his family tomorrow."

"I must consult the magics," she said, her voice sounding faraway. "I need to see into the obsidian, find what went wrong here. And we need to capture Carvahl fast—before he can rebuild his army." Her gaze softened and she laid her hand against Kendra's shoulder. "But Carvahl isn't what's gotten you so upset. You were upset when you arrived. Please, tell me why."

Kendra inhaled sharply and stared at Hekalie a moment. "It's like Shade said. He's my cousin."

"What? How can that be?" Hekalie demanded, hands on her hips.

"My great grandmother was Aeryn O'Riley, a Katorin who left here to escape the Eidolon. She came to my world."

"Oh, my," said Hekalie, a hand to her mouth. "Mallora's grandmother."

Kendra nodded. "She had another daughter. My grandmother, Emmaline Martin."

"There was a story about that one." Hekalie's brow furrowed. "Emmaline. I'm almost sure of it."

Kendra was already nodding. "Yes, Gem's father was Fey."

"Aye, that's the one," said Hekalie. "But surely there's something that can be done here."

Kendra shook her head and rose from the step. "Not unless one of us can change our genetics." She gripped Hekalie's arms. "Please, send me back now. I can't bear to look at him one more time and know that I can't love him anymore."

With sad eyes, Hekalie nodded and led her into the house.

22

S hade felt the emptiness in him expand as he rode with the Katorin forces through the grey hills, yellow sky darkening, and toward the thick darkness of the mountain pass. Toward Eidolon. Toward the oblivis. He had to hit the prison now, while Carvahl's forces were in chaos.

And free as many prisoners as he could free.

The oblivis stood stark beyond the pass, a round structure carved out of basalt rock. It cast a rough, bleak shadow across the golden plains. The air was dry and smelled of sweat and horses as the Eidolon guards scattered before them. He rode beside the captain of the Katorin guard, storming through the oblivis' dark, open gates as the Eidolon forces scattered across the fields and roads.

No doubt scrambling to locate Carvahl. He dreaded telling his mother that all of this wasn't over—that Carvahl had faded into the gate and entered the veil using Shade's wilding magic.

That stung. But it was the only way that bastard could have opened the gate and passed through the veil. It was a one-way trip, but he'd come within a breath of not existing. Something that Shade regretted not finishing. For now, he'd free all the prisoners that Carvahl had amassed during his reign of terror in Katori.

He wheeled his chestnut roan around and gingerly dismounted, his left leg still painful from the beam that had nearly broken it this morning. As he limped down the dank, winding trail that spiraled deep into the earth, he could only think about Kendra.

His chest ached at the memory of her sun-washed raspberry scent, her bright laugh, those fiery eyes. All this time, he'd fooled himself into believing that she'd be waiting for him in Hekalie's study, arms wide to enfold him.

His heart felt like it had been smashed into splinters, but he kept moving down the trail out of sheer stubbornness. He wanted to lie down and melt into the earth. For his father, he would get him out of this sewer.

Shade moved toward the great iron doors leading into the oblivis and its pitch-black confines.

Four soldiers with axes and picks pounded the hinges out of the great door and used a wagon and eight horses to pull it off its jamb. Shade staggered behind the other forces that carried lanterns and called out to the chained prisoners. Pounding apart chains and releasing every prisoner they encountered.

Everyone was leaving the oblivis today.

He searched alongside the Katorins, feeling sick at the filthy hole his father had been in all this time. Was the man even still alive? Had he made this trip in vain?

"Shade!" someone ahead shouted through the darkness.

"Over here," he answered, the spiral of dungeon and endless rows of dark cells confusing in the dim light.

The air smelled like sulfur and ammonia.

A young Katorin in sparkling plate mail rushed up to him, smiling.

"Your father. We've found your father."

"Show me!" Shade shouted, grabbing hold of the man's shoulder.

"This way."

Shade hobbled through the tangle of bedraggled prisoners, weak and draped in rags as the Katorin soldiers unchained them. He turned right down a short corridor and then veered left into a long dark hallway. Halfway down, the young, brown-haired soldier turned left. He followed, seeing a line of murky, dank cells on the left. They were more holes in the earth than chambers.

His father stood in front of the second opening. Shade sucked in a breath. Overcome with relief.

Father's ebony hair was long and matted, face thin and smeared with dirt. At seventeen, he'd always seen his father as tall and strong. Invincible. After so much time had passed, he seemed shorter somehow. And a little frail. But those light blue eyes ran with tears and he held out reedy arms.

"My son," said Braeden Flettcharon (Eidolon for House Charon) in a hoarse, raspy voice.

"Father!" Shade rushed forward and put his arms around the emaciated man, once so tall and strong. Weak and unsteady, he folded his arms around Shade, holding him close.

"I've dreamed of this moment," said his father.

"So have I," Shade replied, his voice cracking.

For most of his life, he'd dreamed of the day when his father would leave this hole. The man had endured a hellish existence all this time—to save Shade's life. His breath caught, his eyes stinging, chest aching as he held his father. He could never atone for this man's suffering.

At last, Shade let him go. "Let's take you home."

His father raised an eyebrow. "Where?"

Shade smiled. "To Airell. We liberated it this morning from Carvahl and his army." He bowed his head. "But father," he whispered, stepping closer. "Carvahl escaped through the old obsidian gate in the temple. I couldn't stop him."

His father pulled him into a tight hug again. "You freed Airell from his control, son," he whispered. "For now, that's enough. Tomorrow, we'll deal with Carvahl. Tonight, we rest and bury our dead."

Shade nodded as his father patted his shoulder and let him go. "Home to Airell. At last."

His father nodded toward the line of cells surrounding him. The oblivis was a big place.

"As soon as they're all free."

"We'd better get to work then," said Shade, patting his father's shoulder.

IT TOOK A DAY AND A HALF TO FREE ALL THE PRISONERS AND CART THEM in wagons across the plains to Katori. They traveled past the dark, menacing edge of Eidolon that crouched in the distance beyond the oblivis. In chaos now that Carvahl's plan to enslave Katori to the west had failed.

The grey haze dissipated as they crossed the steep, rocky pass back into Katori. Under crisp yellow skies the color of daffodils, they rode through silvery green meadows carpeted with purple, blue, and red wildflowers that rolled toward Airell's once sleepy streets. Deserted and empty for so long.

A handful of Katorins danced in those streets today, stringing garlands of red roses and vivid white daisies, royal blue ceanas and lavender star flowers. The air was drenched in the ceanas' brown sugary sweetness as Shade led his father down the lane that looped around the village. Toward the two-story grey stone house where he'd grown up. With its curved walls and cupolas dotted with rose and honeyed quartz, windows draped in pale mint green curtains, it had hardly changed.

Father opened the white wrought iron gate and stepped through it. Shade followed behind him, letting him gather his thoughts and prepare for this long-overdue reunion.

Shade's mother threw open the red front door and ran down the path toward them.

"Braeden!" she shouted. "Oh, Braeden!"

Father hobbled ahead, throwing his arms around her as she sobbed and laughed at the same time.

Jaxon barreled out of the house ahead of Shade's sisters,

screaming for his father. Father had room enough in his arms for all of them until even Shade wiped back tears.

"Shade, come here," Braeden said, motioning to him.

He hesitated a moment, then limped toward his father. The man reached out and ruffled his hair then pulled him into a hug among his siblings.

"Now, Braeden, let's get you inside to a hot bath and all the food you can stomach," said Shade's mother, his sisters scurrying around him.

Jaxon hung back, hands in his back pockets as he stared at Shade in silence. His little brother was a head taller now, almost as tall as him. He filled out one of Shade's old yellow tunics, but his dark trousers were a little too short. The squirt had longer legs and would need a trip to the clothier soon. When it was safe and Katori's villages and cities had recovered. He'd see to it.

"I never thought it would happen," said Jaxon, staring at him.

Shade sighed. "I don't want to fight with you, Jaxon."

"I never thought you'd keep your word." The young man paced around him a moment, stopping within an arm's reach. "But you did. You brought Father home and you stopped the Eidolon march over Katori." His eyes narrowed. "I hated you when you left."

He hadn't stopped them yet. Only slowed them down. And Carvahl was still out there. Plotting. Stalking. Preparing.

"Why?" Shade asked, shaking his head.

Only then did his younger brother's voice crack. His bottom lip quivered, his eyes misting.

"Because I—I didn't want you to leave." He toed the ground a moment. "Now, I want to say I'm sorry that I doubted you."

Shade grinned and grabbed Jaxon by the neck, pulling his kid brother into a hug.

"We haven't exactly won yet, but we've liberated Airell. It's a start. All's forgiven, kid."

He felt a weight lift off his shoulders when he felt Jaxon's arms fly around him. The kid muffled a sob and then let go of him. Shade ruffled his hair.

"Let's go get some of that food before it's all gone."

Jaxon nodded, smiling as Shade slid his arm around Jaxon's shoulders and led him inside.

LATER THAT EVENING, SHADE SAT ON A TAN SOFA IN FRONT OF THE family hearth, feeling restless and distant. The soft sunset-colored walls and rough-hewn beams overhead made the hearth feel warmer, scent of Mother's famous meat pies sizzling in the oven, savory scent of roasting vegetables filling the house. The warm scent of custard tarts and yeasty bread made his mouth water. He hadn't been in this house since he was seventeen.

He loved this house once, but with Carvahl still out there and worse—without Kendra, he felt empty. Except for the raw ache in his chest reminding him that he was still alive, the facts made his body hurt all over.

Carvahl had escaped and Kendra was gone.

No matter how much he loved her, she was out of his reach. And no amount of Fey, Katorin, or Eidolon magic could change that. It was forbidden to court or marry cousins in Katori and Eidolon. And in most of Kendra's world, too.

A hand fell onto his shoulder and he looked up. Father.

"Feeling better?" Shade asked as his father sat down beside him on the sofa.

His father studied his face with those probing blue eyes, making Shade uncomfortable. The man could see a lie from a mile away and he knew when someone was miserable. Shade couldn't hide that fact.

"I am, but you look worse as the night drags on." He squinted. "What is it?"

Shade shrugged. How did he tell the man that he'd lost the love of his life?

"That kind of look is only over a woman, son," said his father, a hand on his shoulder.

He nodded, glancing at the big, rectangular feasting table where the rest of the family sat playing Arcana. Cards and pegs clattered against the wood surface, shouts and giggles filling the house. Flames crackled, the smell of woodsmoke soothing. But it didn't soften the ache in his chest.

"Want to talk about it?"

"Nothing to say," he said finally, not looking his father in the eye. "I've already lost her."

"Lost who?"

"Kendra," he said, her name lancing his chest. "Kendra Martin. She comes from Aeryn's line, Father. The tempering magic that everyone thought was gone from the world. I found it in Kendra. She saved us all. Alone, I'd have died. Couldn't even stop Carvahl from escaping."

"And you love her."

He looked at his father, not caring how much of his anguish bled through now. He couldn't hide it any longer.

"More than my own life."

His father studied his face for several moments then smiled. "So why are you sitting here on this sofa?" he asked. "Why haven't you gone after her?"

"She's from Aeryn's line." A sigh rattled through him. "We're cousins."

"Oh, no," said his father, sinking back against the sofa cushions.

Shade nodded and dropped his head in his hands.

"There was a story about Aeryn's children...what was that?" His father fell silent, gazing into the fire.

"Something about a child of faerie, according to Mother," said Shade. He slid off the sofa, picked up the poker, and speared the hearth logs, sending spirals of ash and sparks into the flume.

"Yes, child of faerie, child of fortune, that's what it was. Shade! That was it!"

His father's shout startled him and he dropped the poker. The man leaped up from the sofa and grabbed Shade's arms, turning him around.

"What's the matter?" Shade asked.

"Child of faerie, child of fortune!"

Shade frowned. "What's that mean?"

"One child fathered by the Fey and the other by fortune. A foundling. A Katorin foundling." He gripped Shade's arms. "Don't you understand? Aeryn found that child. She didn't give birth to it."

Shade pushed back from his father, staring at the man, a sliver of hope stinging his eyes. He was afraid to say the words, afraid he was wrong, that he'd misunderstood.

"Shade, your grandmother isn't blood kin to Aeryn. You're not related to your Kendra."

Shade grabbed his father by the shoulders, unable to hold onto his resolve. "Are you certain? How do you know this story?"

"From my grandmother. She knew Aeryn and her daughters. She used to talk about one of those girls that had a strange gift."

"What gift, Father?"

"She could make anything appear out of thin air. Anything—on a whim. Her mother, Aeryn had been shocked by the strangeness of her Fey child. It wasn't Katorin. The magical gift only worked where she felt at home. Truly at home."

Shade let out a belly laugh, his eyes stinging. "That's my Kendra." He threw his arms around his father, spinning him around. "Thank you. Thank you!"

His father laid a hand against Shade's face a moment, smiling.

"I've got to leave for a while, but I'll be back soon," said Shade.

He ran for the door and threw it open, stopping in the doorway.

"Think Gran's still up?" he asked. "I need a ride to Indiana."

His father frowned, shaking his head. "Indiana? Where's that?"

Shade smiled. "Home," he said and limped out the door, headed toward town.

23

Kendra loaded up her suitcase and carried it out to the silver Volkswagen. Toni Ambrose leaned against the Jetta, standing beside Maddie. Both of them looked as sad as she felt.

"Why do you have leave tonight, Kendra?" Toni asked. "I still want your help with my business plan."

"You've got everything you need, Toni. You'll be fine."

Kendra closed the trunk, her red Keds scuffing across the driveway as she headed inside. A quick run through the house to make sure she hadn't left anything and she'd be out of here. She never wanted to see the place again. First, she'd lost Gem. And now, Shade.

It was too much.

The air smelled corn-sweet from the nearby factory, the husky scent of woodsmoke mixing with fresh mown grass. Darkness had settled like a warm blanket over the sleepy country lane, the crescent moon high in the sky, making it easier to hide how sketchy her eyes looked after crying over Shade all weekend. She loved being here with him, but now, every time she looked across the field at that dark house, she'd remember being in his arms, making love to him in a bed of wildflowers.

Or she'd remember every time she looked up at the moon.

No. It was worse than that. She'd remember what she could have had. What she'd lost. She had to get out of here. Now.

Maddie followed her inside, Toni's heels clicking behind her.

"Kendra, please," said Maddie. "At least wait until morning. It's nearly nine o'clock."

"I'll call you both tomorrow," she said in a tight voice. "Let you know that my stand-by flight arrived in Baltimore. If you're ever in the neighborhood, stop by. I'll show you my patio garden." She walked through to the kitchen and leaned against the back door, staring out at the faerie garden that gleamed with magical creatures. "Of course, it's nothing like Gem's garden."

"Kendra, I won't let you leave like this," said Toni. "You're clearly upset and it's not right."

Kendra turned around, staring at Toni's long face and the worry shining in Maddie's eyes. She smiled at them and walked into the kitchen. She put her arms around Maddie and hugged her. Then she hugged Toni.

"Thank you, guys for everything, but I have to go now."

Anywhere but here! It hurt too much.

The knock on the back door startled her.

She turned around and glanced out the dark window. Across the field, a porch light gleamed from Shade's place!

Her heart skipped a beat.

When she looked out the door, Sebille, the queen of faerie stood on the welcome mat, beckoning her outside. That light on Shade's porch was the protection spell that the Fey had placed there. Not sure why Sebille had lit them again, but she probably knew that Carvahl had escaped hers and Shade's killing blow.

Was probably a precautionary spell to protect the garden. She didn't know what would happen to the garden after she left, but she couldn't stay. She couldn't stare across the field at Shade's empty place every single day and ache for him.

That would be unbearable.

Her heart sank as she opened the door and stepped onto the patio. Toni followed. Maddie couldn't see the faerie lights in the garden. To her, Sebille probably looked like another neighbor. She sighed. An insanely beautiful neighbor.

"I'll call you tomorrow, Kendra," said Maddie, patting her shoulder.

"Thanks, Maddie," said Kendra as Maddie turned around and left the house through the front door.

"We heard you were leaving us," said Sebille, her tone solemn, sadness in those luminous amethyst eyes.

"I'm so glad you're all right," said Kendra, laying a hand on Sebille's arm.

Sebille smiled, patting her hand.

"This garden means a lot to us, Kendra. As do you, kin to Emmaline. We've come to ask you to stay."

Kendra looked around at the sea of Fey and faerie gathered around the patio, elven folk beside them. Satyrs and centaurs stood beside the griffins and unicorns, Gabriel and Lenora on the other side. And beside Gabriel stood Nevar, Sebille's husband and the king of faerie.

She smiled and bowed her head. "I'm touched by your request and if it was within my power to stay, I would. But I—I can't. I'm sorry."

"Not even for me?"

She glanced up at the sound of that achingly familiar voice.

Shade stood at the edge of the patio. He hesitated a moment and then limped through the gathering of magical beings to stand in front of her.

Her breath caught. "Shade!"

A fierce ache stabbed her heart as she looked at him, wanting to throw herself into his arms. Seeing him now, especially now, hurt much worse than it had inside that Katorin temple.

"You know why I can't," she said, her voice breaking as she looked away.

He took hold of her shoulders. "Child of faerie, child of fortune," he said.

She frowned, staring at him, her eyes burning. "What does that mean?"

"It means that you're a child of faerie and I'm a child of fortune."

His hands sizzled against her skin and she longed to feel his arms around her and his love again.

"It doesn't change anything, Shade."

That patient, arctic blue gaze didn't waver, a smile playing on his lips now.

"Your grandmother was born of the Fey," he said, the corners of his mouth curling into a grin. "Mine of fortune—a foundling. Found by Aeryn and raised as her daughter." He grinned, lifting her into his arms and spinning her around.

Kendra felt the tears against her cheeks. "Does that mean we're not cousins?"

He nodded. "There's no blood relation between us, Kendra! None." He let her feet touch the patio again. "And I never want to be away from you this long again. Those two days were brutal."

"Not a chance, Shade Fletcher," she said, matching that devious grin on his face.

He leaned down and kissed her hard on the lips. She pulled him against her, smashing her mouth against his in a frantic, urgent kiss.

She let him go finally, gripping his hands.

"Your place or mine," he said with a wink.

"Let's start with mine," said Kendra, pulling him into the house. "We'll go to Katori in a day or two. I'm sure Sebille can protect the house for a couple of days. Until we're ready to deal with Carvahl."

He nodded. "I'd like to show you those flower-drenched meadows and crystalline skies. Then we'll deal with Carvahl."

She looked forward to seeing more of Katori and hoped to catch a glimpse of Gem's flower-drenched meadows and crystalline skies. But tonight, all she wanted was Shade Fletcher.

He gathered her into his arms, pulling her into another burning kiss. "And tomorrow, I need to tell you about the moons."

Her hand snapped to his chest, holding him back a moment. "The moons?"

He sighed, nodding at her. "Eidolon magic is ruled by the moons."

"Like the ebony moon?" she asked.

"Ebony, strawberry, winter—all of them change the magic in subtle ways," he said, brushing a lock of brown hair out of her eyes. "The ebony moon allowed Carvahl to hunt me and those with the tempering magic in the shadows. Now, he's injured and separated from his army."

Kendra nodded. "Hope he stays that way, too—and goes into hiding. Hunted like he's hunted so many for so long."

But Shade was already shaking his head. "He still has one chance to recover the magic that he lost."

From the patio, Toni gasped and pressed her hand to her face. "Carvahl lives?"

A buzz of voices erupted through Gem's garden, terrifying Kendra.

Shade glanced over at Toni and then nodding, he fixed Sebille with his steady gaze.

"He escaped me in the Katorin temple and fled through the obsidian gate—activating it with my own magic," he said with a groan, glancing from Kendra to Sebille and finally, Toni. "But after discussing it with Hekalie, I think I know where he's gone."

Sebille stepped forward, Nevar at her elbow as the vampires and centaurs shuffled closer.

Kendra grabbed him by the arms. "Shade, tell me what's going on —now!"

"Carvahl's gone back to the point when I arrived in this world and became the Green Man," he said and she began to worry.

"But what does that mean, Shade?" she asked, studying his hot, sexy face.

"It means he's been studying the moons," said Shade as he cast a nervous glance throughout the garden. "Hekalie thinks he's planning to extinguish all the magic in your world through an Eidolon ritual. To refuel the magic he lost."

"When?" Sebille demanded, a hard edge around those glowing hazel eyes.

Shade squirmed. "On the next Blood Moon," he said. "Into the past—that means old world Ireland, Kendra." He sighed as gasps filtered through the garden.

Old world Ireland? Was he serious? Was that even possible?

"Is that like castles and druids, Shade?"

He nodded.

"What are you doing for the next few centuries, Kendra?" Shade asked with a smirk. "Ever see a Medieval Blood Moon ritual before? Even if you don't follow me there, you'll all see the aftermath here."

Murmurs rose through the garden.

"Dammit, Shade!" Kendra snapped. "Explain it in English! What do you mean?"

She studied that poker face of his now.

He pulled in a breath, his gaze encompassing the garden that had fallen deadly quiet now.

"Through that ritual, Carvahl will try to extinguish all magic in your world, absorbing it himself. To take back what he lost on the ebony moon. It's the only way he can equalize the overwhelming magic against him. Tonight, he's still licking his wounds. Soon, we have to follow him through the obsidian gate, Kendra. And stop him."

"Soon," she said and pulled him against her. "For tonight, all I want to follow is you, Shade Fletcher."

She planned to spend the night in his arms, loving him.

He wrapped her in his arms and held her close as she opened the door into the house. She led him up the stairs to the bedroom.

Blood Moon. Extinguish all the magic from her world? She winced, wanting to block those words out of her head right now. Would the light from this blood moon illuminate the end of everything?

Together, she and Shade had to follow Carvahl through the gate and find out.

The End of EBONY MOON: Prismatic Moons, Book 1
The story continues in...
BLOOD MOON: Prismatic Moons, Book 2

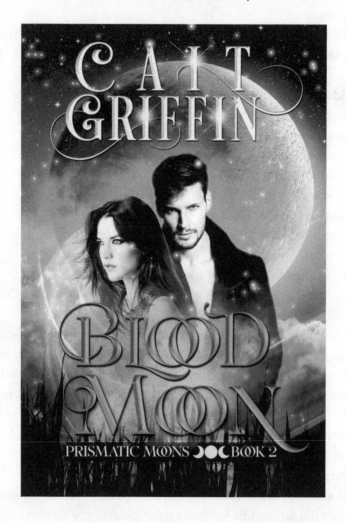

ABOUT THE AUTHOR

CAIT GRIFFIN writes paranormal romance and urban fantasy. She lives in the southwestern United States and this is her first novel. Find Cait at: CaitGriffin.com

---

Before you go, you are invited to please leave a **review of this book**!

Reviews are a wonderful way to help an author. They are also an exciting opportunity to share your honest thoughts with other readers, so **please post yours,** in as many places as possible!

Thanks for reading! We appreciate your support!

f facebook.com/cait.griffin.author

⊙ instagram.com/caitgriffinwrites

𝓟 pinterest.com/caitgriffin

CPSIA information can be obtained
at www.ICGtesting.com
Printed in the USA
LVHW012303260721
693792LV00001B/47

9 781955 197168